"BRILLIANT POLITICAL DIGRESSIONS, FIRST-RATE WIT . . . If John le Carré is the Henry James of suspense fiction, Mr. Buckley, if he chose, might be the Evelyn Waugh. . . . *The Story of Henri Tod* does certainly entertain us."

—*The New York Times*

THE STORY OF HENRI TOD

William F. Buckley, Jr.

"FORMIDABLE WIT AND UNCANNY UNDER-STANDING . . . [Buckley's] skills as a mimic are equal even to the demands of Khrushchev himself."
—*Los Angeles Times Book Review*

"RELENTLESSLY PACED SPY FICTION."
—American Library Association

"IF YOU COUNT GOOD SPY THRILLERS AMONG LIFE'S LITTLE PLEASURES, you will be pleased to know that William F. Buckley has been graduated triumphantly from the company of gifted amateurs to the thoroughly professional."

—*Cosmopolitan*

THE STORY OF
HENRI TOD

William F. Buckley, Jr.

A DELL BOOK

Published by
Dell Publishing Co., Inc.
1 Dag Hammarskjold Plaza
New York, New York 10017

This is a work of fiction. Some of the figures who appear, however,
do so under their own names.

Dell ® TM 681510, Dell Publishing Co., Inc.

ISBN: 0-440-18327-8

Reprinted by arrangement with Doubleday & Company, Inc.

Printed in the United States of America

First Dell printing—January 1985

For Nika Hazelton

ACKNOWLEDGMENTS

I am grateful to the studies of several authors and historians whose books helped me greatly with the factual material. They include *The Ides of August*, by Curtis Cate; *Kennedy and the Berlin Wall Crisis*, by Honoré M. Catudal; *The Wall: A Tragedy in Three Acts*, by Eleanor Dulles; *A Thousand Days*, by Arthur Schlesinger, Jr.; and *Khrushchev Remembers*, by Nikita Khrushchev or whoever else wrote the book, a controversy I wish to be left out of. Some liberties have been taken with the chronology, but not many. I must mention the joy of word-processing on my Kaypro II.

I gave the manuscript to my family, friends, and colleagues. To my wife Patricia, son Christopher, sister Priscilla, and brother Reid. To Charles Wallen, Jr., Thomas Wendel, Sophie Wilkins, Marvin Liebman, and my agent, Lois Wallace. To my colleagues Frances Bronson, Dorothy McCartney, and Susan Stark. To Chaucy Bennetts my thanks for her splendid work, as also to Joseph Isola, as ever. Dorothy McCartney, my researcher, relied heavily on the generosity of Ingeborg Godenschweger of the German Information Center, who knows so much about Berlin she might have founded it.

To them all, for advice, correction, encouragement, research, proofreading, and typing, I am profoundly grateful. I must especially acknowledge the work of my old friend Sam Vaughan, and my new friend

Kate Medina. Their editorial suggestions were superb, their patience and good cheer exemplary.

And finally, in connection with my stay in Berlin, I owe thanks to Nona Oeynhausen, to Dr. Otto and Mari Ann von Simson, to Mr. Ernest Nagy of the American Embassy in West Berlin, and to Ambassador Rozanne L. Ridgeway in East Berlin and her colleague Günther Rosinus, the press and cultural attaché. Fine counselors, friends, and cicerones.

Stamford, Connecticut   W.F.B.
July 1983

THE STORY OF HENRI TOD

1

The *Marlin* was all right—when you have wife, children, nurses, Secret Service, four aides and one doctor. But he liked, every now and again, to remind the company that this was his *father's* boat, not his. *He* liked to *sail.* He could still do so, once in a while. But not when there was a goddam caravan going out. Like today. Lunch, picnic at Great Island.

Oh, it would be all right, and the day was one of those special sunny-blue-warm-crisp days that make the Cape stand out as first contender for Center of the Natural Universe. Why couldn't Washington have Cape Cod weather? Ah, *he* knew why Washington could not have Cape Cod weather. Because there hadn't been a Presidential Task Force constituted to inquire into the question. He must remember to put that on the agenda, call in Admiral Albuquerque; good old Albuquerque, who thought it impudent even to smile in the presidential presence. "At ease, Admiral." Then maybe he'd look at his watch and say, "Smiletime! Ten seconds!" The President could get away with that kind of thing, because his genial informality drew the sting.

Let's see. He should make his point about powerboats versus sailboats. To the mate, standing discreetly under the wooden awning that extended out toward the open cockpit where his wife and Paul and Gatty were seated, on the deck chairs. In a voice loud enough for them to hear: "Sam. Tell the skipper to cut down on the rpm." And then to Paul,

"Noisy, these power buggers. So we cruise at twelve knots instead of fourteen, so what?"

Paul looked up from his book, *Franny and Zooey*. "So what? Why—" Paul was coaching himself not to refer to the President of the United States by his first name, never mind that they had been roommates at college, and never mind that most emphatically during the first few months, though less and less now, resigned as the President had become to being The President, he had been urged to continue calling him "Jack." Paul had progressed to the point of being able to handle "Mr. President," so mostly he addressed his friend without cognomen of any kind. "—why, if we go at twelve knots instead of fourteen, that means we'll arrive at Johnny Walker's dock at 12:48 instead of 12:44, and Plessy will grow old with worry." Plessy, the adjutant who coordinated the President's minute-by-minute movements, fretted each time the President departed Point A headed for Point B.

"Plessy won't grow old unless I tell him to," the President grumbled, and released a half smile, which was when the Secret Service man walked into the cockpit and said, "Sir, we must head back to Hyannis Port."

"What?"

"Yes, sir. The duty officer radioed. He said it was top priority for you to return."

"Tell 'em to send a chopper to Great Island, pick me up there."

"The duty officer, sir, ruled that out. He said they need you *right away.*"

His wife now raised her eyes from her book, and the silence was general.

"All right," he snapped, and the Secret Service man quickly went to the helmsman.

They traveled now at the *Marlin*'s full speed, just over sixteen knots, so that it would have been difficult to communicate other than at full voice. In a way the engine noise made it easier, because even if it had been silent on deck little would have been spoken. Had Caroline been three years older, she would probably have said what was on everyone's mind: "Daddy, why are we going back? Daddy, *why?*" But grownups don't do that in straitened imperial circumstances. Bad form. What is a President supposed to say? "I don't know, dear. Could be the Indians have seized Fort Knox. Could be the Mississippi River has decided to flow east at St. Louis. Could be the Secretary of Defense has flown off to Russia with all of Daddy's secrets. We'll just have to wait and see." Paul and Gatty and Jackie returned to their reading, but a close observer would have noticed that pages now were turned more slowly than they had been on the outbound journey.

The duty officer was waiting for him with the telex. The President bounded onto the dock and took the folded paper, reading it quickly. He turned to his wife. "Go on back out to the picnic. Maybe I'll be able to join you later. If not, I'll see you when you get back."

"All right," she said, as Paul and Gatty looked up at him. Their expressions were a question mark. He paused, and then said quietly, "Berlin. They're partitioning the city."

2

"**O**h my darling boy! My beautiful Blacky!" Blackford Oakes noted that his mother had not changed in the year since he had last seen her, and that was 95 percent good news, he thought; make that 85 percent. References to his good looks had been unbearable when he was sixteen. At thirty-five, he could more easily let them pass as maternal endearments if only they were rendered, as now they were, in private. The trouble was that his mother was perfectly capable of going on about her son's pulchritude in the company of relative strangers. "Mother," he had said to her the last time she trespassed, "if you keep this up I swear I'm going to have a gold ring put through my nose, and a couple of fingers chopped off." But there was no taming her.

"You would *still* be beautiful, Blacky."

"Okay," he had said. "Okay. If you're talking about my *soul*, Mother, you may say it's beautiful, which is a very sweet thing to say. And easier, since you're not my confessor. On the other hand, nobody is. I haven't poped since I last saw you, Mother." Lady Carol sighed with pleasure.

"Alec home?" Blackford asked after his stepfather, while removing his overcoat.

"He's out, but he'll be here for lunch. He knows you're coming. He had to go to a meeting. It's all very difficult, apparently, because it has to do with the widow of his old sergeant, Heathcliff. She remarried after Heathcliff was killed and her new husband is very rich. Very, very rich, Blacky. I think he owns soap."

"What do you mean, 'he owns soap,' Mother? Do you mean he owns a soap company?"

"No, dear. He owns soap. Every time you wash your hands, Sergeant Heathcliff's ex-wife's husband—I can never remember his name—gets some money out of it. Oh, not so very much, I would say. Maybe as little as a farthing. But you know, when you take into account all the people who wash their hands—though it's true, we have to face the fact that there are some lazy people in this world who don't wash regularly—but also, Blacky, we have to face facts, some people who perhaps can't afford to buy soap—anyway," Lady Carol led the way up the staircase at 50 Portland Place and eased her son down on the sofa opposite the fireplace, whose neatly placed logs and tinder she leaned over to light as she continued her story, "anyway, you can see that that amounts to a great deal of money."

Blackford, a graduate engineer from Yale University, with practical experience in architecture and other serious pursuits, decided he would simply accept unconditionally that his stepfather's ex-sergeant's ex-wife had married the man who had invented soap; and let it go, let it go. But he thought to ask, "Why is Alec concerned about the money?"

"Well, you see," said Lady Carol, pouring more milk into her son's tea because she had always thought he did not take enough of it, a stoic self-denial he had picked up as a boy at school, in the early months of the war, "the owner of the soap has died, and left his wife all his money. And now she has said that she wishes to build a monument at her husband's training barracks in Lincolnshire in memory of her first husband, Sergeant Heathcliff."

"Well I think that's very nice of her."

"Yes, dear, it's very nice of *her*, but the gift is entirely unsuitable, Alec says. Sergeant Heathcliff's widow has specified that her late husband's heroism should be described

on the statue she wants to commission and donate, and she
proposes to use as the text for the statue the letter she
received from Alec in 1918."

"Well, I see that there might be a problem there. If Alec
was writing to someone just widowed, he might have written a little—floridly. He was only—what, twenty-two years
old himself in 1918?"

"It isn't merely that your stepfather wrote floridly about
Sergeant Heathcliff. It is that he apparently wrote things
about the sergeant which simply were not true."

"You mean Sergeant Heathcliff *wasn't* killed in battle?"

"He was killed in battle—your father has explained it all
to me—but not by the Germans."

"Why?" Blackford looked up from his teacup.

"It appears that after the first platoon of your stepfather's company charged the German line, just before dawn,
the second platoon was to follow, ten minutes later. As the
light broke, one of them spotted a figure behind a large
tree, and thinking him a German sniper, opened fire. It
turned out it was—Heathcliff, hiding behind the tree while
his men charged forward against the Germans. Your stepfather saw no need to describe to Mrs. Heathcliff her husband's cowardice, you know—he is so kindhearted, Alec—
so that night he sat down with his fellow officers, and apparently they had got hold of a bottle of whiskey. So when he
began to describe the end of Heathcliff, Lieutenant Beaure-
gard—you never met him, he was a splendid man—began
to, well you know, began to embellish the truth. And then
the major chipped in. And by the time your stepfather had
finished the letter and"—Lady Carol sighed—"I suppose
the whiskey bottle, the end of Sergeant Heathcliff appeared
most fearfully heroic. And it was all your stepfather could
do, in the weeks that came later, to explain to Mrs. Heathcliff why her husband had not been recommended for the
Victoria Cross."

At that moment the heavy clomp of Sir Alec ascending

the staircase was heard, and Blackford rose to greet his balding, portly stepfather, dressed as usual in striped pants, morning coat, and stiff collar. They shook hands warmly, and Sir Alec accepted the tea from his wife and sat down on the sofa opposite.

"I say," he said distractedly. They waited. "I say," he repeated. "It was jolly rough."

"How did you manage it, dear?"

"Well, I, hrrm," Sir Alec cleared his throat, "I told Lady Sparrow—"

"Sparrow, that's the name, Blacky—forgive me, Alec—"

"I told Lady Sparrow that Heathcliff had left behind a missive addressed to king and country praying that in the event he should perish, no public notice was to be taken of his death, that he wished to be remembered only as a humble and dutiful servant of his sovereign."

"It worked?"

"It worked. But her tears very nearly overwhelmed us all. I say, Carol, some sherry, please . . . And Blackford, my boy, what brings you to London, if I may ask?"

At this point Sir Alec Sharkey looked over with meaningful concentration at his wife, to reassure her that they were not to inquire too exhaustively into the nature of Blackford's work. It was almost ten years ago, when Blackford first returned to London after graduating from Yale, six years after being decorated as a fighter pilot in the last days of the war, that Sir Alec had sniffed out that Blackford's vague involvement with foundations, engineering firms, and other cosmopolitan concerns, which had taken him twice, for protracted periods, to Germany, and once to France, was best not investigated in detail. He liked Blackford, approved of him; had firsthand knowledge of his mettle when as a schoolboy, freshly in his stepfather's care, he had acted courageously in reaction to the bullying of a sadistic headmaster. Even as a very boyish boy, Blackford had had a manner preternaturally adult, Sir Alec reflected.

Even when munching a candy bar, he had been very much composed. So Alec Sharkey simply assumed that his stepson, now thoroughly grown up, was honorably engaged, and that if it was convenient for him to speak vaguely about his professional life, Sir Alec would not inconveniently press him on the nature of his duties. Quickly Sir Alec took the occasion to move the conversation to more public matters.

"Terrible business, that Bay of Pigs, what?"

"Yes," Blackford said. "Terrible. It was quite terrible." His memory moved, under its own inertia, to the final meeting with Sánchez Morano, at the waterhole-restaurant opposite the military airfield outside Miami. It had been very hot, humid. They had dined together, and spoken of D-Day. Sánchez Morano's skinny frame made his dark brown eyes especially luminous, and his excitement was palpable. But Sánchez and Blackford circled about the question of what day exactly the operation would go forward, as though the date had not yet been specified. In fact Fidel Castro knew the day, and would be waiting for Sánchez. What was not known to Sánchez, or to Blackford—or to Fidel Castro—was the paralyzing ambiguity in Washington of the commitment to Sánchez's mission. In pursuit of which mission he died. In a manner not to be confused with Heathcliff's, though both died of bullet wounds fired, so to speak, from their side of the line.

Blackford left his mother's house and soon discovered that his memory of London's streets lingered sufficiently to point him the way to Park Street, where at Number 74, nine years earlier, he had been given his first assignment. He knew that CIA safe houses were regularly changed, and wondered offhand how it came to be that he was now headed for the same address. Perhaps the houses were recycled—he didn't know.

The April wind was brisk, and as he fought against it he found himself idling, as he often did when in search of distraction, with mathematical calculations: How many safe houses would the Central Intelligence Agency need to have occupied in the course of nine years, assuming that the Agency required—he didn't know just how many safe houses the Agency had in London, even though Blackford Oakes was more now than a mere agent in the field, and so he would take an easy figure and guess—ten. So. How many houses in total would the Agency need to occupy over the course of nine years if each house were abandoned after two months (that, he had been taught by one of his instructors in Washington, was the rule of thumb)? That would be ten houses six times per year, equals sixty per year times nine years equals 540 houses. Enough to house the entire Russian secret service, given the cubic feet assigned in Moscow per family. Fascinating. To whom? Ah, Blackford, you are a cunning old bird. To nobody, that's to whom.

He was walking down Park Lane, and the streets began to look thoroughly domesticated as he approached the residential district in Mayfair. He looked at his watch. Time had not withered away the sacrosanct habit. The meeting had been called for 4:14, at which time, exactly, he would knock on the door. He was a minute early and so walked past Number 74 until he judged the interval correct. He stooped to tie his shoelace, and when he arose walked back in the direction he had come from to the entrance of Number 74 and knocked. The door was instantly opened.

Blackford permitted himself, if many months had gone by without seeing Rufus, to embrace him in the rather formal way in which grown men greet their fathers. Rufus instinctively resisted anything that suggested explicit affection, but a few years ago Blackford had said, "Rufus, I know it's unlikely in our line of business that you would ever be awarded a Nobel Prize, but suppose that you were: What would you do when the King of Sweden, with a check for forty-five grand in his pocket, approached you with a royal embrace?"

Rufus had replied only with his little half smile, saying nothing, as was his habit. Today, Blackford thought, Rufus almost reached the point of returning the embrace. Such was the impression Rufus gave when remaining motionless.

Rufus's notion of foreplay, Blackford thought, amusing himself; and said, "Great to see you, Rufus, you old super-spy!"

Rufus winced—but he had endured worse. When tortured by the Nazis, in the early days of the war. Before his legendary escape, and his rise to eminence in his profession as the intelligence officer Ike trusted most.

Blackford had not seen Rufus since the funeral. Burying Rufus's wife had been a complicated affair, the Director acquiescing in the arrangements only after Rufus had agreed that the ceremony would be held at a small church in the Virginia countryside whose identity and location the dozen men closest professionally to Rufus were advised of only late in the morning. They were ready to set out to wherever the funeral would be. If any Soviet agent was there to photograph a dozen top American intelligence operatives among the mourners, he'd have had to be one of their number. And, of course, no one was permitted whose identity as a member of the Agency was not already known to the others. Over the course of nine years in the Agency, if you're involved in covert operations, Blackford reflected, you do get to recognize only about a dozen people.

Rufus had tried determinedly to retire, but after his last return to duty, the year before, his wife had said to him that she doubted he would ever be able to say no to a special plea by the Director. The very next day Rufus had pointedly refused to meet with the Director, who had proposed driving out to the country "just for a little casual visit." Proud of his determination, Rufus rushed out to the rose garden to tell his wife, who was lying on the lawn, rose shears in hand, dead from a heart attack. After the funeral, Rufus returned the Director's call.

"Come in, come in," Rufus now said to Blacky, pointing to the door of the living room. Beside the fireplace sat a gentleman very tall and thin, his bony cheeks pallid, eyes gray and a little sad. He rose, to just more than Blackford's six-foot-one-inch height, extending a long and tapered hand.

"Howdyoudo, Oakes."

Rufus introduced Sir Basil Monk, and pointed to a chair. A clerk brought in tea, asking Rufus and Blackford whether they took milk or lemon. He did not need to ask his superior, who drank everything straight.

Sir Basil sipped his tea and lit a cigarette. "Oh, I'm so sorry," he extended his cigarette case first to Rufus, then to Blackford, both of whom declined. "Habit I got into during the war. After the winter of '43 we all agreed not to share our cigarettes. Too scarce. Got into the habit. You Americans never did, by the way."

"We even share our secrets," said Blackford, cheerfully. His reference was to the American code dispatcher from the Pentagon who, a few weeks ago, had been convicted of selling materials to Soviet agents. Sir Basil looked up.

"Rufus, you have spoken to Oakes here about *our* problem?"

"Basil, I haven't seen Blackford for a year."

"I see, I see. Very well, as my headmaster used to say, let us get into the business at hand *in media res*. Does the name George Blake mean anything to you?" He was addressing Blackford.

"No sir."

"Well, we have just now got on to him. He has been serving as a double agent for eight years that we know of. And he has been attached to our military intelligence in Berlin. Moreover, we have established, belatedly, that Blake has been in possession of information that emanated from your embassy in Moscow. The chap declines to tell us how he got that intelligence. We have not given up on the effort to get from him that, er, information—"

"You are appealing to his patriotism?"

"We are appealing to his—how would my headmaster have put it?—*joie de vivre*. Meanwhile," his mien was now totally grave, "we have got a most frightful problem. The crisis of Berlin is coming, there is no final agreement among the Allies about what is to be done, the PM has conferred with President Kennedy, President Kennedy has conferred with De Gaulle, I would not be surprised if President Kennedy and Mr. Khrushchev will be meeting, and the Soviet ultimatum is reiterated with increasing distinctness. You may as well be advised, Oakes, that I have been in charge of Her Majesty's intelligence in Berlin for over eight years."

"You were Blake's boss?"

"I was Blake's boss. And if I were otherwise situated, I would devote my energies to forming the Committee to Restore Hanging for Traitors. But let me review the situation."

Sir Basil might have been delivering a lecture on diplomatic history to a class at Oxford, Blackford thought. Although in the art of exposition, Rufus was no slouch. But he didn't have the rhetorical flair. With gusto, Sir Basil was back at Yalta, and then Potsdam, and then describing the *de facto* arrangements reached between General Lucius Clay, representing the Allies in Berlin, and Marshal Zhukov, representing Stalin.

"Let me attempt first a juridical summary, after which I shall follow with a geopolitical summary. But this I do on the understanding that the latter issues from my own understanding—which does not necessarily reflect what I certainly hope will be a crystallizing consensus among the leaders of our respective countries.

"Under formal agreements, signed by all relevant parties

—our own countries, plus France—the City of Berlin, an enclave within East Germany, is jointly governed by representatives of the four occupying powers. No unilateral step taken by any occupying power suffices to abrogate that agreement.

"Second, all occupying powers enjoy the right of access to the City of Berlin. The whole world is aware that that right of access Stalin attempted to block in 1948. And the whole world knows that President Truman's airlift prevailed, and that the right of access to all of Berlin, was in effect revalidated, however grudgingly.

"Third, although not by written agreement but by evolution, early during the occupation civil authority over what is now called East Berlin was ceded to the Soviet Union, while authority over what is now called West Berlin was ceded to the Western powers. Now implicit in that *modus operandi* was the acknowledgment of the right of internal access. Those who live in East Berlin are free to go into West Berlin, and those who live in West Berlin have been free to go into East Berlin. And, of course, the crisis that's been generated is the result of the overwhelming traffic of East Germans— not merely East Berliners—into West Berlin. And from West Berlin, to West Germany. That drain is a social, economic, and psychological drain the Kremlin is certainly not willing, and probably not able, to continue to endure."

"And their strategem," Rufus volunteered, "is wonderfully elegant. The Soviet Union will proceed to consummate a peace treaty with East Germany, which thereupon inherits sovereignty over all of Berlin. Thereafter, Mr. Ulbricht, or more correct, Mr. Khrushchev's Mr. Ulbricht, proceeds to make all the decisions having to do with what may or may not take place in Berlin."

"You know," said Blackford, "I've actually forgotten—I was a student at the time. Why did the Allies go along with the fiction that East Germany was a separate country? Because it would logically follow that it could conclude any treaty it desired to with the Soviet Union, right? Or do I sound like Joe McCarthy?"

"I will handle that one, Basil. Blackford, in answer to your question: a) Yes, you do sound rather like Senator McCarthy; b) East Germany's ostensible sovereignty is subordinate to the antecedent rights of the occupying powers. Just as West Germany, although it is in most respects sovereign, would not have the authority, let us say, to deny us facilities for Radio Free Europe, so East Germany cannot deny us rights to Berlin we won in the course of winning a world war."

"Bravo, Rufus," said Sir Basil, standing and stretching his long frame. "I could not have put it better myself. The Sophists would have awarded you a first prize."

Blackford had not spoken to Rufus since the Bay of Pigs, and wondered how the Sophists would handle that one. But retroactive diplomatic resourcefulness didn't help in handling current problems.

"Our instructions are very clear, gentlemen." Sir Basil was still standing,.and might have been addressing a regiment. "We must repair the damage done by Blake. Above all, we need intelligence. Our objective: *Find out what Khrushchev actually plans to do.* Find out what he plans in the way of using force if needed to accomplish his purposes, which are to seal off Berlin and stop the stampede from East Germany. And, if possible, find out exactly *when* he plans to move."

And then, addressing Rufus, he picked up his umbrella and coat at the corner of the room. "You will call me tomorrow—correct, Rufus? And I will leave you now with Mr. Oakes. Gentlemen," he said, letting his voice frame the desired cadence as he opened the door and stepped out, followed by his clerk.

Rufus and Blackford sat down opposite each other.

"Want more tea?" Blackford asked.

"No. Thank you."

There was a pause. Blackford stood and began to pace the floor. "Seems to me, Rufus, that those bastards are always on the offensive. It would be nice for us to move every now and then, right?"

"We moved at the Bay of Pigs, Blackford."

Blackford stopped. He thrust his hands into his pockets and said nothing for a moment. "Bull's-eye, Rufus. That's right. We took the offensive in Cuba."

"Remember, Blackford, our friends in Moscow enjoy advantages we don't enjoy, in this case the fiction that East Germany is an independent country. And they are closing in. They have been talking now for months and months, laying the background. 'Peace treaty' . . . 'peace treaty' . . . 'peace treaty.' That itself has an impact, like the repeated use of 'disarmament.' Khrushchev is mobilizing right now, and he plans to move. Exactly when and exactly how are what we have to try to find out."

"I wish it followed that if we did succeed in finding out, our people would come through with the right strategy."

"That's not our business."

"Oh hell, Rufus. I don't need to talk to you as one agent to another agent. Why don't we agree that once every five years we can take off our official hats and exercise normal American freedoms to analyze public policy?"

Rufus said nothing. In saying nothing he definitively cooled Blackford, who said now, with resignation:

"We got big assets in Berlin these days? Haven't been there for a while."

"The biggest asset we have in Berlin at this moment is Henri Tod and his Bruderschaft. We have our own contacts too, but Tod's people are something. And that is the principal mine right now. Your first stop. You will need an extensive briefing on Tod. A very unusual young man. There is a great deal to do."

"Do we have anybody—over there?"

"You mean in the Kremlin?"

"Well, come to think of it, yes, in the Kremlin."

"If I answered that question, Blackford, you should turn me in to the Director, who would—quite properly—fire me."

"Rufus, old shoe, if ever they fire you, I'll defect and we can start our own country. Meanwhile we might use our sources to lay on an atom bomb or two, so that we can be impregnable."

Rufus permitted himself to smile.

3

The bell on his desk rang timidly, almost hesitantly. As if especially trained to be obsequious. Walter Ulbricht, Chairman of the Council of State of the German Democratic Republic, and First Secretary of the Socialist Unity Party, responded. Responses were available in any of a number of combinations. If his secretary saw a single green light, that meant that she had permission to relay her message into the little loudspeaker on Chairman Ulbricht's desk. If she saw a red light, that meant that she must abandon, until exactly thirty minutes later, any attempt to communicate with Chairman Ulbricht. Thirty minutes later the executive secretary had instructions to begin again, from scratch. If, in response to the little buzzer, two green lights were flashed, that meant that if the visitor Chairman Ulbricht was expecting had arrived, he should without further ado be admitted, always assuming that the secretary had established that the visitor outside his door was, undeniably, the person expected. If a green and a red signal were shown, this meant that the visitor, or the message, was to be passed along in exactly five minutes—i.e., that the Chairman could not, for whatever reason, be interrupted *at this particular moment*. If *both* red lights were shown, that meant that the Chairman had changed his mind about seeing the visitor to whom an audience had been granted, and his secretary was to tell the visitor to seek another appointment at another time. On the other hand, if the initial ring had been other than for the purpose of announcing a visitor, then the secretary, upon seeing the green and the red lights, was to re-signal the Chairman, by ringing again the anemic bell. "Why don't you get those little machines that make the lights blink on and off, Uncle Walter?" Ulbricht's personal aide-de-camp, Caspar Allman, had asked him a few days before. "That way you could double the number of messages you could give Hilda."

"I have thought about that," Ulbricht replied, not looking up from his desk, and wondering for the one thousandth time why he had agreed to take on his widowed sister Ilse's impossible son. Walter Ulbricht was certainly making up for executing the boy's father, he thought, though Caspar's extraordinary fluency in five languages protected the Chairman from charges of nepotism. As if Old Pointy Beard, as the Berliners referred to him (not in his presence—the Chairman would have tattooed his nose, if Lenin had), needed to protect himself from anybody this side of the Kremlin. "And I shall think about it some more if I incline to think about it more. Does that answer your question?"

"Yes, Uncle Walter," the young man said, leaning back on his chair by the mini-desk at the corner of the office, and swatting at a fly that had got on his beardless face, but missing it.

Today being Monday, Chairman Ulbricht looked with particular resignation at his watch. The time was exactly eight o'clock. This meant that he would now be briefed by his chief of staff. He depressed both green buttons, and Herr Erik von Hausen opened the door and came in.

Von Hausen was a small man, fastidiously dressed, in somber blue. He wore pince-nez which, every few minutes, drawing his handkerchief from his side pocket, he would wipe, carefully refolding the handkerchief and replacing it in his pocket.

Ulbricht motioned him to the usual chair, a gesture von

Hausen acknowledged with a "Good morning, Mr. Chairman." And, to one side, "Good morning, Caspar."

"Good morning, sir," Caspar replied.

The Chairman said nothing. He leaned back slightly in his straight chair, the signal that von Hausen was to begin, which he did.

It was the day for the weekly report the Chairman dreaded most hearing. An account of how many East Berliners, and East Germans, had emigrated to West Berlin. The figure for the third week in April, 1961, was an astonishing five thousand and fifteen. Of these, 42 percent, von Hausen went on, had resided in East Berlin. The balance had come into East Berlin from outside the city to one of the eighty-eight transit points, whence they were taken by the West German police to the great processing center at Marienfelde, where they registered their desire either to stay in West Berlin or to fly west, to West Germany.

"What is the current count on the number of East Berliners who work in the Western sector?" Ulbricht asked, tapping his finger on his desk.

"The figures are not exact, Mr. Chairman. Between 53,000 and 53,075."

"Can't you get more exact figures than that?" Ulbricht needed to express his exasperation in some way.

"Those figures strike *me* as pretty exact," Caspar Allman volunteered.

The Chairman turned his head slowly in the direction of his nephew. "Your views on the matter are neither solicited, nor interesting, nor welcome." Caspar shrugged his shoulders, reached over to pick up the copy of the *Neues Deutschland*, and said nothing.

"I tell you, von Hausen," the Chairman declaimed, "pending a final solution to this problem, we have got to increase the difficulties of these cowardly traitors when they set out to desert their fatherland."

"Do you have any suggestions, sir?"

"Run over for me what we are currently doing to discourage the traffic."

Von Hausen leafed through a black notebook, adjusted his glasses, and began to read: "Respecting the flow of citizens from outside Berlin, we have sharply limited the schedule of buses and trains entering the city. The service is erratic, punctuality is discouraged. It is no longer possible in East Germany to count on making any connections if the objective of the voyage is to travel to Berlin."

"Good."

Von Hausen went on: "When passengers board trains or buses, their traveling papers are inspected. Any irregularity is instantly taken as disqualifying, and the passenger is let off at the next station."

Caspar turned down the paper he was reading. "Why not stop the train and make them get off wherever they are? That would make things much more inconvenient for them, wouldn't it?"

Ulbricht's instinct was once again to rebuke his nephew. But before doing so he gave thought to his proposal. "Not a bad idea, von Hausen. Not a bad idea. They might find themselves, with their baggage—which I assume is extensive—fifteen or twenty miles from the nearest telephone. Yes, yes. Good idea, Caspar. What about the day workers coming over to this side?"

"Well, sir, as you know, we have done the following. We do not, effective last week, permit them to buy anything at any East Berlin store unless they pay in East Berlin marks for it, and of course East Berlin marks are trading on the black market at six to one. So if they want to buy something here, they need to pay six times as much for it. What would you think, sir, of adding an additional requirement, that they produce working papers to show that they have earned their marks in the Eastern sector, and also show an exchange slip certifying that any Western marks were exchanged at the official one-to-one rate?"

"That is a capital idea, von Hausen," the Chairman said.

"Why not tattoo all workers who cross the border into West Berlin?"—once more, Caspar Allman turned down his newspaper.

The Chairman stared at his nephew. It occurred to him that the suggestion was ironic. But then it occurred to him that perhaps it was not. From time to time during the months his nephew had been taken on as personal aide, he had shown a rather ingenious turn of mind. The Chairman decided to be patient.

"That would not be feasible, Caspar. In the first place, the exercise is elaborate. In the second place, it would attract entirely too much attention. It isn't as though it could be done to all fifty-three thousand East Berliners in one evening. There is the further problem that tattoos are not easily erased, making it difficult for the traitors to become integrated after their rehabilitation."

"Just trying to be useful," said Caspar, going back to his newspaper and resuming the crossword puzzle.

"We need"—the Chairman began to stride along the length of the room, his head bowed in concentration—"more public . . . emphasis on the nature of the treasonable activities of the Germans who go over to the capitalist-imperialist side of town. I have studied the breakdown you gave me last week. The number of doctors. Of engineers. Of technicians. We are a society of only seventeen million people. Who, at the rate at which this lesion is proceeding, will build our bridges tomorrow, cure our ills, repair our telephones?"

"Could we perhaps hire them to work here?" Caspar volunteered.

"You *idiot!* Hire *our own workers* to come back to *their* native country, and to do there their *own work!*"

He reached his desk chair and sat down, in silence. "The problem," he said, his voice steady, "is the problem of Comrade Khrushchev. He must be made to recognize this.

Meanwhile we must do what we can do, pending a final
solution. . . . Von Hausen, assemble your staff and come
up with supplementary discouragements we might use. Either at the border-crossing points or this side of them. I
want that emigration figure halved during the month of
May. Halved. We will discuss other matters at our afternoon
meeting."

"Yes, Mr. Chairman." Von Hausen bowed his head
slightly, and left the room.

The Chairman turned to his nephew. "Ah, Caspar. The
problems of governing are sometimes of very near super-
human difficulty. What we must do, of course, is close the
Berlin border. Permanently."

"I thought that was illegal under the postwar arrangement?"

"What is illegal and what isn't illegal is a matter of defini-
tion. We have excellent legal interpreters here and in the
Soviet Union."

"What if the legal interpreters in the United States and
Great Britain and France decide that their understanding of
freedom of movement throughout Berlin is the correct understanding?"

"We would need to disabuse them, Caspar. We would
need to disabuse them." Walter Ulbricht looked out his
window in the direction of the border. "I see there," he
said, "a great wall."

"Oh Uncle, walls don't work anymore. Walls were for
Chinese, way back when."

The Chairman paused, considering whether to expand
on his thoughts in the matter. He decided against doing so,
and instead called the meeting to a close. "Tell your
mother I am expecting her tonight at the reception at the
House of Ministries for the winners of the bicycle tourna-
ment. She is to present the main cup. She should be here"
—the Chairman looked down at the time schedule on his
desk—"not later than 5:45. I am lunching with the Polish

Ambassador, and we are conferring during the afternoon. I won't be back here until tomorrow. Get done whatever work you have pending, and take the afternoon off."

"Thank you, Uncle Walter."

"Is that you, Caspar?"

"Yes, Mother. He let me go early today."

"Well, sit down and read. Lunch will be ready in a half hour or so. No, don't sit down and read. Fix the light in the radio. I've asked you to fix it ten times. It's an awful bother at night to tune it."

"I don't have the right bulb for it."

"Did it ever occur to you to go *get* the right bulb for it?"

"Yes, Mother. It has *occurred* to me, but it has not occurred to the German Democratic Republic to requisition any bulbs of that kind. I would need to go to the other side."

"Well"—Mrs. Allman materialized in the doorway of the kitchen, wearing an apron. Her hair had been blond. She was stoutly built, like her brother; and, like her brother, was of imperious turn of mind. But in her face there was a softness that showed through the lines. She looked at her son while slowly, almost absentmindedly, rubbing the frying pan with a little ball of steel wool.

"Darling Caspar, a week ago I said I wouldn't bring it up again, but how are you going to accomplish *anything* in your life with your present attitude? The only thing you know is language. If it is necessary to go to the other side—to West Berlin—to get a light bulb for the radio, why do you not *go* to the other side? The radio the other day said that there are an average of 250,000 crossings every day. Why cannot there be 250,001? I talked with Walter about you just yesterday, and he tells me that you loaf your way right through the day in the office. You are clearly not aware of the advantages you have as a young man working for your uncle, right in his private office. He has always been very indulgent toward me, and he tells me that he likes you personally. But you cannot expect him to tolerate you forever unless you are actively helpful to him. You do understand, don't you, Caspar? You are almost twenty-one years old, and except for your languages, you failed your work in the university. Your father—" but instantly Ilse Allman sought to make her way back: Caspar's father's name was not mentioned in the household. Someday, perhaps, she would talk to her son about his father. Perhaps. For now, she would depersonalize her reference to his dead father. "—Your father's people, you know, were all very industrious. Four brothers, one doctor, one architect, one engineer, one academician. It isn't as though you had been genetically deprived."

"Yes, Mother," Caspar said. "I will certainly try to please my uncle. Remember that I read the Russian and Polish papers for him. And since we have the afternoon off, I will go this very day to Müllerstrasse and get that bulb. What is there for lunch?"

Ilse Allman looked down at her son and returned to the kitchen, the frying pan still in hand. Her voice, the tone resigned, floated back: "Roast pheasant, fried chestnuts, pâté de foie gras, and will you be taking champagne or burgundy?" Caspar smiled and sauntered into the little dining room, a magazine in hand, and sat down, ready to be waited on with the sausage and sauerkraut.

After lunch, Caspar told his mother he was going out "to walk around a bit." She looked at him, exasperated, as she dried the dishes. "And I'll try to get a chance to go to the other side and get you that light bulb." Caspar's young face, with the elfin ears and small, pointed nose, brightened, in his search of indulgence. "Say, Mother, could I borrow a hundred marks?"

His mother put down the dishes, walked upstairs to her bedroom, and came down with the money.

"Stay away from you-know-where and from you-know-who."

"Mother!" Caspar smiled at her, pecked her on the cheek, took up his wool jacket and, before closing the door, called out: "Have fun at the House of Ministries. Don't get run down by any bicyclists!"

Caspar walked out to the quiet, drab street, and to the stationery store on the corner with its public telephone. He nodded to the old lady behind the counter, who declined to return his greeting even as she had declined to return anyone's greeting since that day, eleven years ago, when she was informed that her stationery shop had become public property and that she was to stay on but as a civil servant on fixed salary. She had made it a point to reverse exactly the habits of a lifetime, arriving now fifteen minutes late, and leaving fifteen minutes early. Caspar went to the far corner of the shop and opened the telephone door. He dropped a 10-pfennig piece and dialed Claudia's number. The central operator at the Railway Division of the German Democratic Republic, Berlin Division, answered, and he asked to be put through to Claudia Kirsch, in the office of Herbert Kohl. She answered the telephone.

"Office of Mr. Kohl, Miss Kirsch speaking."

"Is this the most beautiful twenty-one-year-old girl in the socialist world, by any chance?"

"Mr. Kohl is busy at the moment, sir. Might I take a message for him?"

"Yes. Please ask Mr. Kohl if he has any objections if the handsomest boy in East Germany makes love to the handsomest girl in East Germany at 5:30 this afternoon because, frankly, the handsomest boy in East Germany simply cannot be kept waiting any longer."

"I will deliver that message, sir. And where can he find you?"

"He will be waiting in the usual place. He would find it
most convenient if Miss Claudia were to bring along a
bottle of wine. Say a Johannesberg '59? It should be chilled.
There will not be time to chill it before 5:30. In fact, by 5:30
it will be impossible to chill anything. Mmmm. Mm-Mm-
Mm—" Caspar smacked his lips into the mouthpiece, but
quieted down when he noticed that the old lady was looking
suspiciously in his direction.

"I am sure he will do what he can."

Claudia put down the telephone, reached in her purse
for her lipstick, and felt her heart beating. She opened the
middle drawer on the left, felt with her fingers under the
pile of type B envelopes, and pulled out his picture. She
stared at the boy, standing in his swimming trunks, his left
hand raised, leaning casually against the birch tree, the
head slightly bent. He was smiling that languorous smile
she found irresistible. His hair was long, and framed his
pleasant young face. She looked gracefully over his young,
lithe body. "Ah, Caspar," she whispered. "At 5:30. And
again at 6? Who knows." She shivered with anticipation,
and found herself wondering whether the stallmaster at the
commissary would let her have the wine today, even though
the week's coupons did not mature until the following day.

But where had Caspar called in from? Hardly the office.
He had a marvelous knack for idleness. He seemed never in
a hurry—well, except when experiencing certain undeni-
able, understandable needs. She reflected that she did not
know much about him, really, except that he worked for a
government bureaucrat somewhere, and lived alone with
his widowed mother, whom she had never been invited to
meet. They had been seeing each other ever since meeting
at Beetzsee the preceding summer, and she suspected that
notwithstanding his age, he had got about a bit as on one
occasion, answering the questions of a British tourist, he
had spoken to her in English; and, inside Sans Souci, the
former summer residence of Frederick the Great, he had

translated for her Latin and French inscriptions on a number of *objets*, though when she asked him about his language skill he would smile and lazily change the subject, though once he muttered that an uncle, an academician, had taught him a few words in other tongues. He seemed to have no interests other than self-indulgence—and the car. At first this struck Claudia as decadent. But Caspar's good nature overcame her, and she found soon that she had ceased caring about what he did outside the little retreat to which they most generally repaired.

It lay there, forgotten except for its file number, in the northeast quadrant of the old station, on a siding. One of over two hundred similar railroad cars, their exteriors indistinguishable from one another, a dirty, rusty tan. Probably they had all been constructed in the same factory: probably at the Karl-Marx-Stadt Locomotive Works. Claudia did not know when last any of the moldy old cars had actually been pulled out of their siding. They were deemed antiquated. They had been pressed into special service during the war, and were not suited to such traveling as was encouraged since the foundation of the socialist state.

It was after their summer meeting, in September, that he had come one day to the Ostbahnhof at noon during the lunch break, with the two sandwiches and the thermos of tea. He had no trouble in gaining access to the large old station, which abutted the offices of the GDR's Railway Division, with his category Z identification card. They lunched picnic style, sitting on one of many benches near the station's side entrance. After lunch, Caspar had said to her that he would very much like to have a look at car 10206, if it was by any chance in the station.

Why? she asked, but he didn't answer. He simply took her by the hand, and they headed into the dark interior of the sidings in the dusky station, lit only by such daylight as

sifted through narrow skylights running along the long
sides of the building, revealing only amorphously the
shapes of the railroad cars, ancient, abandoned, seemingly
immobile. The venerable caretaker appeared to confine the
little interest he had in his soporific occupation to the eastern end of the station, near the activity of the office building, and the commissary, in the tunnel between the two
structures. Caspar had observed the watchman and, on the
three or four occasions when he and Claudia had lunched
in the station or the commissary, had made it a point to
greet him, however lackadaisically.

Claudia asked how on earth she would know where car
10206 reposed. Caspar had said there were two ways of
finding out. One was for Claudia to search out the relevant
office, and establish by looking at the archives where the car
in question lay, if it was in Berlin. But probably simpler, he
said, would be by touring, and looking at the numbers. He
had a pocket flashlight.

Which they needed, because the dim daylight was insuffi-
cient to permit them to read the identifying lettering at the
bottom right of each car. It was an exasperating business.
There was no evidence of any apparent plan in laying up
the cars. No one number logically preceded, or succeeded,
another. But, she reflected, in fact it had not taken them
very long. The car was the fourth, on the fourth siding from
the westernmost. About two thirds of the way in from the
office building. On track 22, out of 29 tracks.

Caspar tried the door, which was locked. He ducked
under the coupler and tried the door at the other side.
Then he went to the other end of the car and did the same
thing. But all the doors were locked. "Well," he said, "I'll
have to think about that." Claudia had been amused, but it
was time to get back to the office, and so they strolled out
together, and Caspar bade good afternoon to the old
watchman, seated at a cobwebbed ticket stall, reading his
Neues Deutschland.

The very next day Caspar called to suggest another lunch "at the station—like yesterday, okay?" She noticed that he ate his sandwich less indolently than usual. "You want to go back to the car?" she guessed. Yes, he answered; and again he led her, half-eaten sandwich in her free hand. This time they walked, past two dozen tracks, directly to the car. Caspar took the precaution of establishing that the watchman was nowhere in sight. He reached into his pocket and pulled out a shiny bronze key. It required a little coaxing, but the door opened. He stepped up the gangway and reached down for Claudia. The main door into the car was not locked.

Inside, it was black, no daylight seeping through. Caspar switched on his little flashlight and they found themselves in a narrow corridor. There was heavy dust everywhere they flashed the beam. With his index finger Caspar rubbed a line along the bulkhead, revealing, beneath the dust, a soft, shiny rosewood. He flashed the light down and lifted the old newspaper on which they were walking. It hid a thick red carpet. She remembered the catch in her throat when Caspar told her, "We are in Hitler's private railcar."

It became their project to clean the car of its sixteen-year accumulation of dust. It transpired that Caspar knew something about railroad cars, and about the means by which they received electricity, because on the Saturday afternoon when Claudia did not need to work they spent the entire time on their adventure, and while she mopped and cleaned inside, Caspar ran an inconspicuous cable from a socket under the car to a ground connection which, fussing over a fuse box opposite the lead car on the adjacent siding, he contrived to energize. Immediately he tested the blinds and discovered, to his satisfaction, that Adolf Hitler's private railroad car shed no more light today than it had during those nights when the Führer traveled the length of

Germany while British and American bombers preyed
overhead. They were secure.

The following Saturday Caspar addressed himself to the
problem of heat. He hoped at first to be able to introduce
electric heat from the central supply source, behind the
fuse boxes; but this would have required a complicated
recircuiting operation on the old supply station outdoors,
and this he declined to risk. So they settled for four electric
portable heaters, which they brought in one at a time, made
to look like baskets from which they plucked their sandwiches and apples. "These things burn maybe 150 watts
each, that's 600 watts. Added to what the office building
uses, that won't even be noticed," Caspar reassured Claudia. So that when it got really cold, in late October, they
simply left their electric heaters lit when they left the car. It
was mid-November before they deemed their restoration
completed. That morning Caspar telephoned Claudia and
told her not to appear at the car until five o'clock—she had
her own key by now—as he wished to surprise her.

He certainly had done so. Preoccupied as she had been
with details of cleaning and immediately protecting her
work with newspapers, she had not really before gazed at
the car, now repristinated.

The car was divided into four areas. At the far end was a
salon that could be used as a dining room around whose
table twelve persons could sit, or as a meeting room. The
woods were of splendid hue, the carpeting, though obviously worn, was rich. Vertical antique brass strips decorated
and gave shape to its opulent but utilitarian dimensions.
Settees ran along the length of the room on either side of
the table, which could open to full length or to smaller sizes
and, running on a track almost invisible in the carpet, could
slide back behind one of the settees. The second, slightly
smaller, area could be closed off by a sliding door or left
open. It was a comfortable lounge in which the Führer
evidently sat, a wooden desk-tray available to him folding

out from its vertical chamber. One of the two seats that faced each other had clearly been the Führer's private preserve, because an elaborate Nazi symbol, in ivory and red velvet, was fixed just above head level. Opposite were two more padded reclining chairs, and at either end, large bulletproofed windows. Two small but clearly precious chandeliers perched above the two sides of the salon, crystal spiders holding the little prisms rigid, to keep them from jangling. To the right of the Führer's seat was a cabinet, within which were two telephones and a control panel. Beneath it was room for stationery. And in a drawer lined in green felt there were still papers, which neither Caspar nor Claudia had yet bothered to examine. ("Perhaps they are Hitler's secret diaries," Caspar commented teasingly. "In that case," Claudia said, "we could sell them to an American magazine and be rich!") Obviously the car had been only cursorily examined by the Russians, and then evidently mislaid, sitting all those years with the ugly duckling troop cars from which it was indistinguishable.

Now Caspar led her to the bedroom. Two small candelabra sconces at either end of the headboard framed the husky bed, made up now with fresh sheets purloined from Caspar's mother. The headboard was of red leather with a golden swastika sewn into the material. The foot of the bed pointed in the direction the car was designed to move. It lay snug along the bulletproofed, reinforced bulkhead, though Hitler could, if he wished, open a blind at waist level to look outdoors without ever exposing his face to view. To the right lay a night table with three open trays, the first supporting a signaling device and telephone, the second and third available for books—there were several still there. There was ample standing closet space, a desk, a large bathroom. The walls were lined in leather. They resolved to christen the car "Berchtesgaden" after the beautiful mountain retreat of its nefarious owner.

The bed was made, the heater lit, the wine chilled. Cas-

par turned down the near light and tendered Claudia an
invitation to go around the world with him. She laughed,
delighted, and between the sheets Caspar soon permitted
himself to wonder that so much pleasure could be experienced on a bed of a man who had given so much pain: a bed
that sat in a railroad car especially designed by Caspar's late
father, for his Führer.

4

On March 28, 1961, at 7:45 P.M., the door at the Georgievsky Hall of the Kremlin opened. No one had ever been able to pinpoint the means by which Nikita Khrushchev announced his impending presence. There were no buglers. The lights did not go out. The waiters with the cocktail trays did not suddenly stop. What did happen was that everybody suddenly froze. Not for as long as they'd have done back when Stalin would come into a room. But somehow—whether by smell or by intuition—Khrushchev's arrival was communicated. And, of course, he was instantly the center of attention. On one occasion, six months earlier, when for over a full hour he had not emerged as the center of attention, he had taken off his shoe and banged it on the desk at the General Assembly of the United Nations, which had served instantly to reorder the Assembly's sense of hierarchy. There was no need to do that in the Kremlin; indeed, very little need to do that anywhere Khrushchev went.

He was in an excellent mood, and he greeted with equal effusiveness the leader of Poland, the leader of Hungary, the leader of Romania, the leader of Bulgaria, the leader of Czechoslovakia, and the leader of the German Democratic Republic, at whose virtual insistence Khrushchev had brought together his proconsuls to discuss, of course, the crisis of Berlin. Khrushchev had decided what would be the outcome of this meeting, but he had developed, for international and domestic reasons, the techniques of democratic practice; indeed, he rather delighted in them. "Eh, Comrade Kadar, and what do you think of our five-year plan?" as if he cared what Comrade Kadar thought about Khrushchev's five-year plan, though he'd have cared to know if Comrade Kadar harbored any disloyal thoughts about Khrushchev's five-year plan, or about anything else Khrushchev had determined upon. Still, after all the cult-of-the-personality business involving Stalin, and the jockeying to oust Malenkov, Khrushchev liked it this way, and was never more confident than during this season, notwithstanding that the non-invitation to Enver Hoxha of Albania seemed finally to certify that that *idiotic* man had fallen for the malevolent inventions Mao Tse-tung was dispensing about the Soviet Union.

Yes yes, he reassured Gheorghiu-Dej, he had greatly enjoyed his visit to Romania in 1959, and he wanted Gheorghiu-Dej to come to Moscow under circumstances less hectic than this one. Would Comrade Khrushchev be scheduling a meeting with President Kennedy? Well, he didn't yet know, not for sure. Yes, he said to Ulbricht, who was anxious to make at least *one* comment in the course of the two days that did not relate directly to Berlin, yes he was indeed very pleased and very proud that the Trans-Siberian Railroad had been electrified between Moscow and Irkutsk. And no, the spy trials in London of Gordon Lonsdale and George Blake and the Krogers, four anti-imperialists who loved mankind better than native fascist rulers, would *not* result in the cancellation of the planned British trade fair scheduled to be held in Moscow. "I occasionally feel the need to cancel a *summit* conference," Khrushchev said jovially, referring to the disaster in Paris the preceding June, "but I am very selective about my cancellations." Khrushchev then tried to cheer up Walter Ulbricht, whose general glumness was affecting the natural gaiety of the company. "Did you hear the one, Walter"—Khrushchev was given to using first names, after initial formalities—"about the couple sitting in Gorky Park, and the boy says to the girl, 'It's raining.' And she replies, "No, Rudolf, it's *snowing.*' And he says to her, 'Sonya, Rudolf the Red knows rain, dear.' " Khrushchev laughed uproariously, as did everyone within earshot. Ulbricht forced a chuckle, and then said he wondered whether the joke translated into English, and Khrushchev retorted that it had not yet been established even that Marxism translated into English! The crowd roared. The chairman of the party in Bulgaria said he would like to make a toast, and the two dozen guests politely stopped the chatter, and then Todor Zhivkov said, "Chairman Khrushchev, this is the year in which Yuri Gagarin from the socialist motherland will stun the world by orbiting the earth in a satellite, while the leader of the imperialist world hopes only to transport a Mr. Alan Shepard from Cape Canaveral to Nassau!" There was a general clamor, hoots of derisory laughter, and then Chairman Khrushchev led them to the other end of the room, where the buffet had been prepared. He had privately decided against a seated dinner, on the grounds that in such circumstances business matters tend to come up, and business matters he wished to put off until the morning. Meanwhile they would eat the smoked salmon, and the caviar, and the fresh bread, and the cucumbers, and the roast duck and the vodka. It was somehow understood that the host did not want raised the subject of Berlin.

It was a very different Chairman who, the next morning in the stately Chekhov Room, brought to order the Warsaw Pact's political consultative committee. He came right to the point, and said that the assembly would listen to Comrade Ulbricht.

Ulbricht stood and delivered his carefully thought-out speech. It lasted for very nearly one hour, and told of the seductions with which the imperialist forces were coaxing away into West Berlin, and then on to West Germany, what threatened eventually to add up to the entire professional cadre of East Berlin. He permitted himself an occasional hyperbole. How, for instance, could one set out to build a gibbet if every carpenter in the Democratic Republic of Germany had gone West? He gave the figures for the out-flow—two hundred thousand in 1960. This was something, he said, that threatened the very life of the country. And to the extent that his country was threatened, so were his partners in the Warsaw Pact. Indeed, so also was the mother country, the Union of Soviet Socialist Republics. For that reason, he wished to make a proposal.

The leaders looked to the head of the table. Khrushchev said nothing.

What was the proposal? someone asked.

Well, said Ulbricht, he wished to call to the attention of the present company something some of them may have known and forgotten. Back in the early fifties, when the unpleasantness had taken place and there had been a strike against the government, he and Wilhelm Pieck had in-structed engineers to devise a plan physically to partition the City of Berlin. In fact, when American intelligence offi-cials became familiar with that plan, they dubbed it "Oper-ation Chinese Wall." The plans for that operation were highly detailed. The exact boundary had been traced, mak-ing a line twenty-eight miles long. Along this line, Ulbricht explained, would be erected a barbed-wire barrier. Passage points between East and West would be reduced to three. Perhaps two. Conceivably just one. Only that way would the hemorrhage be stopped. Ulbricht did not divulge that Operation Chinese Wall called for erecting a wall made of brick and mortar over the barbed wire. Save that bit for some other time.

There was silence. Khrushchev was also silent. But Khru-shchev knew that the silence would not last. He had planned ahead. Comrade Kadar of Hungary rose to say that he thought the move certainly provocative, probably dangerous, and in any event drastic in its potential for propaganda exploitation by the West. Ulbricht replied that Kadar's Hungary had, apparently without mortal psychological difficulty, survived the border controls operated by the Hungarians along the Austrian frontier. Gheorghiu-Dej of Romania said that it was obvious to him that the West would simply not tolerate what would amount to a repeal of Western rights of access into East Berlin and, by inference, the right of East Berliners to go West. To precipitate a crisis with the brand-new American President—who had campaigned in part on the necessity to be tough, and who in his warmongering inaugural address had said that the United States would pay any price, bear any burden to—he forgot just how Kennedy had put it—to further imperialist interests—to challenge such an American President who had made so straightforward a commitment—would be foolhardy.

At this point Chairman Khrushchev spoke. He said he had listened carefully to the exchanges that had now gone on for almost two hours. That his own view was that it was unwise to challenge the Americans in a local theater; that the Warsaw Pact powers were better off with the ultimatum the Soviet Union had delivered: namely, that before the year's end the Soviet Union would, with or without joint action with its wartime allies, conclude a peace treaty with East Germany. But, said Khrushchev, it was necessary, before proceeding practically with that demarche, to weigh its consequences. To confuse the grander strategic idea of a peace treaty that after all would give to the German Democratic Republic the right to run the *entire* city of Berlin, with the lesser issue of East Berlin itself, was not, in his judgment, a good idea. However, said Khrushchev, he would certainly be guided—he would certainly be *advised* by—his *partners* in the Pact. So he would like for them to take a vote. He would not, he said, himself participate in that vote.

He went around the table.

The vote was unanimous to reject Operation Chinese Wall.

Khrushchev announced that lunch would be served in the adjacent room.

He called Ulbricht over to the corner and lowered his voice. "It will not be made public knowledge for a little while. But I am going to see Kennedy. After I talk with him, I will have a better idea of how we can deal with him. Meanwhile, you have my word for it that we will increase our troop strength in the Berlin area." He patted Ulbricht on the back, there's a good fellow. Ulbricht was silent during the lunch, after which the consultative committee broke up, and Ulbricht flew back to Berlin, and instructed his Minister for National Security, Erich Honecker, to begin to assemble, but with the utmost secrecy, a huge deposit of construction materials.

5

At the corner of Breite and Mecklenburgische Strasse Blackford Oakes got off the bus. It had been a year since Blackford had lived in Berlin, on assignment, and he knew the city, through which he had roamed so thoroughly, well. He was pleased that his German, studied and practiced so intensively in the fifties, continued to serve him. Not a bad idea to search out *something* pleasing to him, he pondered. Little else was going well, professionally or personally. The quarrel with Sally in Washington, about which he had got so inflamed, seemed now trivial in the lowering threat of a new war in Europe. On the other hand, what strikes some as trivial, others will die for. Ten million people were inflamed enough to die in the first world war, and Blackford had to reach into the recesses of his memory to remember exactly what *that* war was all about. Die against Hitler, yes. But the Kaiser? Worth dying to frustrate the Kaiser?

On the other hand, some people were saying the same kind of thing even now. Worth dying mainly to frustrate the Kremlin? Sally simply didn't think so, never mind that she was briefly swept up in the enterprise. But her ultimatum had been firmly stated: he must leave the Agency—or leave her. He wanted her more than he wanted the Agency, but he could not leave it under such circumstances.

Besides, he reasoned, his desire for Sally was personal. His desire to frustrate the Kremlin was also personal, but also something else—what exactly, he could not say. Was he, he taxed himself, experiencing an afflatus? Oh dear.

Just about everybody he knew with a personal sense of mission was something of a bore. Was he becoming a bore, he wondered? He wasn't preachy, true. On the other hand, engaged in black operations for the CIA you could hardly go around carrying a sandwich board reading, "DO YOU WANT TO HEAR ABOUT THE LATEST SOVIET ATROCITY?" And the men and women with whom he mingled didn't feel the need to opine, regularly, on the subject of why it was they were engaged as they were. He knew that one or two, or maybe ten times one or two, of the men he had worked with were simply working at this job instead of working at another job. But he knew also that this was not so with such as Rufus, or Anthony Trust, who had got him into the Agency as a senior at Yale. They did understand themselves to be engaged in the organic job of maintaining peace, and freedom. And they *were* engaged in important work. So why, Blackford wondered as he entered the house on Mecklenburgische Strasse, did he need to reiterate this to himself at this point? Because, he conceded, the long ache for Sally needed to be sublimated.

Useful word, that. What word did they use to describe that phenomenon before Freud came along with sublimate? He would think about that. As a matter of fact, he probably could find out from Henri Tod. After six hours with him yesterday, Blackford Oakes was satisfied that Tod knew just about everything there was to know about the operation of the Democratic Republic of Germany, and probably knew most of everything else.

Really the most unusual young man Blackford had ever run into. Young? Well, Rufus's dopesheet said Henri had been born "December 1927"—which made him exactly two years younger than Blackford, who was thirty-five. At some point, Blackford thought, I must ask him whether Henri was also born December 7—Blackford's birthday and a day that will live in infamy; only it won't, Blackford smiled to himself. The guy who led the raid against Pearl

Harbor had recently visited Pearl Harbor and was practically treated like a hero.

Blackford rang the bell for apartment 3B, and a woman's voice came out over the little loudspeaker on the bell panel: "Who is it?"

Blackford replied, "This is Mr. Eccles. I'm expected."

The identification had been given him when he dialed a number that morning. The buzzer released the lock, he climbed up three flights of stairs and again rang the buzzer on the right-hand door, and was admitted.

He smiled at Sophie, and said good morning. She returned the greeting and led him past the sitting room and dining room to the study. To the study of Henri Tod, who was sitting in his easy chair, reading the East Berlin daily. Tod motioned Blackford to a chair and said, "My sources have informed me that Gromyko met with Thompson yesterday, and the day before. And now the Soviet Foreign Minister and the American Ambassador to the Soviet Union have agreed that their principals will meet. Early in June."

Tod spoke in English with only a trace of a German accent, though the British accent was pronounced. He was dressed in gray flannel pants and a crew-neck wool sweater. His face was Semitic in general appearance, olive-skinned, long fine nose, brown eyes, his hair dark, lank. His teeth were pearl-white, his words were intensely articulated, but quiet in modulation. Blackford had struggled yesterday to recall whose voice Tod's reminded him of, but gave up after a while . . . Was it the man in *Casablanca?* Ingrid Bergman's husband, what's-his-name?

"The Bruderschaft certainly gets around. I am crestfallen that you have not ascertained the exact place and day in which they are going to meet."

Tod smiled. "The exact date has not been set. But it will be early in June."

"Where?"

"Vienna. Khrushchev wanted Helsinki, but Kennedy held out for Vienna. Thompson stressed that after all, Vienna has been faithfully neutral, and therefore Khrushchev shouldn't object. Kennedy has got a memo from Secretary McNamara on the Berlin situation, but I don't know what's in it. Yet. Now, Blackford, what do you have for me?"

"Nothing you don't know. The military people—General Watson, Colonel von Pawel—are waiting for Washington to formulate a range of responses. Maybe the McNamara report you're talking about will flesh out policy. As things now stand, our people don't know what the exact response is going to be to whatever it is Khrushchev and Ulbricht come up with. And we're supposed to tell Washington exactly what it is that they *are* going to come up with. If you want the truth, Henri, I think it's this simple: The United States does not *have* contingency plans addressed to the sealing off of the Berlin border. Our contingency plans, I think, relate to grander stuff. A Communist ring around West Berlin. Isolating the city again; 1948. Does the Bruderschaft have contingency plans?"

Blackford only half playfully referred to Tod's organization of secret young operatives as though it were a foreign army.

"Let's go to lunch."

Several things about Henri Tod became clear to Blackford in the weeks that followed, during which they were so frequently together. The breadth of Henri's operations went far further than those of Blackford. The Bruderschaft he had organized was on the order of a resistance movement. And for that reason, no formal affiliation with official Allied operations was permissible. The Bruderschaft, indeed, engaged in activities in East Berlin and East Germany that were plainly unlawful under Communist law, and would have been even under Western laws, had they applied. But the Bruderschaft and Allied intelligence agencies had very much in common a desire to know one thing, namely what did Khrushchev intend to do in and around Berlin; and when did he intend to do it? How the West would respond was of course of vital interest to Henri Tod. But he never gave the West's representative any reason to believe that he would be bound by the West's conclusions in this matter. Henri Tod therefore desired a certain explicit alienation from Western operations; and Western operators desired an equally explicit alienation from the operations of the Bruderschaft. This dichotomy figured in the relations between Henri Tod and Blackford Oakes, and Blackford was formally careful not to inquire into the operations of the Bruderschaft, even as Henri drew the line carefully in his questions to Blackford. But the obsessive question being the one that brought them together—What would Khrushchev do?—there was much to share, and reason to spend many hours together.

Blackford saw in Henri signs of the disciplinarian. But it was not gratuitous, reflecting rather his sense of what was expected of him, not least of what he expected of himself. There was, Blackford noted one evening when the conversation digressed, a haunting distraction there. Something that lay in the back of the mind of Henri Tod. Conceivably, not even Tod knew exactly what it was, or exactly what hold it had on him. The devotion to him of his colleagues was not only an act of gratitude for the spirit he represented— the unity of free Germans—but a recognition of Tod's personal courage. He regularly put himself on the duty roster, engaging in dangerous activity, armed always with the cyanide capsule in the event he was captured. But he would be detected in acts of personal kindness. There was the widow of young Ochlander, who had been captured, tortured, and executed. Although she had removed, with her young son, to France to live, she regularly received personal letters from her late husband's leader, and these she took to copy-

ing and sending to her husband's closest friends. They in
turn gave the letters discreet circulation. And in them
Henri, who had known the widow only slightly, gave evidence of his great reserves of sympathy, of his desire to
assuage suffering, of his determination to convince Hilda
that her husband's sacrifice had made an important contri-
bution. Several times when a member of the society, fighting for his life in a hospital bed or—when the nature of the
operation that had caused his wound kept him from a hospital—lying in a safe house, tended to by Bruni or by other
doctors brought in, the companion posted to sit by the
patient during the night would, at two or three in the morning, look up to find Henri Tod, silently entering into the
room, who would nod the attendant out. "Go and get some
sleep. I will stay here."

Blackford at first only admired Henri Tod. But very soon
after, he began to like Henri Tod. In the end he would come
to love him. And now he accepted without resentment the
boundary beyond which Henri would not admit him. It was
primarily, Blackford reflected, a professional boundary.
And Blackford was right in supposing so. Because Henri
Tod had vowed many years ago that he would not again
impulsively reveal information that should be kept secret;
not again, that once having been more than a lifetime's
ration.

6

Henri Toddweiss (they called him Heinrich in those days) and Clementa (Clementina) had always shared the same bedroom, and did so even now, aged thirteen and eleven. It wouldn't be until the following year that they would get separate quarters, their mother said: so it had been in her own family, and in that of her husband. Henri and Clementa had privately sworn never to sleep other than in a single room. Moreover, they swore according to the sacred rites of a society so secret that it had only two members, Henri and Clementa, and even beyond that, so secret that no one else in the entire world knew of its existence, not even Hilda, who knew most things about her little charges, and in whom they confided most things. But not about their society.

They called it The Valhalla, because everyone who was a member of it was, if not quite a god or a goddess, a king or queen. Clementa, when she was ten, had presided over the coronation of Henri, and it had been a most solemn occasion, conducted in the bathhouse outside the swimming pool at Pinneberg, where they lived then. And the very next day, King Heinrich had presided over the equally ceremonial investiture of Queen Clementa. Each now had a staff of office, for which purpose they had taken two golf clubs from a discarded set of their father. Clementa had complained that her wand was unwieldy, but Henri had reassured her that she would grow into it: so at least twice every week, usually on Wednesday afternoons and Saturdays, they convened the royal court—not, during the summers, in the bathhouse, which was otherwise engaged. But their court was mobile, and met sometimes in the attic, sometimes outdoors, in the little glade at the end of the property. On such occasions they heard petitions from their subjects, discussed matters of royal moment—for instance, whether Hilda should postpone the hour at which she turned off their reading light. Always, they would refer to themselves with proper respect. "Is Queen Clementa satisfied with the service Her Majesty is getting, or does she desire King Heinrich to behead anyone?" "Sire, I would not go so far, but Stefan [Stefan was the groom] I think should be given forty lashes, because he was not properly dressed yesterday when Her Majesty went to the stable to ride." King Heinrich would write in his notepad, and move his lips as he spelled out the sentence he would mete out: Stefan, 40 lashes.

Every Saturday morning they were given their spending money, and in recognition of Henri's seniority he got two marks, while Clementa got only one mark fifty. But Clementa knew that she could confidently expect to find, that Saturday night under her pillow, an envelope with twenty-five pfennigs. And, written on the envelope, with crayons of different hue, a note. Last week's was, *His Majesty King Heinrich has ordered that this purse be put at the disposal of Her Majesty, the Queen.*

The messages would vary. And once, when Clementa was eleven, she found on the envelope a note advising the Queen that her purse this week would come to only twenty pfennigs, because His Majesty had seen her eat an American hot dog at the school picnic, and at age eleven the Queen should know that Jews do not eat hot dogs, under any circumstances. But the King added that he did not intend to report the infraction to their parents.

They didn't know what time it was that night when Hilda roused them. They had been asleep, and it was dark outside —it might have been eleven in the evening, or four in the morning. Hilda had turned on the lights and quickly placed on their beds a set of clothes and told them to get dressed instantly, not to utter a single word, that she was carrying out the instructions of their parents, and that the success of the enterprise absolutely required that they utter not a single word. "We will talk later," she said.

Confused and bleary-eyed, but with a sense of adventure, they dressed, and looked at each other, exchanging The Valhalla signal pledging secrecy to their proceedings. Hilda had two suitcases in hand, and outside a car was waiting. Not one they had ever ridden in before, or even seen before, and the driver was a stranger to them and spoke not a word, even as Henri and Clementa kept their silent pact. What was distressing was the near ferocity with which Hilda embraced them, each in turn, as she shoved them into the car. "I will see you tomorrow," she said. But when the car drove off Clementa whispered to Henri, "Hilda was crying!"

"Shh," Henri said, removing himself to the corner of the seat. By the time they reached Tolk, a two-hour drive, it was dawn. Clementa began to cry, and so the spell was broken as they drove, finally, into the little farm where they were met by the Wurmbrands.

Mrs. Wurmbrand told them that they would be staying here at the farm for a while, that such were the instructions of their parents, who would be absent for a spell, but soon they too would come. Meanwhile, Mrs. Wurmbrand had said, they must refer to their hosts as Aunt Steffi and Uncle Hans. Now they must go to bed, and she would talk to them more later in the morning.

If asked when did he and Clementa realize that they would not again be seeing their mother or father—or Hilda —Henri could not answer. For the first few months, Aunt Steffi simply kept postponing the day on which they could expect to see their parents. When, after the first fortnight, Clementa had asked why her parents had not written a letter, Aunt Steffi said curtly that where her mother was, there was no post office. At the time, Henri had not known how to interpret this retort. Aunt Steffi was kind, but not demonstrative—but this time she had put down the telephone in the kitchen during dinner, after an exchange of only a couple of minutes, during which she had contributed practically nothing except to say, "Yes . . . Yes . . . I understand . . . Yes." She had then, inexplicably, leaned down and embraced first Clementa, then Henri, and had left the kitchen so quickly that, though Henri could not absolutely swear on it when he and Clementa discussed the episode, he thought she was in tears; certainly there had been a noticeable heaving of her bosom. By the time Henri had reached age fourteen, he had guessed that that was the conversation at which Aunt Steffi had got news of his parents' annihilation. When he was fifteen he would find out: at Belsen.

In those early days, Uncle Hans told them that the war had brought on a number of difficulties and hardships, and that it was important to take certain precautions. For instance, under no circumstances must they discuss politics, not with anyone. This instruction Henri found extremely easy, because he didn't know anything about politics, except that there was a war going on, and Hitler was the head of the country, and Henri was quite certain his father didn't like Hitler. A few weeks later, Uncle Hans told them he was going to enroll them in the little school at Tolk. He told them that—"now listen to me very carefully"—they were to pass as orphans, the children of a Danish mother and Uncle Hans's brother. Their parents had died in a car crash when they were very young children, they had been brought up by a cousin near Hamburg, and when that cousin died they had been brought to Tolk. Their surname was Tod.

This deception they managed without difficulty, and without difficulty they mingled with the children, most of them, like Uncle Hans, sons and daughters of farmers. The schoolmaster, after two months, was called away to serve in the army, and passed along the teaching job to a widowed sister, who was a proficient disciplinarian. Her attention gravitated toward students in whom she detected curiosity, and before long Henri was reading special books assigned by her, and handling English with considerable fluency, as was Clementa.

And so it was that, gradually, the profile of Nazi Germany transpired in his mind, and Henri gradually came to know what it was all about. He and Clementa were Jewish; they were being protected, for some reason he did not know, by "Aunt" Steffi and by "Uncle" Hans, and if it were known that they were in fact Jewish, they would be taken away, perhaps to wherever it was that their mother and father had been taken. All this he passed on to his sister, but only after he had thoroughly digested the data and it had become clear to him that Clementa could take the news with fortitude.

They were never apart. The schoolhouse had only the one room for the forty-odd students. When they returned from classes they worked, side by side, helping Uncle Hans with the cows or with the hay; or Aunt Steffi, in the kitchen. She quickly noticed that they liked to be together, and for that reason did not separate the chores by assigning kitchen work to Clementa and outdoor work to Henri. They were put to work together, indoors and out. When it got dark they went into Henri's bedroom, which doubled as a study, and did their homework, Henri helping Clementa with her work, she, occasionally, with his. Supper was increasingly unimaginative fare, as shortages multiplied, but they were

never hungry. After supper they would resume their homework and then, for one half hour, they were permitted to
play games, and there was a checkers set, and some playing
cards. After a year or so they were permitted to listen to the
radio, which broadcast news of one Nazi victory after another, although they did finally conclude, after a few weeks
of trying to sort it all out, that the Nazi army had *not* undertaken an amphibious operation against England; and de-
scriptions of enemy bombers shot down suggested that
there were considerab!e Allied air raids going on. In Tolk,
so near the Danish border, it wasn't often that they saw
enemy aircraft overhead, although blackout precautions
were rigorously observed.

One day, two months before Henri's sixteenth birthday,
just before noon, the children heard the sound of a motor-
cycle, the roar diminishing to the whine, then the little
stutter, as the engine was turned off. Directly outside the
schoolhouse. There was no knock on the door. It opened,
and an elderly man—someone had once pointed him out to
Henri as the mayor of Tolk, also its postmaster and under-
taker—escorted in a hulky young man dressed in a Nazi
uniform.

The mayor approached Mrs. Taussig at her desk in front
of the blackboard and whispered to her. The Nazi officer
was meanwhile scrutinizing the children and taking notes.
He said nothing. Mrs. Taussig addressed the class. "Children, the gentleman from the army here has been sent to
check on draft registration." She was interrupted by the
officer, who spoke to her in a quiet voice that could not be
heard. Mrs. Taussig then transcribed the order: "The captain wishes all the girls to leave the room."

They did so, rather in a hurry. Clementa managed to grip
Henri's hand on the way out.

Now the captain took over. He was very young, perhaps

twenty-five. His brown hair was clipped short, his frame husky, his voice metallic. "How many of you are sixteen years old or over sixteen, raise your hands."

Two of them did so. "Move to that side of the room." The captain reordered the seating.

"How many of you are fifteen years old?" Henri and one other boy raised their hands. "All right, the rest of you are dismissed. Wait a minute"—he pointed to a boy leaving, who looked older than the others—"you. What is your name?"

"Paul, sir."

"Paul what?"

"Paul Steiner."

"Steiner? Stay here."

The captain was interested in four things. He wanted to know by documentary evidence whether either of the two boys who had given their age as fifteen might actually already be sixteen. And he wanted to know whether Steiner was Jewish. Concerning the first point, the captain wanted supplementary proof other than that which school enrollment records provided, so Henri and Siegfried were sent home to consult their parents. Steiner, with the name suspiciously Jewish, was asked where he had been baptized. He replied that he didn't know. Mrs. Taussig intervened and said that the boy's parents were Lutherans, to her certain knowledge, as she regularly saw them in church on Sundays. The captain was finally satisfied, and now needed from Steiner only proof that he was not yet sixteen.

Uncle Hans had two years earlier foreseen the need for papers. Having through sources established that St. Bonaventure's Church in Hamburg had been bombed and all its records destroyed, he procured on St. Bonaventure's stationery a baptismal certificate, dated December 7, 1928, which listed Henri's birthdate as one year earlier. In longhand he wrote that his nephew had been born in Denmark, at his mother's home, and that when Henri's mother and

father were killed in the auto accident, they had merely
been visiting in Germany, so that no papers concerning
their son and daughter were in hand, and that he had never
known where his dead brother had kept such papers. "Give
this to the captain, and if he wishes to see me, tell him I am
here, at work, and would be glad to see him."

It worked. But the captain had made careful notes, and
told Henri, Siegfried, and Kurt that they would receive
notices within thirty days of their sixteenth birthday telling
them where they were to report for induction into the army.
The senior boys would be receiving their notices right
away. He put away his writing materials, bowed perfunctorily to Mrs. Taussig, and left the schoolhouse.

After dinner Uncle Hans informed Henri that he needed
to talk with him. The spring evening was warm, and Uncle
Hans said they might take a little walk. It was then that he
told Henri that he must go abroad, that contingency plans
had been made to take him to England. The following day,
right after dinner, a resistance member would pick him up
and take him to Tönning, on the North Sea. He would be
delivered there into friendly hands, and by the end of the
week he would be in England. Once there, a Mr. Wallenberg would look after him. When the war was over—as,
Uncle Hans said, surely it would be over, within a year or so
—he would be reunited with Clementa.

Henri, up until now compliant in attitude, stopped dead
in his tracks. What? Leave without Clementa? He came
close to hysteria. He would do no such thing, ever ever ever
ever. Uncle Hans replied calmly that he had no choice in
the matter, that resistance leaders made such decisions,
that they had evidently reasoned that Clementa, as a girl,
was in no danger, unlike Henri, who stood to be drafted in a
matter of weeks. Henri replied that he would rather be
drafted than leave Clementa. Hans Wurmbrand replied

that to be drafted would hardly put him any closer to his
sister. Henri threw himself into a mound of hay at the side
of the pathway, and half swore, half cried that he could not
leave Clementa. Hans Wurmbrand reasoned correctly that
he should let the matter drop for the moment and confer
with Clementa.

And of course he did; and of course Clementa went to
Henri and told him that if he truly loved her he would leave,
and be safe, until the war was over. He had cried, inconsol-
able at the thought of their separation; but agreeing, finally,
to go. They stayed up until early in the morning, talking,
exchanging endearments. At school that final day he could
not bear to look in her direction, or she in his, and halfway
through dinner, after removing the soup plates, Clementa
crept upstairs and shut her door. Aunt Steffi handed Henri
a note. He opened it. Clementa had written, "You must not
say goodbye to me. I will see you very very soon. I know I
will. Besides, that is the royal command of Queen Clementa, who loves her King Heinrich so very much." Henri
lunged out of the door, and wept uncontrollably until the
car came, and after hugging his adopted parents he went off
with the stranger and two weeks later was enrolled in St.
Paul's School in London as a boarding student.

Mr. Wallenberg told Henri that he had been a friend of
Henri's father, that he would look after Henri until the war
was over, that Henri was to be extremely careful not to
divulge to anyone the circumstances of his departure from
Germany or give any clue concerning the practices of the
apparatus that had brought him to safety, and above all he
was not to breathe a word of the existence of his sister, or of
the Wurmbrands. Special arrangements would be made to
instruct him in the Jewish religion, but this was to be done
during the vacation period because his Jewish background,

combined with the obvious fact that he was German, might arouse curiosity in someone capable of making mischief.

To all of this Henri of course assented, but he was astonished on being told that there was no way in which he might communicate with Clementa, that the resistance was simply not willing to run risks in order to deliver correspondence. The day he heard that—the day before entering the school —he resolved that he would write her a letter every single night and, after the war, he would give her the whole collection to show her that he had not let a day go by without thinking of her.

St. Paul's School could not remember when last it had received a student of such energy and talent. Although the curriculum was very different from what he had got used to at Tolk, it was only a matter of weeks before the necessary adjustments were made. Before the semester was over, Henri was receiving all A's—in Latin, Maths, English, Geography, Greek, and History. He was permitted to stay at the school during the summer vacation, during which he studied and did chores twenty hours every week. By the beginning of the Michaelmas term he was jumped in grade to the fifth form. Several months later, soon after his seventeenth birthday, he was elected school captain, his office to begin in the Lent term, after the holidays of December 1944.

That was the night. It was traditional that the captain-elect and his prefects should be taken by their predecessors to the Aldwyn Chop House, next door to the school, a favorite and handy restaurant for visiting parents. It was the unspoken tradition of the school that on that night the captain and outgoing prefects would entertain their successors and dip deep into the Aldwyn's inexhaustible supply of ale. The headmaster of St. Paul's had himself staggered out of Aldwyn's sometime after midnight thirty years ago, and so—on that one night—the school's stern rules were, very simply, overlooked.

Henri had not tasted beer before, but of course as captain-elect he was the special object of the revelers. The incumbent captain rose with toast after toast to Henri Tod, the German boy who in a little over a year had had such a meteoric career at the same school as the great General Montgomery—Montgomery, who would be the first to reach Berlin (cheers!), by God, and show those Krauts (nothing personal, Tod) who was who, and maybe General Montgomery would bring back Hitler's mustache to frame in the school's museum (cheers!). Are you willing to drink to that, Tod?

Henri lifted his glass solemnly to the defeat of Hitler. To the defeat of Hitler *and* the Germans, corrected Espy Major.

Wait a minute, wait a minute, Henri smiled, jug in hand, there *are* some good Germans, you know, please don't think that they are all like Adolf Hitler.

Well, said Espy, there are certainly a lot of Germans who are taking orders from Adolf Hitler and a lot of Germans who have been cheering Adolf Hitler all these years. Perhaps, he said, Tod was so engaged in his studies while in Germany that he didn't have a chance to find out what was happening to other people?

Henri at this point could not quite focus, either on his companions or on the question. But he felt a compulsive need to straighten Espy out, and so, as the boys began filing out to cross the street to the campus and to their dormitories, Henri approached Espy and asked him to come with him for a minute to the corner of the room, as there was something he wished him to know. Espy good-naturedly did so. "But first," Henri said solemnly, trying to remind himself how one was supposed to look when one looked solemn, "first, you must promise me that you will never tell anyone what I am about to tell you." Espy promised, solemnly, that as long as he lived, Tod's secret would be safe. Well, said Henri, he *had* suffered. He was a Jew. His parents had been taken away and killed in a concentration camp. He had a sister, her name was Clementa. She hid out in a town called Tolk, with a family called Wurmbrand. They pretended that Clementa and Henri were their niece and nephew. They had looked after them since he was thirteen, and they were in touch with the Resistance. And the Resistance had brought him safely to England. Was this not evidence that there were indeed good Germans?

Espy Major whistled, and whispered that he'd had no idea that Tod had gone through so much, and that he wished immediately to modify any suggestion that Tod had not known danger. Whereupon they shook hands, rose, and Henri was very sick. Espy led him to his bed.

Three weeks later, Henri was surprised to be called out of his Greek class. Mr. Wallenberg had secured permission of the headmaster to interrupt him, and was waiting for him in the reception room.

He was pale, and told Henri that he needed to talk with him privately. And so they drove to The Boltons, at Number 7 of which Wallenberg lived. Inside, he told Henri to sit down.

"Have you spoken to anyone about the Wurmbrands and your sister?"

Henri's lips quivered, and for a moment he did not reply. Wallenberg repeated the question.

"I told one boy."

"When?"

"The night I was made captain. Three weeks ago."

Wallenberg turned his face to one side. "The day before yesterday, the Gestapo went to the farmhouse. They took the Wurmbrands out and shot them. They took your sister away in their car. She was driven to Hamburg and put on a train with all Jewish people rounded up in a general sweep. The train left Hamburg, and headed toward Poland."

Henri Tod left St. Paul's the next day and took a job in Leeds as a coal miner. His curiosity about Espy was limited, because he knew that Espy himself would not wish harm to come to Henri's sister. He did inquire about the profession of Espy's father, who was a journalist, wholly engaged in covering the war. It crossed his mind only fleetingly to ask Espy Major whether he had told his father (or anyone else) the story of the new school captain's secret family in Tolk, but decided against doing so. Of what use that line of questioning? On whom could the blame be put, other than himself? And so all he did was to collect, wordlessly, his personal materials, and leave a note in the headmaster's office. He did not leave a forwarding address with Mr. Wallenberg, whom he never saw again.

In the spring of 1950, he knocked on the door of the dean of admissions at Trinity College in Cambridge and said he would like to enroll to do advanced studies in philosophy. The dean looked at the young man, deferential but proud, mature beyond what the dean had experienced in young men of twenty-three or -four. He was clean-shaven, strong, even-featured, brown-eyed, with perfectly shaped white teeth, slender nose and lips. The dean told him, somewhat more courteously than he'd have addressed a young man less striking in appearance and behavior, that there were conventional ways of applying for admission to graduate schools—where had he attended college?

He was surprised to be told that the applicant had not even completed his public schoolwork at St. Paul's, five years earlier. However, the applicant said, he had done concentrated reading while working in the coal mines, and was prepared to submit to examination. Rather intrigued by all this, the dean excused himself, left the room, and telephoned to the taskmasterish Russell Professor of Philosophy, James Jamison, and told him he would be grateful if Jamison would examine an applicant who was there under unusual circumstances.

Three years later, with an advanced degree in philosophy, Henri Tod recrossed the Channel he had only once before crossed, as a frightened fifteen-year-old sick at heart at leaving his sister who, however, had promised him she would be seeing him soon, very, very soon.

7

John Fitzgerald Kennedy sat in the Oval Office. He had one hour before he would need to go upstairs to dress for the state dinner for what's-his-name, the little hypocrite. Dulles told me he's stolen maybe forty, maybe fifty million, and he is always poor-mouthing about his people. Damn right they're poor. He stays in power another ten years, what's-his-name (he must make it a serious point to get his name straight before dinner—why aren't they *all* called Gonzalez? I mean, most of them are as it is), ten more years and his "people" will have nothing at all left. Ah, but if only the worst problems were Latin American. Chiquita Banana, da-da-da da-da—how does it go? . . . But he was putting off what he had scheduled for himself—more hard thought on Khrushchev, the bastard, and Berlin. He couldn't remember whether his dad had told him that all communist chiefs of state, like all businessmen, were s.o.b.'s. Maybe he thought I'd simply take that for granted. Nobody knows what Khrushchev's after and nobody's going to find out, not even Arthur. . . . (Arthur! That might be fun! Say in 1986, on the twenty-fifth anniversary of the Bay of Pigs. I'll be . . . almost sixty-nine. We'll arrange a big public seminar, and someone will say, "Mr. President, in his study of your presidency, Professor Schlesinger writes that you were said to have simply shrugged off the Bay of Pigs as just one of those misjudgments that occasionally happen. Would you comment on that?" I'll pause . . . look a little pained. Then I'll say, "Oh dear. I was afraid someone

would ask me about that book someday. The trouble is,
Arthur really *never understood.* . . .") He stopped and
hooted, just audibly. Cut it out, Jack. I mean, Mr. President
—back to the problem. It was true that no one had understood how deeply he felt about the screw-up at the Bay of
Pigs. For their sake *and* his. Yes, he had said publicly it was
his fault. Yes, he had got plenty of people friendly to him, in
plenty of places, to suggest it was really the fault of the CIA,
and the Pentagon, and Ike, and Tricky Dick, and Sagittar-
ius, and Marilyn Monroe. But let's face it, it really *was* my
fault. I know I'm as bright as anybody. Nobody, really, is
any brighter than I am. But being bright isn't enough. You
need to make the correct decisions, and sometimes dumb
people can make sounder decisions than bright people, I
mean, look at Ike on the one hand, Adlai on the other hand
. . . God, what will they talk to each other about in eternity
—Joe McCarthy? That's about the only distaste they have in
common. . . . In two weeks he would have met with Khrushchev. Was there any human being who had met Khrushchev, studied Khrushchev, defected from Khrushchev,
that he, the President of the United States, hadn't either a)
spoken to, b) read the works of, or c) been lectured to by?
Was it possible to count the number of hours he had spent
with Dean Acheson? Good old Dean, he wants just one
little world war before he dies. On the other hand I could
take Walter Lippmann's advice, in exchange for which
Khrushchev can have Europe. I've talked to every ambassador alive who has ever served in Moscow. What do they
say? Pretty much the same thing, give or take this emphasis
by Bohlen, that emphasis by Kennan. I've studied the minutes of—what? God. Geneva summit 1955—I wonder what
that one solved. Then there was Camp David 1959. And
Paris 1960—he aborted the damn thing on account of a U-
2! That was vintage Khrushchev, right! Especially the press
conference he gave when he stopped over in Vienna. Said
maybe Ike was just a little cuckoo. . . . Brings up an inter-

esting point. One of the things I have to ask myself is: How far do I let him go? I mean, if he starts to scream and yell, what do I do in the cause of Peace with Honor—God, I wish that phrase had never been coined. Fact is, you don't that often get both at the same time. You make up the honor, like the Japs after Hiroshima saying they had to have their emperor. They'd have imported the people who did in Mussolini to take care of their emperor if we had said to them we had one big beautiful one left over after Hiroshima for Tokyo . . . OK, so what's he up to? Seriously, what is he *up* to? Jack old boy, I mean, Mr. President, old boy, let's start at the other end. What's he *not* up to? He's not up to beginning a nuclear war. Among other things, Poppa Marx wouldn't like that. A nuclear war with maybe only Patagonians left over isn't going to do much to validate the Marxist theory of class struggle. Okay, at what point do we start dropping nuclear bombs? A hell of a question to ask, but I'm the one who's going to decide. Well, since you can't argue with hypotheses (quote unquote; old Strausshaven, Harvard, Philosophy 10ab—nice guy, and little Miss Hilda Strausshaven was, well, what's that word—synesthetic? Was she ever. He was a little nuts, but most of them are), then I can't argue with the proposition that Khrushchev doesn't want nuclear war. So he's got to know that nuclear war is exactly what is going to happen if . . . if what? That's the problem . . . He depressed a button on his desk. "Get me a Coca-Cola, please." He smiled. Ken Galbraith once said that when Jack Kennedy really got excited, he would order a Coca-Cola. Never booze. So, he was excited? Correct . . . So they don't want a nuclear war. But they do want to press on. After all, there isn't any believable sense in which they are acting in order to end an aggression *we* are responsible for. The only thing *we're* "responsible" for is giving shelter to East Germans who are moving out of the workers' paradise. That's hardly *our* aggressive act. Khrushchev might try demanding that we deport them. Not that it would be the first time. Ugh, 1945, 1946. God, let's not think about that. He knows he can't ask us to keep people from going from East Berlin to West Berlin. And once they're in West Berlin, what are we supposed to do if they tell our processors at Marienfelde they want to go on to West Germany? That they can't go to West Germany? The refugee stream into West Berlin is the only ongoing East-West phenomenon that's in any way destabilizing. Laos has quieted down. The nuclear testing issue is on track. Now, how bad *is* it in Berlin? Is Khrushchev up against something he literally can't stand and *must* do something about? Or is he simply looking around to make a little hell, and push the old revolution up a peg or two? In the last three weeks he's talked to maybe six ambassadors or foreign ministers or whatever, and talked about how nuclear bombs might be necessary if I'm intransigent. *Me*, intransigent. All *I* want is a continuation of the status quo, that's all. But [he was looking out on the Rose Garden at this point, where Caroline was arguing with her nurse] I'm not going to draw a line and then redraw it. That's what happened in Cuba. It hurt me. It hurt me with Europe, it hurt me in America, and it hurt me inside. The whole point of the exercise is to find exactly where that line should be drawn, and make it absolutely clear that that line is not to be moved. We can't simply give them Berlin. But we'll have to give them other things, things that don't really matter, if possible. Question: What doesn't matter? That's what I've got to find out. De Gaulle will have one idea on this, Adenauer another, Macmillan another. And Khrushchev, gee . . . He thought. Was it really a good idea to agree to see Khrushchev? Hell, to *ask* to see him—that, really, was how it had gone, en route to this summit, though the history books will be appropriately murky on this point. Khrushchev can scream and yell, and what he does is acceptable as packaged behavior—a) his people don't have any say in the matter;

and b) those few of his people who do have a say in the matter don't seem to attach much importance to decorum. They want their satisfactions. Funny thing: it shouldn't really make any difference, as I understand their phony-baloney doctrine. It's action that matters; but theater matters a lot too. I wonder whether Suslov—good example, Suslov, the tablet-keeper of Marxism in the Kremlin—I wonder what he thought when Khrushchev banged his shoe on the table at the UN? Or when he went crackers in front of De Gaulle, Macmillan, and Ike last year? If Khrushchev is just being Khrushchev, then the boys have got to weigh whether just being Khrushchev is the best way to advance their cause. And the only means they have to measure that is—me. How do *I* react?—that's the question. How does John Fitzgerald Kennedy, President of the United States, maximum leader of the imperialist powers, react. And what will I come up with, in my search for something we can give them, that we can do without?

The special telephone on his desk rang, to which, at the other end, only one person had access.

"I'm coming, dear."

8

Leonid Ustinov came into his office in the massive new building in East Berlin. Soviet agents who did not wish to hunker down in the principal dwelling of the Soviet Embassy were more comfortably inconspicuous in one of the side buildings within the huge compound, and accordingly it was in one of them that Ustinov elected to locate the intelligence ganglion that had heretofore squatted in the embassy. From this side building subsidiary terminals went out to the safe houses sprinkled about East (and West) Berlin.

There were two entrances to his office. The conventional entrance, through which he, his secretary, and various aides entered. And a back-door entrance, used only by Ustinov. This led to a large room which, from the outside, appeared to be a kind of windowless concrete blockhouse, housing giant furnaces or what-have-you. Radio equipment and a detection-proof electronic insulation system covered the entire room, which measured twenty feet by thirty feet. Access to it other than from Ustinov's office was by elevator. The elevator that went from the ground floor of Building H to the fourteenth floor listed G as the bottommost stop. A special key inserted in the elevator's push-button panel impelled the elevator down to a subterranean level, the elevator exit opening on a door that could be opened by working a safe lock, or by using the little telephone to announce one's presence. Ustinov was pleased with the expeditious means by which he was able to carry out his normal administrative life and, without going through the boring rigors of buses, taxis, subways, umbrellas, goatees, what-have-yous in order to meet with his agents in scattered safe houses, he could actually bring them to Blockhouse H, as they came to call it.

Ustinov, age fifty-one, had been deputy intelligence officer in Berlin from 1947 until 1953. He was recalled after the June uprising in 1953, on the general principle that whenever there is an anti-Soviet demonstration or strike or riot, that means that the cadre of Soviet officials supposed to prevent that kind of thing has been in some way negligent. Since the uprisings were in June, and Stalin had died three months earlier in March, Ustinov felt lucky. Moreover, he had early on mastered a principle taught him by his mentor and patron, the legendary Pupskavitch, for a brief period himself a protégé of Josef Stalin. That was just after Stalin had exiled Trotsky, who had been Pupskavitch's original patron. Pupskavitch resolved, at age twenty-eight, that he was really too young to die, and so he elected to build up a personal dossier documenting the surreptitious treacheries of Trotsky, whose treacheries went so far beyond anything Stalin had thought possible to contrive that he instantly demanded to see the author of this political grand opera, promoted him on the spot, and gave instructions that he was to be attached to Stalin's personal staff. In what capacity? Stalin said he did not care. And then, on reflection, he suggested that Pupskavitch become the Trotsky expert, in charge of counteracting Trotsky's propaganda and that of Trotsky's janissaries. This Pupskavitch did with wonderful ingenuity, and remained in the Kremlin right up until Stalin succeeded, in 1940, in contriving the assassination of Trotsky.

In the early thirties, Pupskavitch had brought Ustinov into his staff, partly because Ustinov read and wrote English and Spanish, two languages through which Trotsky was sending out high-voltage anti-Stalin material all over

the world, and partly because Pups, as in informal circumstances his staff liked to call him, was a Stakhanovite homo-
sexual, and young Leonid, whose sense of priorities was
never tormented, had no problem whatever in electing to
feign reciprocal ardor for Pups in return for a private apartment in which he could keep his mistress. During the seven
years Ustinov was a part of the Trotsky Bedevilment Team,
Pups fell out of favor twice: once when Stalin, quite without
reason, held him personally responsible for not having got
hold of, and destroyed, Lenin's so-called last will (it was
always referred to as Lenin's "so-called" last will) in which
he had warned against Stalin. And, again, Stalin was infuri-
ated when Trotsky provided evidence to the John Dewey
Commission set up to investigate the validity of Stalin's
purge trials. Pups had on both occasions taught Ustinov
what he called the Principle of Evanescence. "You simply
cease to exist, my dear Leonid; it is that simple. You will
note that all communications to Comrade Stalin will be
signed other than by me, never mind that I wrote them. All
suggestions will be made by others. For all intents and
purposes I shall be dead. Except!—I can be made to rise
again! By whom? By the great Stalin. Who, one day, will
say, 'Where is Pupskavitch? I said, *Where in the name of God is
Pupskavitch!'* And within fifteen minutes I shall appear;
'Comrade Stalin, you were asking after me?'

"That is the way to proceed, my dear Leonid. Not the
scheming and the counterscheming. Remember that," he
said, stroking Leonid's head as Pups sat, and Leonid lay, on
the couch.

So that after the June uprising-riot-strike-demonstration
and Leonid Ustinov's recall, he never raised his voice in
such a way as to remind his superiors that in the course of
five years' duty there he had become thoroughly familiar
with the Berlin scene. But there were those who remembered. And so, early in the critical year of 1961, he had
been discovered—doing routine security work for the In-

ternational Atomic Energy Agency in Vienna. It had hardly
fitted Pup's Principle of Evanescence that a few years after
his being assigned to Vienna, the replacement as Soviet
representative to that agency was none other than Vyache-
slav Molotov. To find himself serving as an assistant to the
man who, after Stalin, was for a number of years the most
conspicuous Communist leader in Russia was less than the
total Evanescence on which Leonid had planned when he
insinuated himself into the atomic agency. On the other
hand, he consoled himself, the idea had been to give Molotov the single most ignominious assignment around. It
would follow that anyone who was subordinate to Molotov
was less than nothing, correct?

Correct, he concluded; and he'd have called Pups to
check this out except that, neglecting his own advice, Pupskavitch had put in with Beria in 1953, and twenty-four
hours after Beria was executed, Pupskavitch was executed
—moreover (or so the story got out), by an executioner so
hideously deformed that Pups could not possibly have succeeded in sublimating the ordeal in one of those masochis-
tic reveries to which he had introduced a startled, if docile,
young Leonid twenty years earlier. Poor Pups.

At 10:20 exactly, Leonid would enter by the back door of
his office, having twirled the safe-opening device and
opened the door. From the moment he left his desk to exit
the office by the back door, his secretary knew to say to
anyone who inquired that Comrade Ustinov was not in his
office. There was an emergency signal—a rudimentary device that rang from her bottom right drawer directly into
Blockhouse H. She would depress that button only if Moscow—and she knew who, in Moscow—quite simply demanded it. Otherwise, Comrade Ustinov was—unavailable.

At 10:20 Leonid Ustinov found Felix Zimmerman waiting
for him. Zimmerman, a forty-year-old, lithe, dark-skinned,

sallow-complexioned, mustachioed, middle-sized, middle-weight polyglot, was, Ustinov could never quite decide, primarily a profound and extensively experienced brainy intelligence agent, or a chain-smoker. Ustinov, who did not himself smoke, could coexist with colleagues or subordinates who smoked casually. But Zimmerman was in this respect (to be sure, also in others) quite extraordinary. One time, exasperated after sitting for one whole hour in a restaurant on the lee side of the airflow that brought Zimmerman's smoke into Ustinov's nostrils, Ustinov had asked the question: "Felix, are you *ever* without a cigarette?"

"Yes," Zimmerman had answered. "When I dream of hell, I am without a cigarette." Ustinov had sighed, and resumed the conversation on how to contrive the fatal accident of Witterkind, the troublesome labor union leader.

Already, Blockhouse H smelled as though it were a tobacconist's . . . tasting room? Abattoir? Cave? Ustinov went through his hand-to-the-throat-I'm-choking gesture, which Zimmerman accepted as a form of handshake. They sat at the table, Ustinov at the head of it, Zimmerman to his right. Twenty people could have sat around the table. Zimmerman began.

"I have some very interesting news for you, Leonid." Ustinov winced, as usual, though he did this only the first time he heard Zimmerman refer to him by his first name. It was Zimmerman's way of reminding Ustinov that in no hierarchical sense was Ustinov the superior of Zimmerman. Z. was a free lance. Once, when after a long night of record searching they had drunk together, and Ustinov had said orotundly something to the effect that socialism was the intellectual mother of all creatively good things, and didn't old Zim agree, Zimmerman had put down his glass of schnapps and said, "Leonid, old boy, you forget the rules. As far as you are concerned, I am for all intents and purposes the natural son of Leon Trotsky, and you concerted the killing of dear old dad"—Zimmerman at this point wheezily exercised his handkerchief, sobbing but so noisily that Leonid passed quickly through the threshold of alarm into amusement—"so don't ever ask me these things, or try to anoint me in your ideological mysteries. I make a living, did so precociously under Hitler, comfortably under Stalin, and affluently under Khrushchev. Khrushchev will one day have a successor, and I permit myself this sole note of sentimentality, my dear Leonid. I hope that Khrushchev's successor will be—Ustinov. Comrade Leonid Ustinov." Felix stood at attention, only the cigarette in his lips marring the general impression of the martinet. "Ladies and gentlemen," he boomed, "I introduce Chairman Leonid Ustinov, First Secretary of the Communist Party of the Union of Soviet Socialist Republics." Felix, who wore rings on both hands, rat-tatted them on the table, to simulate a drumroll.

"All right, all right. What've you got on the Bruderschaft? Better make it good."

"What I have got," said Felix, talking through his cigarette, "is a good deal on the identity of their leader. I do not know where he lives. This may surprise you, Leonid, but I am not sure that anyone knows exactly where he lives. But I do know how to get a message through to him. And I know about his background. And there is something there that your people are going to have to investigate, and then maybe clue me in.

"It's this simple. He goes, as you know, by the name of 'Henri Tod,' explanation forthcoming in due course. A German Jew, born in Hamburg in 1927, spirited away in 1940, parents to Belsen, exit parents. Schooled between thirteen and fifteen, along with sister, one year younger, in countryside, in Tolk, near Denmark frontier. Getaway to England. Betrayed. Foster parents shot, sister taken to Hamburg, put on train with that day's Jewish harvest, sent east, as far as I can gather to Auschwitz. We are talking, Leonid, mid-January 1945, and as we know, the flesh became a little weak along about that time, and what was

supposed to happen on Monday didn't always happen till—
Tuesday? Thursday? Sunday? Question before the house:
Was this sixteen-year-old girl, who went by the name of
Clementa Tod, actually executed? Because if she was not,
she could be very important to us—if we can find her.
There is a correspondence . . . between the boy and the
girl. Charming. Not written by Henri to Clementa from
England. If he wrote from England at all, we have no evi-
dence of it.

"No, the correspondence we have is letters—dozens,
hundreds of them, written by Henri to Clementa *while they
were living in the same farmhouse!* I assume that because they
were apparently well-supervised, well-brought-up kids,
they did not engage in incest, but believe me, Leonid, eroti-
cism is the only thing missing from these letters. They were
in the farmhouse when they took the girl off and shot the
foster parents. I've read them.

"So, my friend, I am telling you now two things which
will cost you, each of them, ten thousand marks, and I do
not mean ten thousand of your marks, I mean *their* marks.
One of them is that I have isolated the figure of the story of
the head of the Bruderschaft. Born Heinrich Toddweiss. I
know that you will pay for the first. The other is that I can
probably devise a means of trapping him. This will be much
easier if Clementa Tod is alive. Especially so if she is willing
to cooperate. If she is alive and is not willing to cooperate—
why, my dear Leonid, advise me when that uh—what a
useful word!—disability has been cured; then we will plan.
If she is *not* alive," Felix said, shrugging his shoulders, "we
will simply have to make other arrangements."

It was Ustinov's turn to be agitated. "Listen, Zimmerman. You talk about Tod and his Bruderschaft as though
you will figure out a way to prune the branches after the
seedlings have grown up a few years down the line.

"Tod's organization, three years ago, consisted of two or
three people. We don't know how many people are in touch

with the organization now, but if it were one thousand people I would not be surprised. Do you know what they did yesterday, here in Berlin, outside Pechnow Prison?"

Zimmerman, who fancied himself well informed at every level, was obliged to say that no, he did not know what had happened yesterday outside the Pechnow Prison.

"A young woman came in, regular visitors' door, was searched by the woman guard, passed through. Put in to see Zinsser, the writer up on sedition charges. They are taken to one of the private rooms for political prisoners. Girl suddenly 'faints.' Woman guard shouts at regular guard to go for nurse. They come back three minutes later. All three gone! Walked out—*our* guard escorting them! *Our* guard, working for the Bruderschaft!

"That was just one item, yesterday's caper. This Tod has a magical effect on his people. Their faces turn a sickly golden hue when his name comes up."

"I can imagine, Comrade Ustinov, that those faces look somewhat different when you are through, uh, making them up?"

Ustinov spat on the floor. "I am talking about men and women who are—most often—buried. We have tried and executed thirty. But the situation grows worse. Every day. And the fever is catching. No one has a picture of Tod, and none of his colleagues is permitted to carry a camera in his presence. The point is, we have got to get him."

"Is it your estimate that the Bruderschaft would cease to exist without Tod?"

Ustinov's mood became pensive. "I have to be careful. The removal of Tod would be a crippling blow. Whether it would be a *mortal* blow we don't know. Not until the removal of Tod is effected. Which reminds me that this is your mission. Our resources are extensive. But I've worked with you, and I know that yours are unusually good, so I'm expecting concrete and useful information from you, and I am expecting that information sometime before the apple-picking season in the fall."

Felix Zimmerman stood up, and now he began speaking in the voice of a stockbroker struggling against a deadline. "Do you think you can have that information for me on the sister within a week?"

He pulled from his jacket pocket a sheet of paper and handed it to Ustinov. "That contains everything collectible about Clementa Tod, born Clementina Toddweiss, April 1, 1929, Hamburg, admitted Tolk Common School December 12, 1940, living with 'foster parents' Stephanie and Hans Wurmbrand, at Lochse Farm, Tolk. Seized by Gestapo January 20, 1945, taken by auto to Hamburg, relinquished to SS-Depot 297A at 9 P.M. January 21, assigned to Group C18, destination Auschwitz, departure scheduled for noon January 22. There is also a picture of the girl, taken from one of her letters to her brother on her fourteenth birthday."

Leonid stared at it. "Interesting face. She looks older than fourteen. She would be beautiful. She . . . was"—he put the picture down—"beautiful." He walked toward the coatrack. "Anything else for me, Leonid?"

"No," the head of the East German Intelligence Division, KGB, said. "I mean, no, except for one thing. Do you know where Blackford Oakes is?"

Felix turned around, his rhythm interrupted.

"Is Oakes in Berlin?"

"Yes."

"Well!" He was then silent for a moment. "And do I take it that another of my commissions is to find out where he is staying?"

"Perhaps with Henri Tod." Ustinov leered. "How much?" Ustinov knew that coming right to the point with Zimmerman was, well, a good idea.

"Five thousand to concentrate my mind on the problem. Fifteen thousand if I find him."

"Okay . . . Out of curiosity, Felix," Ustinov was smiling now, "what are you going to do with all your money when this is all over?"

"In answer to your question, Leonid: 'This' will never be 'all over.' Answer number two, I shall buy more cigarettes. A lifetime supply. That will depend in part on you."

"The cigarettes?"

"No. The lifetime. I move very carefully, Leonid. But I am engaged in a profession in which I cannot dictate the movement of others. And some of those moves impinge on my own. Understand?" He blew a shaft of smoke into Leonid, who stood up and, coughing exaggeratedly, stretched out his hand.

9

It had been a long day for Blackford Oakes, one of those long days that tend to get left out in the telling of how covert operations people spend their time. At thirty-five, after almost ten years, Blackford wondered whether he might not be able to prove, if he had to, that he had spent more time, or as much time, monitoring fixed sites as a traffic policeman; as much time looking at people's records as the FBI; as much time going over old files, clippings, and books as a filing clerk. Well, sure, he had done the other kind of thing too. But for instance, here he was in Berlin. Mission? To find out exactly what Ulbricht was going to do, or had been told to do, and when. The place was crawling with people who were willing to tell Oakes (sometimes *pro bono publico*, sometimes for a price) about this or the other hot lead. Some came forward with exact schedules. Khrushchev was going to announce a peace treaty on August 1. One week later, East Germany would announce that all Allied troops must evacuate West Berlin. Five extra Russian divisions would move to the western border of East Germany. Or—another version—Ulbricht was going to be sidetracked, and someone else would come in who would defuse the crisis; Khrushchev didn't want confrontation right now. Watch for his speech to the congregation of Communist Party heads in late July.

And everything in between. And—of course—a number of the people he spoke to, a number of the reports he read, had in them something that was true. Something that he should ship out with his imprimatur to Rufus, and on to Washington. But after three weeks he began to intuit another possibility. And this, he recognized, he could not have done ten years earlier. It was something that came with a development over the years of the relevant senses. He came to the belief that there *was* no inside plan. At least not yet. That the Berlin business was one of those mounting crises concerning which *neither* side knew what steps the other side was going to take, and, in fact, didn't know what steps *his* side would take. Should take. Could take. What would be the corresponding action of Side A to Initiative X taken by Side B? Blackford came to suspect that Side A—which was his side—had not even scheduled hypothetically the corresponding action, or even reflex action. Or does one schedule reflex actions? Interesting point. You don't schedule a yell when you fall out of a window, right?

All morning with that guy Rodino—funny name for a German. Rodino said his companion had access to a woman who worked in the office of Ulbricht, and what she needed was just a little encouragement to get her started: she was really very, very close. And so on.

How much?

Well, just to begin with, a couple of thousand . . . Blackford interrogated Rodino for four solid hours. Rodino had been a Nazi, but only under stress. (Blackford wanted, before he died, to meet *one* German who had been a Nazi because he thought Hitler was terrific, thought Nazism a wonderful philosophy of life and the Jews a menace to humankind. Just one.) Rodino had got wounded on the eastern front, was sent back to a military hospital, fell in love with the chief nurse, who was a hustler, a sure-enough hustler. And in return for her monitoring his therapy in such a way as to guarantee that he would fail any test that might result in his being sent back to the front—and those tests were less and less exacting as German resources were depleted—he had set up the nurses' brothel, attending, so

to speak, to the business end of things, which was the easi-
est money, said Rodino frankly, he had ever made, because
soldiers who were up to a little physical activity in the
hospital were hardly hoarding their money, expecting as
they were to be sent back the next day or the day after to the
front to have one more fling with the Russians, so why not a
compensatory fling in the hospital?

Rodino rather enjoyed describing the mechanics of his
operation, which involved taking over one third of one
entire wing of the officers' section of the hospital, ostensibly there for wounded field-grade officers and higher. Finding himself with no less than twelve rooms, suddenly he
contrived to make them off limits to the regular medical
staff, on the ostensible grounds that there patients were
sequestered who might have infectious diseases, ha ha ha,
that's exactly what a lot of them went on to get, said
Rodino, his little mustache bounding about his ruddy skin,
his mouth open in a huge smile. He and Eva had got away
with it for an incredible four months, in part because they
judiciously dispensed favors to this or that itinerant inspector or surgeon general; and in any event, one or two
higher-up military people had passed the word discreetly
that to permit a little of this kind of thing was really a part of
R and R.

Of course, said Rodino, despite everyone else's Rest and
Recreation, eventually he and Eva were caught, both were
sentenced to courts-martial, convicted, and then led off to
prison. "But we're talking March 1945." Rodino had very
simply informed his jailer that twenty thousand marks was
his upon Rodino and Eva's achieving safety. Not only did
the jailer agree to help them escape, he escaped along with
them, and they all three managed to get to Austria by the
time Hitler did his Götterdämmerung. Rodino and Eva
were rich!—until the devaluation of the mark by Ludwig
Erhard that just plain wiped them out.

So they were back in the business of making a little

money, and this time Eva was coming close to Ulbricht via an old girlfriend, and Blackford could check on every word Rodino had said, but he did need a little sweetener for Eva to work with, feel her way around. In part on impulse, Blackford went to the adjacent room, removed a couple of volumes, and took money from the little wall safe. He gave Rodino instructions, and decided to walk back to his apartment.

It was past spring, really. Just plain summer. Blackford hadn't bothered to put on his light green poplin jacket, matching his trousers. He simply slung it over his shoulder, his yellow tie loosened, his thought turning, for the thousandth time, to his failure to grasp exactly what were the crystallizing forces. *Exactly what would come next?* He was experienced enough to know that the crunch was not far away: this matter of the sharpened instinct. Besides which, on the weekend's visit with Rufus in London, he had seen his old mentor more put off, by the awful impalpability of the problem, than ever before—all those other crises having involved a deadline in part of their own initiative, or a plan over which they had effective control. This time they had no such control, none. It was terminally discouraging to remind himself that his mission was to find out what Ulbricht intended to do but that in all probability Ulbricht did not know what he intended to do, because Khrushchev had not decided what he would permit him to do. Though Khrushchev's post-Vienna rhetoric was more strident than ever, and the inside word was that the old pro had taken Kennedy good and proper. Rufus hadn't wanted to talk about that.

Rufus did want to know everything Blackford was able to tell him about the Bruderschaft and its operations. Every day it became clearer that if there was going on, in East Germany, something that could be called a resistance

movement, Henri Tod had it in hand. Henri Tod. A difficult
man to know, about whose capacity for personal warmth
Blackford knew only abstractly, not as an intimate.

There was no doubting that Tod felt deeply. And on one
reflective occasion he had, without giving out the story, let
alone the details, alluded to "his" nightmare. In fact Blackford knew the story: Rufus had got it from the widow of
Henri's old guardian in London, the story about Henri's
spilling the beans to another schoolboy—which story had
got to the Gestapo, it was assumed, there being no other
explanation for the sudden detection of the Wurmbrands
and Clementa's hideout in Tolk. Blackford doubted he
would ever be told the story by Henri himself. If ever that
were to happen, he would deem it a form of initiation into
the very closest company Henri Tod kept. But Henri's emotional life was clearly imploded into that endless nightmare
of self-reproach—Blackford had discussed the question
with Rufus—at once the fountain of Henri's personal mel-
ancholy and the dynamic cause of his agitated motivation,
as if he intended to live out his life in hectic expiation for
what he had done.

It was nearly an hour before Blackford arrived at the
apartment house, on Rheinstrasse. He didn't know exactly
what he would do that evening. He felt restless, felt like
talking to someone as different from Rodino as he could
find. Though not, he acknowledged, necessarily different
from some of the ladies who, in the past, had dealt with
Rodino. What were the nurses like? he wondered.

He climbed the two sets of stairs to the entrance of his
"uncle's" flat. He had to admit it, the CIA was the most
ingenious foster-parent finder in the history of hospitality.
He could not count the uncles, aunts, cousins, stepfathers
whose apartments, conveniently vacated because they had
gone on extended vacations, had accommodatingly been
turned over to him in the past ten years, no paperwork to
be performed, not even any letters to be sent, no dunning

landlords. "Dear Uncle Jack: It's warm in Berlin. What a pity you had to go to the Antarctic? On the other hand, you were always a little queer for igloos. Love, Blacky." Ah well.

Blackford, unlike Rufus, was not given to rigorous self-scheduling. He managed to keep trim not by daily exercise, but because something within him, every three or four days, would begin to creak, and he would know it was time to visit the gymnasium or, if none such was about, to take his exercise wherever he might. He never knew exactly what book he was going to read next, but knew that when he was finished with his current book, the next one would be right there, intuitively situated in an erratic but ulti-mately dependable assembly line. He had, however, devel-oped such habits as are inculcated in deep-cover agents. He never made entirely casual appointments, he routinely trav-eled by different routes, he was careful what he said over which telephone, that sort of thing.

But one or two habits of a personal kind he did have, and one of these was, almost immediately on coming home to his apartment, whether in the late afternoon or at night, to walk into the bathroom, open the medicine-cabinet door, and reach for his toothbrush: he had got into the habit for some reason of brushing his teeth after getting home from work. This afternoon, stuck cockily inside his glass, the toothbrush protruding from either end of the sealed enve-lope was—a letter. Addressed, simply: "Mr. Oakes."

Oakes was registered, as the inhabitant of his uncle's apartment, as John Jerome, with documents to match. His little apartment was in the Consolidated Insurance Build-ing, subleased by Lloyd's, where independent insurance agents wrote policies, conducted investigations, and made assessments, and a few kept living quarters. His cover had been done with some care.

Now he reacted professionally. Without withdrawing the letter, he let himself carefully out of the apartment. He walked not down, but up the stairs, to the top level, the fifth

floor, which accommodated a single tiny room under the
gabled roof. Designed for a maid, or a grandmother, or a
few trunks. He took the key from his ring, opened the door,
and went to a dusty telephone. He dialed a number. He let
it ring exactly three times, then hung up. The requisite
message was transmitted, and specified contingency arrangements were triggered.

Next he went to the cobwebby little window of the room,
and peered out over the street. He did this for a full half
hour, only then letting himself out the door. He walked
down not into his own apartment on the third floor, but all
the way down, and out the principal door. At the corner was
a restaurant-bar. He stopped and, at the counter, ordered a
beer. While it was being fetched up he went to the telephone and rang a different number, which answered instantly. He said, "Anything for Jerome?" A voice answered,
"Nothing spotted in the area. You are under friendly obser-
vation front and rear. The usual signals will apply." He
returned to the bar, drank half the beer, left change,
bought a newspaper, and went back to his apartment. Inside, he walked to the bathroom and carefully examined the
medicine cabinet before withdrawing the letter. He sat
down on the toilet and opened the envelope, careful not to
mutilate it. The letter was typewritten:

"Dear Mr. Oakes:

"I am a very reasonable man, you will discover. And I like
very much to expedite, so to speak, the desires of different
parties. What I have to offer you and Henri is Clementa
Tod. Yes, she is alive. I enclose a picture of her, on the back
of which she has penned a note to her brother. She advises
me that no further proof of her survival is necessary. I am
willing to do what I can to contrive her liberation. But it will
be very expensive, in every sense of the word. You are
deputized to act as intermediary between me, repeat me,
and Clementa on the one hand, and her brother on the
other. If you wish to pursue this discussion, bring fifty

thousand marks (no tricks, please: Clementa would be terminally disappointed, and other important plans would be frustrated). Come alone with the money to East Berlin to Arnswalder Platz at the corner of Pasteur and Hans-Otto-Strasse at 1605 hours on Thursday, day after tomorrow, and begin walking northwest, on the sidewalk, as close as you can to the curb. You will accept the offer of a ride from the person who, from the car, addresses you as 'Mr. Jerome.' It would be, I repeat, a most awful pity if these arrangements were embarrassed. The sum of money is not negotiable, so be so good as not to appear with a lesser amount. Yours truly,"

The letter was signed, simply, "F."

The color photograph was of a girl severely garbed in a gray pants suit. Her expression was serious, her figure trim, her eyes downcast. She was very beautiful. Blackford turned the photograph around, and read in German, "I long to see Your Majesty." It was signed, "C."

10

It seemed to the President to be over only moments after it had begun, though he knew that, before the century was finished, historians would probably write whole books about the events that began on May 30, 1961, and ended on June 6. Interesting point: end of the century. There was a sense in which the question whether the century would end was affected by the events of that week. Curious question: What happens to a century if there is no one around to record its passage? There was all that business Professor Strausshaven used to talk about—was it Hume? Berkeley? One of those things-don't-exist-unless-you-can-feel-them types. Empiricists. Right. The ones who said that a tree in the forest that falls makes no noise unless someone is there to hear it. Neat point. Provided you have an appetite for neat points of that sort. Not the kind of thing he would discuss with Paul Butler the next time they had a conversation about the electoral vote in Wisconsin. Though come to think of it, he'd have a point that might interest old Paul, who was something of an intellectual in his own politically obsessed way. A vote is, or is not, a vote if the voter doesn't actually record that vote? Isn't that related in some way to the business of the tree and the forest? I mean, Mrs. Jones decides to vote for Kennedy but doesn't get around to doing so. Is her decision to vote for Kennedy the philosophically interesting event, or is it her actual appearance at the polls in order to execute her decisions? Isn't that what Hume was talking about, so to speak? Or was it Berkeley? . . . Anyway, it had been one hell of a week. The arrival in Paris was some spectacle! Charles de Gaulle was obviously curious to know something about me, and no doubt had read everything he could lay his hands on. Not quite everything, I hope. On the other hand, I did homework also, read through De Gaulle's war memoirs. Pretty powerful stuff, gave you an idea of the man's steel. But not a clear picture, the one that emerges. On the one hand he acted, and wrote, as though France would go on forever. On the other hand there was, here and there, an apocalyptic turn of mind sort of thing: Do it our way or, it doesn't matter what happens, the world will burn up. Catholic stuff, in a way. De G. was certainly one of those. I mean, one of us. Not an uninteresting political point, that one. Because if life on earth is merely a transitory business, then it isn't all that important, though God knows I hope I don't have to work as hard to get into heaven as I did to get into the White House. On the other hand it occurs to me that in order to get to place A, as Walt Rostow would put it, I'm going to have to satisfy a lot of people in not quite the same way that I satisfied the people who took me to place B, right? Well, that's merely a politically interesting point. How exactly? Well, goddam it, if Charles de Gaulle, who is nearly a hundred years old or whatever, feels that we can just give Khrushchev an atomic ultimatum, it may just be that his judgment is affected by the Catholic business. I mean, the Christian business. Important point, that; I got hell from Bobby when I slurred it in my speech early on in the campaign to the seminary people. And sure enough, De Gaulle *was* that way. Just as Ted Sorensen had warned he would be. De Gaulle wants me to make *no concessions whatever* in the matter of East Germany and Berlin. Needless to say, none on the matter of the right of our own access to Berlin, but none, either, on the right of access to different parts of Berlin by Berliners. Sure, neat. But then he would spring odd things. For instance, he told me late that after-

noon in that—God, that's a fancy office of his (I'm sorry
Jackie saw it: the Oval Office will never again quite do)—
when we were discussing NATO, and he was off on one of
his metaphysical binges. He's getting ready to pull out of
NATO and we all know this. But he's not *really* pulling out
of NATO, says the wily old bird, because we have to distinguish between NATO the *alliance,* which he has no intention
whatsoever of pulling away from, and NATO the *organization.* And this organization, says the general, is really Made
in U.S.A., patent pending, and this isn't quite right. And so
he says to me—not just the usual thing, about how Europe-
ans could never feel absolutely sure that an American President would push the nuclear button to defend Europe if the
result would be that the Russians would devastate American cities. He says to me, "M. President"—I wonder if even
Mrs. de Gaulle calls him Charles?—"please understand
that I am not reproaching you. I would not, if our roles
were exchanged, guarantee you on my honor that I would
be prepared to sacrifice every American city in order to
defend the cities of Europe." Not all that easy to answer, so
I said the usual things about an alliance being an alliance,
and the son of a bitch reminded me that the language of
NATO authorizes *any* member of NATO, having interpreted an assault on one member as an assault on all members, to retaliate militarily as that nation *"deems necessary."*
That means, theoretically, we might not deem it necessary
to retaliate militarily at all. Maybe we'd cut down that
month's shipment of Pepsi-Cola, and declare war on Don
Kendall. Then he says to me—as a matter of fact, that was
on Wednesday at the lunch in the palace, when Jackie made
such a hit. Good old Jackie. God knows what in French
history she was speaking to God about at the lunch, but
suddenly he turned to me, and he was radiant, and he said,
Do you realize that the conversations your wife has had
with me are on the order of my wife chatting with you about
Henry Clay? I smiled. Appreciatively, you bet. Managed a

wink at Jackie. Thank God Mrs. de Gaulle wasn't trained to ask me my views of Henry Clay, since the only thing I could remember about him offhand was that he was the Great Compromiser. Wish the Great Compromiser had been with us in France. Though he'd have been especially useful at Vienna . . . Oh yes, and then—last words, practically— after that final meeting he says to me, "M. President, stand fast when they tell you they want to change the status of Berlin. That is the most useful thing you can do for the world. And for world peace." All these general instructions and admonishments I get. I was a little pissed off at Averell Harriman charging into the Versailles party, though he'd have been invited if I had thought to send in his name. But what he said was, "Jack, do what *pleases* you. *Relax.* Enjoy yourself. Trust your own instincts." He's about the only one left who calls me "Jack." But then I hear he calls Her Britannic Majesty "Liz." Maybe he'll bring us together again one of these days. "Liz? You know Jack? Of course." What the hell, confusing. But you leave De Gaulle with an eerie kind of serenity, maybe related to that religious business. Arthur reminded me that when De G met with Khrushchev in March a year ago and K was going on and on about how awful wars are, De G said to him that if he didn't want war, then he shouldn't start one. Apparently that really dried K up. On the other hand, when De G says something he means to be the last word on some discussion, his mind visibly walks away from the subject, and you have the feeling that if his last words were: Would you like the Venus de Milo for Christmas? and he intended that to shut off discussion, he wouldn't even hear you when you said no. Khrushchev would probably say no, the son of a bitch. Yeah, he would, I bet, though he'd accept the Venus de Milo if one of his spies stole it for him. Bastard.

11

At Auschwitz, by the time Clementa got there in late January of 1945, the assembly line was running with feverish haste. The commandant had said he would settle for nothing less than one thousand "eliminations" per day, notwithstanding that the routine had been for just under five hundred. This meant all the obvious things—day and night sessions, lengthened duty hours, a general compression of the horror. But it also meant that the victims did not have the time to atrophy that their predecessors had, whose "elimination" often came only after a month or two or even three of near starvation. So it was that Clementa, on the day her execution was aborted by the Russian infantry division, though thinner than normal, had only the physical stress of one week's separation from her pastoral routine with the Wurmbrands at Tolk. Her complexion was healthy, her frame rounded. All the haggardness was concentrated in her eyes, which denoted that she had not only lost weight, she had lost all contact with reality. She went from the place in line which one hour earlier had been moving toward the gas chambers—a line whose links instantly dispersed when the commotion came—to another line outside the Revolutionary People's Club, designated as such within one hour after every German in the vicinity of the building, used for recreational purposes by the authorities who had administered the camp, had been either shot or stuffed into railroad cars headed for slower deaths. Clementa was separated from her dazed, and elated, companions and, with a half-dozen other girls, one or two younger, the others in their early twenties, was taken to a dormitory, and in the course of the evening raped a dozen times. Her body reacted spastically to the pain and the bullying, but she was for the most part without facial expression of any kind.

In eight days she had seen her foster parents executed without warning, been herded into a car and driven silently to Hamburg, then into a railroad car jammed with several hundred shivering human beings, some half her age, some four times her age, none of whom she knew; from them she vaguely learned that they were headed for a death camp. The thought of ceasing to live was the only bright prospect that came to mind, and so she carried out the orders given to her with exemplary docility, and when she was nudged by the old lady who had sobbed it seemed every moment of the five days and nights in the camp, to be told that this was the day designated for the extermination of everyone in that barracks, that the gruesome execution by gas would happen that very afternoon, Clementa felt nothing at all. And then, moments after the wailing company had lined up for their last farewell, there were the scattered shots, the sudden disorder, the flight of the guards, the blare of the radio, the howls from the prisoners. Clementa merely stood, as though commanded to stay in line, outside her barracks, head pointed to the right, toward the gas chamber one kilometer distant.

She had stood alone almost two hours when a Russian soldier grabbed her arm and led her to an improvised processing center at which the captain, looking up, asked her her name, her age, and where she had come from. She replied to none of these questions, whereupon the captain designated her for officer entertainment, in which capacity she proceeded to serve for the balance of that month, before being shipped first to an interrogation center, where she was pronounced dazed beyond the capacity of conventional therapy to extricate her, and then on to Vorkuta, a Soviet prison camp, where she was given menial work to perform.

She had not shown interest of any kind in her sentencing, no curiosity about her crime, whatever it was. She had merely done her work, mostly in the mess hall, cleaning, serving the officers. As the years went by, her status evolved toward a kind of indecipherability that seemed to bother no one in particular. She was sexually obliging to the commandant and to anyone else particularly importunate, but her nervelessness was a depressant to ardor, and after a few years it simply became a part of the accepted convention that Clementa (she had given that out as her name, and said she had forgotten her surname, so she had been given the name Wolf) was left alone. She never initiated a conversation, but she would now reply, giving brief, perfunctory answers as required. Her Russian had become fluent, and it was discovered about her, when she absentmindedly picked up a book in English from the officers' lounge she was cleaning, that she was apparently conversant with that language, because she did not conceal that she read the text without difficulty.

Two Russian officers, one of them elderly—indeed, he had been recalled to duty notwithstanding that his retirement had come in 1939, and now he was nearly seventy— had taken a personal interest in her. The first, a colonel, had told her that there was really nothing in her dossier that presented serious difficulty and that if she wished him to do so, he would attempt to arrange for her release. She thanked him, but said she had no place to go, and would therefore remain where she was. Ten years after she had got to Vorkuta she caught the eye of the second, a spirited Ukrainian captain, a widower, apparently something of a war hero, now attached to the KGB and doing duty in a prison camp because of an informed suspicion in Moscow that three or four of the camp's inmates had histories much more interesting to the KGB than the prisoners had let on at the time they were interrogated and sentenced. This required the captain to preside over extended interrogations that kept him in Vorkuta for almost three months, in the course of which he fell in love with Clementa Wolf.

She treated him like everyone else, but Captain Gouzenko persevered, even as with the prisoners. It did not discourage him that for over two weeks he appeared to be making no headway whatever. But then, on that third Sunday, she suddenly began to go beyond the entirely perfunctory talk to which she was given. What she said was greatly disjointed, but the captain encouraged her to reformulate her thoughts and her sentences. He invented a game they played together, designed to stretch "their" memories. He would supply one datum, on his side of the board, relating to his early childhood, and she would do the same. Gradually there came a reconstruction of sorts. She knew now that she had a family, and knew their names. But the memory of them was purely factual, as if they had been the mother, father, and brother of friends. She remembered that she and Henri had played games together, and remembered some of the practices of those games, but nothing of what once they had signified to her. In a month, he knew her story; and she herself knew it, for the first time in a decade. She remembered the Nazis coming and putting her on the train. She remembered the liberation, and—on this point the captain questioned her most diligently—expressed no resentment at her treatment by the liberators. She had supposed that that was how the Russians were supposed to be; at least that was the impression she had always got—savage and rapacious, like all soldiers who had suffered. She had no complaints to make against those who had rescued her from the Nazis, the murderers of her parents and her foster parents.

On this matter Captain Dmitri Gouzenko showed a most

relentless curiosity, probing as to why she did not resent the raping, the imprisonment, the forced labor. Clementa said she had not really reflected on the matter; she assumed that they were men carrying out orders and obeying instincts, which instincts were certainly preferable to those exercised by the people who had dominion over the society in which she had been brought up.

There was here, finally, the beginning of an analytical intelligence, even if there was nothing left of an emotional memory. Dmitri spent many engrossing hours with his beautiful dark-skinned protégée, whom he patiently, with the help of the commandant's wife, instructed in basic cosmetic literacy. At one point late in the evening, when he had taken much vodka (Clementa consented to taste the vodka, as an act of docility, but did not finish the little jigger glass), Dmitri had led her quietly to his quarters. She knew what was expected of her, addressed no complaint, and in the dim light Dmitri Gouzenko looked down on the body of a girl not quite thirty, whose eyes' glaze he had known; but he saw now, for the first time, something else: a rising sense of keenness, of self-recognition other than as merely a vehicle of others' convenience. He approached her thoughtfully, patiently, tenderly, and he felt for the first time, as indeed it was the first time she had so responded, that there was latent passion there. The following night he knew it, and she knew it. By the end of the week she had experienced passion, and Dmitri marveled at it and at her surprise at finding that she had feelings she could at first just experience, and then begin to express.

One week later they were married, in the office of the commandant, both wearing overcoats because the coal heater was working only fitfully. It proved no problem for Mrs. Dmitri Gouzenko to leave the home she had known the longest of any she had frequented and follow her husband to Moscow, where he was pursuing with such success his career in Soviet intelligence. By the end of the decade he was able to show off his gifted wife, who also spoke German and English and read French, to his little company of intimates. He took pains not to conceal her story, and she got around to listening with stoic resignation to his telling it. People were as people were, was what she had learned; and the Nazis were the worst. The Russians were also bad, but at least one could say about them that their society was at the service of a great social ideal. Dmitri had talked to her about that ideal, and although she had never really studied Marxism-Leninism in any detail, she accepted it, if only because Dmitri did, and as far as she knew, Dmitri's patience, his resolution, his great love of his country and of its ideals, were exemplary.

She wondered, though in ways altogether detached, about Henri. She remembered him, in an abstract way, as having been the light of her life. She remembered this only as an objective fact, as she remembered the feelings Juliet had for Romeo. It was their life together that she remembered, but not the experience of it; a life that had been totally extinguished one dark day. She had not seen him for nearly twenty years, since the night he went away to England, and she remembered even wondering why he had not written to her, though she knew that there had been difficulties. She more or less assumed that—of course—he had been killed, fighting alongside the English, or by a bombing during a raid, or however; her own rescue from disaster was surely unique in her family. When the Nazis came, and the Wurmbrands were made to stand before the riflemen—hands clenched, Uncle Hans holding a Bible in the other hand; all this in front of her, in the garden, at high noon—everything that came before receded in concreteness, and although she could remember scattered details without difficulty (her mother, the last day she had seen her, was wearing a red evening gown, and smelled of lavender), she was in no way involved in her former life. It might have been someone else's. Dmitri had roused her from her traumatic lethargy, and now she had feelings again. But feelings only for what happened now, what happened to her, to Dmitri, to their two-year-old girl, Nina, whom she named after the wife of Chairman Khrushchev, and to the twenty schoolchildren aged fourteen and fifteen to whom she taught German history with emphasis on the terrible reign of the Nazi Party, whose followers continued to dominate the western half of the country. So that when Dmitri came home that afternoon and told her that her brother was in fact alive, she felt only a twinge of curiosity—not, really, much else.

Where did he live? she asked, and what was he doing? Dmitri replied that, unhappily, he had to report to her that her brother was in league with the neo-Nazi movement in Germany, with headquarters in Berlin, and that it was now Dmitri's assignment to track him down. If indeed he is helping the Nazis, Clementa remarked, then he should be tracked down, indeed her very own mother and father would hope that the Russians, and Dmitri in particular, would be successful in any such enterprise. Yes, she said matter-of-factly, patting her little girl on the face to stop her crying, yes, she would cooperate; what was she supposed to do?

12

Henri Tod met with Stefan Schweig at the cellar of Number 12, as they designated this particular meeting room of the Bruderschaft, though meeting room was perhaps inappropriate to describe Number 12, inasmuch as not more than five or six people could with any comfort convene there. It served primarily the function of a mini-armory, where the paraphernalia of the uglier face of covert activity were collected, provided they were small—large machines, suitable for reproducing ugly pictures of Ulbricht, were kept in the roomier quarters of Number 22. Number 12 had the basic lethal weapons, plus a very few that served special purposes—silencers in particular, and telescopic sights. And a cabinetful of this or that drug or opiate or poison, useful but only provided that Sophie was there. As trilingual secretary to an American general who liked to go out and review the troops and other delights, there were times when Sophie, whose father had been a pharmacist, was simply not there, and if one of those times was also a time when the Bruderschaft required some Prussic acid, why, her absence worked to the advantage of the designated consumer.

Indeed, Number 12 was, so to speak, the launching pad for terminal operations. It was not used regularly; but neither was it used stingily. Henri Tod had attracted his disciples around one basic proposition plus another that he described as a corollary to it, in language that might have been expected from a man formally trained in philosophy.

The basic proposition was that when the alternative modes of living were apparent, human beings would choose freedom. He came to this social conclusion, which he believed to be profound, and profoundly believed, as a very young scholar freshly arrived from extensive training in Great Britain. And he had come back to Germany with the end in mind of planting in the public consciousness a second proposition, namely that the Communists were Nazis. And that therefore any apostolic attention given to Communist ideology other than as social filigree was sheer frivolity, a form of autohypnosis exercised by either philosophical naïfs or charlatans. The awe and esteem in which Tod was increasingly held was fortified by the swelling number of Germans who, given the alternative, indeed proceeded to choose freedom. It was that enormous human traffic, westbound, that brought on the crisis everyone knew was now coming to a head.

But Henri Tod's corollary was that history tended to be dominated by the phenomenon of inertia. That unless individuals act decisively, antisocial forces tend to come together and form glacial tides creating their own momentum; thus the tyrannies survive, as the sloth persists; and the people, submitting, becoming the individualists *manqués* the political philosopher Professor Michael Oakeshott had written about. The immediate condition for testing the social law of Henri Tod—that the people will choose freedom if they are given the alternative—was that the alternative had to be available. The mortal enemy of freedom, he generalized, was the inertial conspiracy which denied the alternative. Thus if the alternative had been more dramatically recognized by more people critically situated on July 20, 1944, Adolf Hitler would have succumbed to, rather than survived, the inadequate attempt by Stauffenberg to assassinate him. Indeed, if an alternative to Hitler had been dramatized from the beginning, he would not have accumulated the power he did.

In Berlin, Tod would lecture his growing fraternity on the objective, namely the destruction of Communism-Nazism. He mingled with his young disciples, discoursing with them quietly wherever life was lived—at the corner of the bar with one or two members of the Bruderschaft, drinking schnapps or beer or wine (in the conventional division of Bavarian beer drinkers, Rhenish wine tasters, and Prussian schnapps drinkers, Henri the tea drinker did not fit at all); or in one of the meeting halls, though always discreetly—there were no public meetings. What he told them was at once simple, and complex. What was simple was that Berlin was the key to the future of Europe, as Hong Kong was the key to the future of Asia—and probably the world. Because in Berlin and only in Berlin, the great social point could be dramatically made: the people would choose freedom (and opportunity) over against slavery (and stagnation). If Berlin was kept operative as the permanently open sluice gate for human idealism, then eventually the glue that caused the Union of Soviet Socialist Republics to stick together would dissolve. That substance, Tod would lecture, was no different from what had temporarily mesmerized virtually all of Germany into consenting to follow the orders of the mad and sadistic Hitler. If Hitler's borders, so effectively sealed early in his reign, had been more porous, he would not have lasted.

The purpose of a few men, annealed in idealism, vision, and courage, was then twofold: to keep Berlin open; to help those in Communist Berlin who were especially inhibited by the Communists to make their way across the dividing line of the city.

And the ugly part (Tod always began by acknowledging it as that): to discourage individual acts of sadism against those who chose freedom and to punish, most severely, those who organized most effectively to prevent East Germans from achieving their freedom.

Foremost of these offenders, of course, was Ulbricht. But

Tod, early on, had ruled against killing Ulbricht. To do that, he argued, would be to give the Soviet Union the excuse it most wanted for resorting to intervention. True, the Soviet Union's armed legions were, every day, gathering along the perimeter of East Berlin in greater density. But clearly there was a felt reluctance actually to intervene, as had been done five years earlier in Hungary, and this notwithstanding that it was actually the Russians, not the Germans, who had juridical rights to govern Berlin—the right of conquest, shared with Americans, British, and French. But so great was the investment by Moscow in the pretense that the Warsaw powers were individually governed that it had been left primarily to Ulbricht, to his "council," and to the omnipresent Vopos—the young, uniformed Communist-Nazis—to do the dirty work. Although it might be said that Ulbricht was the principal formal enemy, it was not for such as the Bruderschaft—the growing secret fraternity of young, idealistic Germans—to take on the job of dealing with Ulbricht. It was, however, the responsibility of the Bruderschaft to take on the job of dealing with Ulbricht's most unpleasant agents, and indeed the mission tonight, being planned at Number 12, was to arm in order to effect the elimination—incidentally from East Berlin, coincidentally from the planet—of a double agent, caught out.

Stefan Schweig had been born on the day that Adolf Hitler marched into the Rhineland, which made him twenty-five. His father had been killed, in Italy; his mother had nursed him in the hatred she felt for Hitler, and for the whole monstrous nationalistic atavism for which he stood. When Stefan's father was killed, his mother treated the news as more or less inevitable—or such was the memory of her eight-year-old son. Later, during the awful privations of 1945–48, she protected him by working as a subway janitor and, taking the earliest opportunity, she lectured her son that there were no interesting differences between the

Communists and the Nazis "except for professors, who always study the unimportant things." Stefan had not known what his mother meant by that, and in any event had a problem in reconciling her generalization with the sacrifices she was making to keep him in school, where he was exposed to professors for long hours every day.

But as he grew older, he began to understand. As Henri Tod understood instantly what Stefan meant when he said that the taxonomies of the social scientists were inverted. What Nazism and Communism had in common was that both systems sanctioned the killing and torturing of innocent people, and if one saw that, all else that was sayable about the nice ideological differences of the two systems was, well, trivial.

It was not trivial in the life of Stefan Schweig—notwithstanding that this would not be his maiden killing—that on this night either he or Henri Tod, depending entirely on chance or opportunity, would execute one Aristophe Spender. He needed, in order to satisfy his sense of obligation to the distinctions laid down by his dead mother, to repeat to himself that Aristophe Spender was *not* an "innocent person." Else? Else he, Stefan, was a Nazi, a Communist, a killer of innocent people.

He had had trouble, he confessed one day to Henri Tod, on the matter of "civil authority." Stefan was a Catholic, and a Catholic, he reminded Henri, does not "execute" anyone. A Catholic is permitted to pull the trigger knowing that a bullet will then enter the brain of the man whose head lies between the crosshairs. But this must be a military act. And the "military" is a duly constituted division of government, as distinguished from the Bruderschaft. To which Henri had said that this was of course in general true, but that a larger view of natural law entitled the individual to deny the civil authority of those who exercised power in East Germany, and that such was the existing situation. After all, did Stefan Schweig believe that those who had

met to murder Adolf Hitler on July 20 had violated the civil
law about which the Scholastics had spoken? Stefan let the
matter go, even though he did not feel that his curiosity had
been entirely satisfied. Was he, tonight, going out as a soldier of an inchoate army of justice? Or had he appointed
himself, or rather been appointed by Henri, a "civil authority"? But no more time for this.

Sophie had brought coffee, and had laid out on the
kitchen table in the cellar the weapons from which Henri
would choose those especially appropriate to the occasion.
They knew the four sites in East Berlin in which their mark
spent, at a guess, 85 percent of his time. There was his
bachelor apartment, on Neue Blumenstrasse. There was
the restaurant-bar he most generally frequented; indeed it
could almost be said about Aristophe Spender that he had
office hours at the Löwen-Eck. Almost every day he visited
his mother, if only for a half hour or so, during which he
watched television and drank the tea his mother brought
him. And, of course, there was the Helsingforser Platz,
where he was the superintending dispatcher of the state
taxi fleet, operated mostly by veterans, many of them partly
crippled, who were also the important sources of the information he sold regularly to the Bruderschaft.

A profitable relationship for both parties, and moreover
a relationship almost three years old. But then last week
Spender had reported that a particular taxi had been re-
served to pick up Lt. Colonel August Hester at 11:30 at the
Schwanenhof at Pankow, a watering place for highly placed
East German gentry, which before the war had also acted as
a discreet brothel, and was now showing signs of recidi-
vism. The Bruderschaft had been looking for an opportunity to settle scores with Colonel Hester, who presided over
what was generally referred to, in plain talk, as the Torture
Wing of the Pechnow Prison, and had, in early April, himself presided over the torturing to death of a twenty-two-
year-old member of the Bruderschaft whose older brother,

aged twenty-four, now claimed the privilege of arranging to
arrive at the Schwanenhof at the same time as the taxi
carrying Colonel Hester. He did; and when, ready to do his
duty, the avenging brother turned away from the news-
stand at the corner at the same moment the colonel walked
out of the noisy bar, the older brother was mowed down by
two sharpshooters who had clearly been waiting for him.
Aristophe had been paid twice that day, and the idea was
that, tonight, he would be paid one final time.

The price on the head of Henri Tod was distractingly
high, and accordingly he consented to Sophie's rather elaborate, but unmistakably effective, ministrations. His fine
straight brown hair was soon gray and curly. His almond-
shaped eyes had now just that little lift that gave them a
squatness faintly oriental. A shadow under his left nostril
suggested a scab not entirely gone. And the tip of his right
front tooth was now gold. He appeared a slender man, in
his mid-fifties, something of a roughneck. He was appropriately dressed, and his documents revealed that he was a
butcher, employed in West Berlin at a large concern that
provided fresh meat for the American garrison. Stefan
Schweig was an assistant who, dressed in a sport coat and
open shirt, looked slightly raffish, and could have been one
of the hundred thousand young Germans who prowled the
streets on Saturday looking for entertainment. Stefan carried a .38 and a powerful tear gas canister in his jacket
pocket. Tod had a hunting knife, and the Hi-Standard .22
revolver he handled as adeptly as a barber a straight razor.
It was a convention at Number 12 that when a meeting was
over at which Henri Tod was present, Sophie would require
that with a single shot he extinguish the candle at the far
end of the room, in the center of the padded section that
guarded the main safe, using the silencer. One time he had
missed the target, the refractory candle continuing to give
out light after the bullet had plugged the mattress behind.
Sophie and company were amused at this unusual sign of

Tod's fallibility. But Tod was desolate, and that weekend he devoted to recapturing his skill, and finished by putting out ten candlelights in a row.

It was still easy, on the S-Bahn, to cross over. Less so if one were carrying packages; so these Henri and Stefan did without, burying themselves, standing, in the smoker, and handing out their identity cards at Friedrichstrasse to the Vopos without bothering to raise their heads from the newspapers they were both reading. In the event either of them was searched, they had contingency plans, centering around Klaus, over in the corner in the oversized raincoat who, if needed, would materialize and identify himself as a Vopo inspector general, taking charge.

It was just after nine, and the killers ambled first to the Löwen-Eck where they sat, ordered beer, and began a game of skat, Stefan removing the playing cards from his pocket. After a half hour Tod asked the waiter whether Herr Spender was expected, as Tod had a message for him. The waiter shrugged his shoulders. "It's Saturday. Probably he'll work late at Helsingforser Platz. If you want, you can tell me, and if he comes in late, I'll tell him."

"Yes," Tod said, bundling up the cards, and to Stefan, "—it's getting late, old boy, let's roam about a bit. Yes, if you see Spender, tell him a friend of Colonel Hester wanted to express his gratitude. That's all," and he put a 50-pfennig piece in the waiter's hand.

They spotted him at Helsingforser Platz. Normally he sat inside the glassed cabin, his knees under the long linoleum table at one end of which was the active radio dispatcher. Tonight he was standing in the cabin for a moment to check with the assistant dispatcher, then outside to resume what was apparently a heated conversation with an elderly, stoop-shouldered man wearing a driver's cap, presumably gone off duty and arguing with the boss. Henri walked past the cabin to the street corner, without looking left toward the dispatcher's box in the large parking lot. Now in the shadows, Henri stopped to light a cigarette and whispered, "Go over there, northeast corner. See the wind current over the chestnut stand? It's moving toward the taxi area. Lob the gas into the area of the back taxis when you see me, in the lead taxi, begin to drive out toward the dispatcher. There'll be a lot of confusion. I'll nail him as my taxi goes by. All right?"

"And then?"

"And then you go back to the bar, get the waiter, and tell him never mind about Spender. Colonel Hester delivered the message himself. Then get the hell back home."

"And you?"

Henri Tod looked at his young confederate, and for a moment said nothing. "My job, Stefan, is to see to it that our people don't worry about me. Only the Communists. I will see you on Monday."

They separated. Henri ambled toward the lead taxi and told the driver he wished to be taken to Oberbaumstrasse. The driver nodded, and then whispered, "Can you pay me in West German marks?"

"I'll split the difference," Henri replied. The East German mark was selling on the open market for one quarter the West German mark, and in any event was not being accepted, by many West German commercial enterprises, as tender. Henri's reply had been conventional: He would agree to pay in West German marks, but he would pay half the taxi bill.

"All right." The driver started the motor.

At that moment a few yards behind him there was a small explosion. It was followed by what seemed like a gusher of smoke, instantly felt by those downwind of it as tear gas, and now drivers, passengers, and pedestrians were yelling, coughing, beginning to run. Meanwhile Henri had rolled down the taxi window as the driver quickly engaged the gear and started out, well ahead of the airflow of gas. He followed the custom of pausing at the dispatcher's gate,

where he yelled out his destination: "Oberbaumstrasse."
As he did so, Henri, his face largely concealed from the
open window, fired a bullet into the brain of Aristophe
Spender.

Henri had not counted on what then happened in quick
succession. The assistant dispatcher dove under the table
and evidently hit an alarm button. Simultaneously a siren
began to scream—and a crossarm gate fell suddenly across
the entrance to the parking lot, blocking entrance, or exit.
Henri's driver had gradually assimilated the events, and
now slammed his foot on the brake just in time to miss
crashing into the gate. He looked back, into the muzzle of
Henri Tod's pistol. Tod looked quickly behind and saw that
there were people on the run headed toward him, fleeing
the tear gas, but perhaps also determined to overtake the
car from which the bullet had done its conspicuous work
under the neon light of the dispatcher's office. Tod opened
the door, slipped the pistol into his pocket, and began a
lope, not wanting to attract attention. When he saw that
three of the pursuing throng deflected in order to follow
him, and that two of these were armed Vopos, he broke into
a full run. He followed the Warschauer Strasse, the least lit
of the two streets he had the choice of running down. But
before he had gone a half block, one Vopo had begun to
fire, and he felt the bullet pierce his back under the shoulder. The tumult behind him increased, and Henri looked
desperately for an alley to run down, found one, and was
gratified that the lights were less frequent. But the pursuit
was hot and, hardly able to see, there being no lighting left,
he ran into a concrete blockhouse. He fingered his way
desperately around its grainy surface. The throbbing pain
in his shoulder suddenly became acute. The wall led him to
a door he did not need to open, because it was already
open. He dove through the black space, breathing hard,
and his eyes, now slightly adjusted to the dark, seemed to
discern huge rectangular bulks. He rushed toward one, and

saw that it was an empty train car. He ran toward the far end of the station and, turning a corner, ran fifty yards and then stopped, breathless. Now he heard noise and saw, reflected on the high, vaulted ceiling of the huge station, the rays from the searchlights with which the Vopos were armed. He heard the shout, "He's in here somewhere! Cover all the entrances! Fritz, follow me!"

Henri leaned against the coach stairs, panting. He thought to throw himself under the car, hoping that his flattened shape would escape detection; but he knew this unlikely, and considered for a moment a firefight, probably suicidal, though he could take five men with his five remaining rounds of ammunition. But the roar that increased in volume suggested that the Vopos had congregated in force. It was then that he heard, from behind, a soft male voice. "Quiet. Step up. Two steps. But *quiet.*"

Henri Tod, pistol in hand, struggled up the stairs of the coach car. He could not see his host.

"Just a formality, but do you mind giving me your pistol?"

Reluctantly, Tod handed it over.

"Now, follow me."

The door to the outside was first quietly locked. Then the door to the carriage was turned, and locked from the inside.

"Follow me."

Henri's host held a tiny flashlight and walked down the railroad car's corridor. After a few steps, Tod found himself in the most luxurious sitting room he had ever seen inside a railway car—stretching fifteen meters. It was lit by small candles, but he could discern the velvet, and the bronze, and the rosewood, and the couches. And the girl, sitting in one of them, the soft light from a sconce shining on her, a glass of wine in her hand.

"Ah, Claudia," his host said, "we have a guest. I know that this violates our rules. But it just happened that he and

I arrived at our Berchtesgaden at exactly the same moment.
He was being pursued by people who sounded most awfully disagreeable, so I presumed that you would agree to
extend our hospitality, just this one time?''

Caspar did not wait for her answer, turning to Tod.

"The lights you see here are absolutely undetectable
from the outside. Not so any considerable noise, though
this railway car is better soundproofed than the average.
Still, hold down your voice, if you have any inclination to
start singing, or whatever. We will, I suppose, in due course
hear our friends attempt to enter the car. They will discover
that it is locked. This will not make them suspicious, because the other 248 cars in this part of the station are also
locked, and it is altogether unlikely that they will rouse the
Chief of the Railway Division at this hour to ask for 248 keys
on the assumption that you were carrying one in your
pocket. They will look for you under the cars, and on top of
the cars. They will then post a guard, and look again tomorrow when it is light. They will abandon the search for
you sometime tomorrow night, Sunday, which will facilitate
our dispersal the following day. Claudia and I are working
people. And what, sir, do you do, when you are not avoid-
ing Vopos?''

Henri Tod managed a smile. But he needed support, and
so reached out his hand and leaned against the wall before
falling on the floor in a dead faint.

13

On the airplane, right after takeoff and the meeting with Macmillan, the President was given his news roundup. Normally he went through this eagerly, circling condensed items he wished to see in their entirety—a column, say, by James Reston, who had a way of making him feel philosophically serene, though that was a hell of a question Reston had asked the day of Inauguration. "Mr. President, just what do you expect to do with the presidency?" What would have been an appropriate answer? "I dunno, Scotty. Something Periclean, I think." He'd read it later, he gestured, easing back the chair behind the desk of the private compartment of *Air Force One*. He had got it a little bit out of his system, talking with Macmillan. And on the flight from Vienna, Tommy Thompson and Chip Bohlen—God, *they* ought to know the Russians if anybody does, time they've spent there, poor buggers—they said to me: Don't be upset. That's just the way "they" are. I said, You don't mean "they" are *all* like that crazy man Khrushchev, do you? Well, not quite. Khrushchev is sort of unique, they felt, but I might as well, they said, have been talking to anyone else who was head of the Soviet state. That's the way "they" talk? Well by God, that's not the way they're going to talk to me. Fuck summit conferences. No, that's the wrong word. Don't want to say anything unfriendly about fucking. To hell with summit conferences. I mean, God knows I *tried*. He comes rolling in over his empire. A train, all the way from Moscow, stopping here and there like the czars, to receive flowers from little girls in countries he owns like I own Boston, and before the first afternoon is over he is sitting there, looking me straight in the face—there he is, with Gromyko, Menshikov, and Dobrynin. The three Russians who probably know the most about America. And there I am, with Thompson, Bohlen, and Kohler, the three Americans who probably know as much about Russia as anybody. And Rusk. And Khrushchev tells me that all the so-called satellite countries are *absolutely* free, and in fact, he doesn't even remember the names of their leaders! I mean, if he had said he couldn't remember the names of all the leaders he's had replaced, or executed, I might have believed him. Oh yes. Later on, maybe that was the next morning—doesn't matter—he looks me in the face again and says that Poland is more democratic than the United States! I mean. He was *sore*—and all I had said was that we all believe in political independence, but that some countries are located so close to our own that we have to look out after our vital interests, and how would he like it if we said there had to be free elections in Poland? You'd have thought I had propositioned Mrs. Khrushchev. No. Nobody would ever think I had propositioned Mrs. Khrushchev. But he really laid it on. Now what is a President of the United States supposed to say, when the leader of the Soviet Union carries on about Polish independence and Polish democracy? I was very polite—everybody told me I was polite. Everybody told me I had held my ground well. They probably told Neville Chamberlain the same thing. Hell, I know I didn't hold my ground well. What would Ike have done? What would Churchill have done? I must find out about that. Was I supposed to say: *Are you going to tell me that the Russian troops that imposed order on Hungary in 1956 were Moscow U. graduate students doing lab work on democracy?* How in the hell would Dean Acheson have replied to Khrushchev? I must get the answer to that . . . You can't talk to him. I say, Look, we don't want war "because of a miscalcu-

lation." Now, was that so offensive a thing to say? You'd
have thought I had questioned Lenin's sincerity. (Was
Lenin sincere? I forget.) MISCALCULATION! he said.
Could I have heard you use that word? Are you suggesting
that when the people respond, as they inevitably will, to the
social forces of history, that that is a *miscalculation*? And is it
a *miscalculation* that the United States, which pretends to be
anti-colonialist, supports the most repressive, reactionary
countries everywhere it can? Is that a miscalculation? And
so on and so on and so on and so on . . . In the afternoon,
before leaving, we walked together and I thought maybe
now he'd ease up. Not at all. Did I want war? he said. *He*
didn't want war, of course not. No Communists want war.
Ask Lenin. Ask Marx. He knew that the *Pentagon* wanted
war, he knew that the Nazi generals in Germany—who are
really running NATO—he knew that *they* wanted war. Well
if we *wanted* war—he didn't want war—that would be that:
We want war? We get war. . . . God knows I tried, on the
Berlin thing. Interesting point he made about Japan, the
bastard. Interesting to a sophomore debate team. A junior
debate team would laugh the position out of court. He says:
You people didn't hesitate to make a peace treaty with
Japan without consulting us, right? Well, why should *we*
hesitate to make a peace treaty with East Germany without
consulting you? How do you handle something like that?
The Russians got into the Japanese war—what was it, two
days after Hiroshima? Two weeks? All *we* did is fight Japan
from Pearl Harbor all the way to Hiroshima, and *we* need to
consult *Moscow* before making a peace treaty with Japan?
But now we're talking about Germany. Berlin. Berlin would
be the capital of Russia if it hadn't been for us imperialist
warmongers. We kept Russia alive. Sure they lost ten million men. Ten million men less for Stalin to kill for other
reasons, big deal. Sure they fought heroically, fought desperately. So did the Nazis, for that matter. So he compares
our making a treaty with Japan with his making a treaty with

East Germany. Neat. And he says: Look, it's sixteen years
since the war was over, this is ridiculous. You people said at
Yalta you'd be out of Berlin within two years. I hadn't been
briefed on that, and no one remembered it when I met with
my troops that night. But the hell with it, he knows occupation arrangements under treaty can only be rearranged by
collective action of the four occupying parties, and he is the
only party that's wanting to change it . . . Oh yes. Forgot.
I made that point maybe five times. Five times? Was it fifty
times? That *he* was the one who was wanting to change
things, that we weren't pressing for any changes, that therefore *he* was responsible for others' reactions to changes he
was responsible for making. And what did he say? I guess I
could have guessed. All life is change, yeah yeah, was that
Heraclitus? Or Plato? Or Jack Benny? One more time I
tried reason. Look, Mr. Chairman, if we let you unilaterally
abrogate our rights in Berlin, then every treaty we've got
will just be considered by our allies as nothing more than a
piece of paper. So he says, what do your allies want? Why
do they want Berlin? Would they feel happier if they had
Moscow? And he looks over at Gromyko, as though it was a
serious point he was making. I mean, serious that what we
really want is Moscow. And Gromyko nods his head. Reflec-
tively. Khrushchev got a great kick at dinner at the palace,
telling me Jackie said she thought Gromyko had a pleasant
smile. Had fun with Jackie about that later on, asked her if
she thought Boris Karloff had a pleasant smile. Then Khrushchev said a lot of people think Gromyko looks like Nixon.
I was a good boy, I didn't say a lot of people think he acts
like Nixon. . . . God, what a relief to be with Macmillan.
For one thing, we can talk about what the *exact nature of the
problem is.* Dean Acheson's got a memo—he thought it
would be useful before I prepared my television address—
that'll be some address. I must remember to ask Arthur
what a historical euphemism for fuck-up is. Acheson, as
usual, has a point, and I got a chance to mention it to

Macmillan. I didn't start off by saying Dean thinks we might actually end up having a nuclear war over this one, which is what he thinks. What caught my eye was this. Acheson said: Look, suppose Khrushchev goes ahead with his treaty, suppose that the government of East Germany now becomes the government that we need to check our passports with, etc. etc. etc., when we send our military convoys over East German territory on the autobahn to Berlin. Suppose that the guards that check the papers at the airports are East German, not Russian . . . well? Granted that is a violation of treaty arrangements. God knows we know all that. But suppose that is *all* that changes? Go to nuclear war over that? No. Acheson suggests we take two divisions over the autobahn, headed for Berlin. See what happens. Prepare for any contingency. But make one thing absolutely plain to Khrushchev, namely that if anybody attempts to keep us from getting to Berlin, we're going to fight. The scale of that fighting is to some extent his doing. And what did he tell me, last words in Vienna: If you interfere with the rights of the sovereign Democratic Republic of Germany after we have concluded the peace treaty, either their land rights or their air rights, we will meet that challenge with force. But Acheson has an interesting point, I thought, and Macmillan likes the idea of pretending nothing really happened, though I have the feeling that was about all he liked about Acheson's memo. Still, it's a breakthrough of some sort— i.e., we're just plain not going to go to war over a change of uniform.

The President rang for his news summary, and said he wanted a Coca-Cola, and get Bobby on the line. Tell him it's a collect call. He'll like that.

14

$\mathbf{R}$ufus didn't question Blackford when, over the telephone, using their code, Blackford told him that it was necessary to consult with him in Berlin. "If you will call Sergeant McCall," Blackford had added carefully, "she can catch you up." Rufus understood from this that on arriving in Berlin he was not to proceed to Blackford's apartment, no longer a "safe house," in the terminology of the trade. "Sergeant McCall" was a number in the regular intelligence office with which Blackford maintained only such liaison as was necessary. The point was to meet under circumstances as nearly as possible secure. Blackford was given by "Sergeant McCall" a new address, at 64 Nollendorfstrasse, and a password. Subsequently he gave the same information to Rufus. Blackford was there a half hour before Rufus arrived, admitted into the apartment by the same elderly German woman who had already admitted Blackford. Rufus had lost weight, and showed signs of a fatigue Blackford had never before associated with him.

"You look tired, Rufus," Blackford said, taking the older man's raincoat and hanging it in the closet. "Martha here has said she could fetch us up anything light. We have"—Blackford now imitated the booming, syllable-by-syllable accents of the vendors that cruised American trains—"choc-o-lates, can-dy-coat-ed ch-ew-ing gum, orange-ade, fresh cof-fee, cash-ew nuts. What will it be, ma'am, sir?"

Rufus smiled and sat down. "Coffee would be fine. I ate on the plane." In German, Blackford asked for two coffees.

Rufus still liked to get to the point. Though in the last few years he had, Blackford noticed, developed a faculty for light philosophical badinage, in interesting contrast with his traditional reluctance to utter one extra-utilitarian syllable. Always Rufus was the professional, but now he would go to the point of permitting himself to display an affection for Blackford, perhaps because Rufus's wife had so very much liked, and enjoyed, the young protégé of her husband. Blackford unabashedly admired Rufus, but never praised him except to Rufus's wife, because to have praised Rufus to his face would have brought on mortal embarrassment. So, sitting down opposite Rufus, the coffee table between them, Blackford began. He told, in chronological detail, the events of the day before.

"I wanted to consult with you before telling Tod about the letter. But I also made inquiries so that we could get hold of Tod later today if you thought we should consult him. And there's been a hitch. Tod is missing."

Rufus looked up. "Missing since when?"

"Missing since night before last, Saturday. Nobody knows where Tod lives. But there has never been a time when, by contacting the 'office,' you fail to establish contact. He simply calls you up, from wherever."

"Has the Bruderschaft grown since we last talked?"

"It has. And is really catching the popular imagination. People don't know what Tod looks like, but they quote him. He is becoming something of a folk hero. The Commies go crazy at the mention of his name, and if one East Berliner gets the clap, they blame it on Tod."

Rufus winced, and Blackford contritely reminded himself that raffish language visibly distressed Rufus. Even General Eisenhower, legend had it, would not permit swearing in the presence of his most valued intelligence officer. One time when General Patton was reporting on developments in Africa, he had, after the report was completed, taken off on a salty digression. In due course General Eisenhower turned to address a reference to Rufus, one of the dozen members of the staff present at the meeting; but Rufus had quietly left the room. "Wonder what Rufus would do," Ike had at a moment of exasperation said, "if he had to decode an intercept from Hitler to one of his generals that said, *'Fuck the 8th Army at 0500 June 8th.'* " Beetle Smith had volunteered that Rufus would probably transcribe the intercept as, "The Nazis are planning to penetrate the 8th Army at 0500 June 8th." Ike liked that and told it to Mamie, but then thought to remark at a meeting of his personal staff that no one was to make slighting remarks about Rufus or to Rufus. Of all of this, Blackford surmised, the wisest intelligence officer in America was undoubtedly aware. Sometimes, Blackford suspected, he snatched a little discreet amusement from it.

"No doubt about it," Blackford continued. "The GDR folks want Tod as much as any man alive. And let's face it, they probably wouldn't have much of a problem trying and executing him. Tod is not at all discreet about certain of his activities. He leaves fingerprints. Intentionally."

"Was he up to anything—unusual—that you know of on Saturday?"

"I'm pretty close to Bruni, Tod's principal aide. And when he told me this morning that Tod was 'missing' I told him that I might have news later on in the day I'd want to communicate to him, and what was the likelihood that his disappearance was sort of routine? Bruni got pretty hot under the collar and said that Henri Tod didn't go in for 'routine' disappearances. He then sat down and said there was no reason for him, Bruni, to have less confidence in me than Tod has shown me during the past couple of months. So he told me that on Saturday Tod had gone over to the Eastern sector with Stefan Schweig on an assassination venture. The Bruderschaft do that kind of thing, you know."

"Of course I know. And I assume you've known that

that's one of the reasons we have dealt so circumspectly with the Bruderschaft.''

Blackford stretched out his legs, accepted the coffee from Martha, and leaned his head back.

"Rufus, we've got the beginning of a big problem here. I've been here now—what, over seven weeks? I've seen a lot of Tod, and no question about it: his intelligence apparatus is the best in town. Knows twice what we know, and he's bankrolled. And unless you're now going to confide in me that you know where he's getting the scratch, let me help by telling you I *don't* know. But I do know that routinely he pays off informers, and I don't know what he's paying them off with unless he's robbing banks on the side."

"I would be surprised if he went in for that kind of thing."

"I would too. On the other hand, if he's gotten into kidnapping, my guess is we'd have heard about it from the friends of the victims, and the only thing the *Neues Deutschland* hasn't charged Tod with is kidnapping. But let's hold that, and focus on other things. Now last Saturday, Bruni told me, Henri and Schweig, who is a youngster—''

"How old is Schweig?"

"Oh, maybe twenty-five."

"How old are you?"

"Me? I'm thirty-five."

"Go on, grandfather.'' Rufus permitted himself a half smile.

"Rufus, you astonish me sometimes. I mean, you always astonish me. Anyway, he went out with middle-aged Schweig to do in a double agent."

"You do mean, to kill him?"

Rufus's penchant for precise language got in the way of idiomatic extemporaneity. "Yes, Rufus. The target was a double who got one of Henri's boys mowed down by giving out information used by the Vopos."

"What happened? Is Schweig back?"

"Yes, he got back late Saturday, after leaving the Bruderschaft's calling card with a friend of the victim so that all of
Berlin would know he hadn't died accidentally, and
Schweig simply assumed Henri was okay. He reported to
Bruni that Tod had made the hit from a taxi, but that after
that, Schweig ran off and didn't see anything more. For one
thing there was tear gas between him and the operation.
For another, Henri had told him to get going after he let the
tear gas go."

Rufus lowered his eyes and entered into one of his mini-
trances, for the duration of which there was no point in
talking to him, so Blackford sipped on his coffee. And in
due course resumed . . .

"Now here is something, Rufus, that maybe even you
don't know. I know you know Tod's general background:
rich Jewish boy and sister, parents to Belsen, taken to foster
parents upcountry, the Nazis get on to them, execute the
foster parents and send the sister away to a death camp.
What you don't know is that Henri Tod's memory of his
sister is something on the order of an obsession. He mentioned her to me only once, in that conversation we had a
couple of weeks ago, when he let it all pretty well hang out.
Anyway, he is convinced that she was the most wonderful
creature God ever created, and you told me you found out
he's convinced that indirectly he killed her."

"Yes."

"And now"—Blackford held out the photograph—"we
discover that Clementa Tod is alive. The impact of that on
Tod isn't easy to predict."

"Do we know it's she?" Rufus said, looking at the photograph.

"No, we don't *know* it. But wouldn't you say the guy who
wrote that letter"—Blackford handed Rufus the document
—"doesn't expect Henri is going to doubt that that girl is
his sister? I also assume that the mumbo jumbo on the back

of the picture is some childhood code word. I think we ought to go on the assumption that the girl is alive."

"And of course," Rufus said, putting down the letter, "the writer of this note desires us to believe that he is a double agent, or even merely a mercenary. And he could be just that. Fifty thousand marks is moderately serious money. More likely, though, I'd guess this was a Ustinov operation. Seems to me that what he cares about is Tod, pure and simple, not Tod and fifty thousand marks. The problem we have is to handle this whole business with some reference to Tod's apparently unmanageable affection for his sister—what's her name?"

"Clementa."

"Clementa. We have got to learn more before we bring Tod in, because he may make hasty decisions, under the circumstances."

"Right. And that, Rufus, is why I brought you all the way from London."

Rufus smiled. "Let's think now about it." And they did, for three hours.

15

Claudia and Caspar stayed up with their patient. They had stocked, at their Berchtesgaden, only routine medications—aspirin, a cough syrup, Mercurochrome, bandages. Claudia stripped the young man, and instantly detected his facial disguise. She located the wound on the back of his shoulder and the corresponding wound above his chest. She whispered to Caspar that the evidence was pretty clear that a bullet had passed through their ward, who was now moaning quietly, slipping in and out of consciousness. Claudia boiled hot water, nursed the wound, cleaned and dressed it, wiped the makeup from his face, removing the gray wig, and then made a little purée of aspirin, which she attempted to get him to drink. He managed to get most of it down and was soon sleeping regularly, though in his sleep he spoke in convulsive jerks, unintelligibly. Claudia left the door of the master bedroom slightly ajar and motioned to Caspar that he should follow her into the adjacent salon.

She busied herself unpacking, on the desk top, sausage, bread, honey, and cheese, while Caspar opened a bottle of wine.

"Well now, Caspar, you have got us into a pretty pickle."

Caspar was visibly excited. "I don't dare go out. I don't know—maybe I could risk it, what do you think?"

"Are you crazy? They've probably got searchlights out there. I hope they don't have dogs. But he didn't trail any blood." She paused. "I suppose they are pretty sure by now that he got away through the open—south—side. That's where he'd have headed if he had been able to see, and he could have run down those tracks pretty fast. Still, I don't think you should go out."

"If I did, I could find out pretty quickly what they want him for. And I think that's probably something we ought to know, don't you?"

Claudia was distracted. "He looked so tired, a little desperate. What a striking face, Caspar. I doubt he is a common criminal."

"He's a common criminal unless he kisses my uncle's ass first thing in the morning when he gets up, and last thing at night before he goes to bed."

Claudia munched on her cheese sandwich and smiled. "You know what my boss said in a letter to your uncle yesterday? He said, 'Sir, the entire railway system is benefiting from your inspired guidance and attention to its problems.'"

"My uncle doesn't know one end of a railroad car from another. Marx forgot to tell him. Well, your boss is no different from everyone else's boss. Uncle Walter believes that all of Germany is in his hands and that the only thing needed to cure everything is to stop the refugees. That and, maybe, the resurrection of Stalin."

"Caspar," Claudia's voice was soft, feminine, and now there was anxiety in it, "did your father actually . . . know Hitler?"

"Yes, I gather he did. In that bundle of stuff in the locker I told you about there's a letter to my father from Asshole Adolf (Heil, Asshole!)." Caspar did the Nazi salute. "Hitler was telling him stuff he wanted in this car. There were some sketches there. Pretty professional. See that"—Caspar pointed to the highly polished wooden slab, waist high, usable as a desk or a little dinette, that stretched out across one half the width of the car, but which could hinge down and over, disappearing against the wall—"Hitler designed that. It is exactly as he specified in his letter to my father."

"But how do you know that your father actually had personal contact with Hitler?"

"Because in one letter my father referred to their 'conference' the day before about the car, and the notes he had taken."

"Was there anything—you know—well, anything—sort of . . . idolatrous in the letter? I mean, did your father go on and on the way the GDR people here do?"

"Actually, he didn't. My mother doesn't like to talk about it, obviously. But once I asked her, just like that, 'Mother, was Father a Nazi?' And she said what I guess everybody says, 'Caspar, your father was a railroad engineer, drafted into the army with the rank of lieutenant colonel. He did what he was ordered to do.' "

"Then why was he shot?"

Caspar looked at her, and paused. She had moved along the settee, pushing away the coffee table with her foot, and was caressing him behind the ears.

"I know why my mother *thinks* he was shot," Caspar said, his voice husky.

"Why?"

"Because the Soviet military tribunal declared him a war criminal on the grounds that he had designed trains that transported victims to the camps."

"Did he?"

"I should certainly think so, Claudia. He didn't spend fifteen years designing custom cars so that he could design this one car for Adolf Hitler. And after he designed train cars, I don't think he put up brass plates: 'NOT TO BE USED TO PROVIDE TRANSPORTATION TO EXTERMINATION CAMPS.' Of *course* he designed trains that were used for that, but he didn't design cars *expressly* for that. As far as I know, they used mostly cattle cars."

"Then why did they shoot him?"

Caspar got up. He looked very young in the dim light,

but the customary raillery was gone now. He looked to one side and spoke in a monotone.

"He was shot on orders from my Uncle Walter, because Uncle Walter discovered that my father had sent railroad coding information to the Americans with a message indicating how the Americans might, by trying to take over three or four critical control centers, regulate the flow of traffic. That was when the Russian and East European refugees were beginning to be shipped back to Russia to be killed. What Father apparently didn't know was that the whole operation had an American stamp of approval."

"How do you know this?"

"That's easy. Because my father wrote it."

"To whom?"

"To me. The night before he was shot. A sealed letter, kept in the envelope with my birth certificate and baptismal papers, with a note to Mother that she was to hand me the letter, unopened, on my twenty-first birthday. I saw the letter last September. The day before I asked you about this car." Caspar was back on the sofa, his head on Claudia's lap. His voice was at once childlike and august. "What happened was that I sniffed out the key to the locker one day when Mother was out. So, of course, I looked inside, and found all that stuff, including the master keys to this car. Then I saw the letter. And, of course, I opened it. Mother was away for a week, with Uncle Walter, at some state function. The last line of my father's letter said he wanted me to know the truth, but that if at the time I read the letter my Uncle Walter was still alive, and if my mother was still alive, I was not under any circumstances to divulge its contents to my mother, as it would only make personal and political problems for her.

"My problem then was to come up with a dummy letter, because often Mother had said to me that when I was twenty-one I would see a letter from my father. Her curiosity about it was terrific. So, using Father's typewriter, I faked a letter. I began by saying that he would pretend to have handwritten a letter from the prison, but in fact he was writing it at home but before going to trial, in case he did not have an opportunity later on. Then I just copied everything in his letter, the kind of thing you would expect a father, the day before his death, to write to a five-year-old son. And, of course, left out the important parts."

"Did it work?"

"No problem at all. On my birthday in May, Mother just cried, and said how beautiful the letter was, and how Father had really been an innocent victim, but that in that postwar atmosphere it hadn't been possible to distinguish the true Nazis from the mere professionals, and so on. I didn't tell her what I thought, which is that the leading Nazi survivor is her brother, my Uncle Walter."

Claudia said nothing. But she began to cry. Caspar, alarmed, took her into his arms. "Claudia, Claudia, why? What?"

"They did it to my oldest brother too, and what I told you about my father being killed in the war isn't true. He was taken on—one of your father's railroad cars—to the camps. My father's crime was that at the town meeting at Leipzig he gave a speech against the practices of the occupying Soviet troops. He was gone the next morning. We never heard from him again, or about him."

Caspar sat up, but without releasing her hand. He pressed it. "Do you know, Claudia," he smiled, "I do believe that you and I are security risks! When I become prime minister, you will be my commissar, in charge of the Railway Division of the German Democratic Republic."

They heard a moan from the bedroom. Claudia went quickly. Henri's face looked flushed. She turned to Caspar.

"I'm going for a thermometer and some medicine."

"No. I'll go."

"Caspar, quiet. In the first place, I work in the railway headquarters. In the second place, I would not fit any description of the man they are looking for. In the third place, if they do find me, I know what to say and how to say it, about what I've been up to."

Caspar smiled, and let his hands down from her arms. "Which, right after you get back, will prove to be correct."

They took the routine precautions as she walked down the steps of Berchtesgaden and, knowing where and when to turn, was soon in the alleyway of the office building. There were more guards than usual. She showed her pass. "I need to get some papers from my office," she said simply to the sergeant who looked at her card, and she walked into the building, and out the rear door. Not to the all-night pharmacy, where an order for antibiotics at that hour might raise suspicion, particularly when she had no doctor's prescription, but to the apartment of her former roommate, Margret Nilsson, who worked in the hospital as a nurse and kept in her house a little of everything. And a lot of what Claudia had needed almost daily since coming to know Caspar during that placid week in that sylvan setting, so far from the impacted grisliness of the offices in which they spent their working lives.

To Margret, Claudia confided that she needed a little help "for this reason or that." Margret, while not probing the confidences of her friend, was as ever loquacious about her own concerns. She readily consented to get the prescription and have the blood analyzed. "Oh Claudia, I am so very much in love. Yes, a doctor. Unfortunately, he is married. I don't know what I will do if we can't live together, forever."

Margret's leisurely rhythm as she described her passion did not synchronize with Claudia's pressing need. But after an hour she had the prescription, her ex-roommate's doctor-lover's signature nonchalantly forged on a prescription blank from a pad Margret kept at home. Claudia did not wish to appear indifferent to Margret's passion, but she managed, soon, to kiss her good night and get on with her desperate business.

16

At exactly five minutes after four in the afternoon a tall man wearing a fedora and a brown suit stepped out at Arnswalder Platz, carrying a briefcase. He turned west purposefully and began a measured stride, looking neither right nor left. He had walked one block when a 1958 Trabant pulled up alongside him. A man seated in the back seat opened the car window and said, "Mr. Jerome?" The man carrying the briefcase stopped and said, "I am a porter from the Hotel am Zoo. I was instructed by a Mr. Jerome to give you this briefcase. He regrets he could not deliver it himself." The porter handed over the briefcase and walked away.

Captain Gouzenko clenched his teeth, and to the driver said, "Go up Pasteurstrasse for one block. Turn right on Greifswalder. Keep the radio on alert. If we are being followed, we will be notified by the time we reach Bernhard-Lichtenberg. If we are not being followed, then go back to Hildestrasse."

Dmitri Gouzenko opened the briefcase. It was empty, except for a single envelope through which a yellow toothbrush protruded at either end. Gouzenko deliberated for a moment whether to open the missive himself or wait and let Colonel Ustinov open it, but decided to go ahead. He took a penknife from his pocket, slit the envelope open along the narrow side, and pulled out a letter.

"My dear F:

"The suggested rendezvous is unsatisfactory, for reasons

I leave to you to imagine. The next time I visit in East
Germany it will not be at the invitation of a stranger.

"I am, as you may or may not believe, not a floating
exchequer for Mr. Henri Tod. I certainly hope that his
sister will be freed, and unofficially I have agreed to accept
Mr. Tod's commission to act as his intermediary in effecting
his sister's repatriation. (Mr. Tod does not question the
authenticity of the photograph.) But of course the details
will need to be worked out, and we shall have to know that
your plans are feasible.

"Inasmuch as I do not plan to visit East Berlin, and you
evidently do not desire to visit West Berlin, I agree to meet
you in Vienna. If you desire such a meeting, telephone the
concierge at the Hotel am Zoo and tell him you wish the
concierge to advise Mr. Jerome, when he calls in, that Mr.
Frank (I am contributing four more letters to your name)
will meet Mr. Jerome as planned. I have checked the schedules, and there should be no difficulty in arriving in Vienna
by Thursday late afternoon. You may proceed by plane or
by train, as may I. When you reach Vienna, call the concierge at the Hotel Regina and ask if Mr. Jerome left an
envelope for Mr. Frank. Mr. Jerome will have done so. The
envelope will indicate where I will meet you, and at what
time. I shall not have a colleague along, and you are not to
have one along either. I will have with me a briefcase, but
this one will have 25,000 marks as a gift from the International Association to Benefit Refugees from Nazism Impris-
oned by the Soviet Union. Another 25,000 will be yours
when Miss Tod reaches West Berlin.

"Oh yes. Spectrographic analysis reveals that the toothbrush is now contaminated, and so I return it. If you decide
not to go to Vienna and wish to communicate further with
me, write in care of the White House. They always know
where to reach me.

"Yours truly,

"O."

Ustinov, in his clandestine office at Blockhouse H, on reading the document confessed his surprise to Dmitri Gouzenko and rang for Felix Zimmerman, who appeared twenty minutes later looking suave and suspicious. Ustinov leaned back in his chair. "I just don't understand it. The reconstruction we made, confirmed by your wife Clementa, about Tod's relationship with her simply does not explain Tod's indecisiveness. He seems almost blasé about her turning up alive. I'd have expected almost immediate action."

"Do we know that Tod has seen my letter?" Gouzenko asked.

"It would seem to me inconceivable that such a discovery would be kept from Tod by his American friends. And Tod is reported here as having verified that the picture is that of your wife. Of course, she *has* changed; perhaps Tod has changed. But I would be surprised. The question now, of course, is do *we* go along?"

"Sir, if I may say something here," Gouzenko spoke. "They don't know for certain whether Mr. 'F' is KGB or a mercenary. Our response at this point is surely going to incline them in one or the other direction. If we *don't* go to Vienna, they'll—"

"Of course we will go to Vienna," Ustinov interrupted.

"I was going to say, Colonel, that the only reason not to go to Vienna is if we conclude that they are not interested in Clementa, and that is inconceivable. And if we don't go, they'll conclude it was definitely a KGB operation, that Clementa is safely in Soviet hands and we're simply using her as bait for Tod. In that case, unless Tod is willing to exchange his own freedom for Clementa's, which isn't likely—he presumably wants to enjoy her company—the whole operation will stall. Among other things, Tod would first need to convince himself about Clementa's condition, and on that point we couldn't be very reassuring."

"You are saying if we don't go, they'll conclude they haven't been dealing with an independent operator. I agree. But what do we think we can get out of the Vienna rendezvous? Other than the money?"

"Well, Colonel, I could maybe stand a chance of stringing him along. I could go and tell him that I worked at the Vorkuta labor camp, that I got to know his sister, who has been in that camp for fifteen years but is not under sentence at this point. I could say that she is a little amnesiac but otherwise quite normal. And that it would be possible for me to return to Vorkuta, and plot with her to effect her release by marrying her. He may even know about Article 118."

"Article 118 does what? Remind me."

"It permits 'rehabilitated prisoners' to leave a camp provided a) they have a family to return to, or b) a job that also provides living facilities. My line—and I think he would swallow this—is that I am willing, for fifty thousand marks, to go back to Vorkuta, take out wedding papers, and bring his sister to East Germany. From there, as we all unfortunately know, it is easy enough to get her into West Berlin."

"On what pretense would you tell him you could get her into East Germany from Russia?"

"Colonel Ustinov! You forget that I *live*, and am employed, in East Germany. Ever since leaving the camp, I have worked for the Amtorg Trading Corporation in Potsdam. Remember?"

"Yes, yes. I remember your cover story. So then?"

"So then my wife brings in Henri Tod."

"Where? How?"

"There are a variety of ways, sir. One of them that appeals to me I would need to discuss with my wife before elaborating. But you must agree we have lost nothing. I go to Vienna for two days. I return with 25,000 marks. In a week or so we arrange to fly my wife in from Moscow. We proceed from there."

"You are quite certain your wife will cooperate, Gouzenko?" Zimmerman broke in.

"I am quite sure my wife will cooperate, Herr Zimmerman."

"Very well." Ustinov put his initials on a form on his desk. "Fill it out yourself, and get to Vienna. If you bring back Blackford Oakes's head, I will put you in for a promotion. Bring the money to me."

"And I'll take it from you, Leonid."

"You get half, Felix."

"We must get Tod," Ustinov turned to Gouzenko. "We most certainly must. That business Saturday on Aristophe Spender. The gall of it! And leaving word at the bar. They might as well have left calling cards."

"We nearly got one of them."

"What good does it do *nearly* to get someone?"

"Good for the morale, sir."

"Yes, I suppose. Good for the morale. Check with me as soon as you get back from Vienna."

17

Henri Tod sat on the large fore-and-aft sofa, its back to one of the train's windows, his left forearm lightly slung, his arm wrapped snugly to his side by the dressing that went right around his chest. It was Thursday and nearing seven in the evening. He and Caspar were listening to the little shortwave radio. It featured, in the local news, Ulbricht's speech to the GDR parliament, in which he announced that henceforward the border crossers, the hated *Grenzgänger*, the East Berliners who worked by day in West Berlin, would be required to register with East Berlin authorities and obtain permission to continue working in West Berlin.

The foreign news spoke of an interview Khrushchev had granted to the English ambassador in which Khrushchev had warned pregnantly of the awful dangers of nuclear war. Khrushchev had, meanwhile, publicly announced that the next scheduled phase in Soviet demobilization had been postponed indefinitely, and that he planned to increase the Soviet military budget by one third. Tod switched to the BBC World News, which mentioned the two Khrushchev items, and also that Chancellor Adenauer planned to visit West Berlin in a few days and had made a statement to the effect that the East German government was showing signs of panic because of the thirst of its own people for freedom. The BBC went on to sports events, and Henri turned the radio off. It had been a strenuous passage to the relative serenity they now experienced.

By the time Claudia had got back to Berchtesgaden, well after midnight of that Saturday, the wounded visitor had begun to show signs of mounting fever. He ranted and he sweated and he tossed about on the Führer's ample bed. Caspar was at his side when Claudia entered with a wet towel, stroking his head and occasionally using force to keep Tod from ejecting himself from the bed.

"He's gotten a lot worse, Claudi," Caspar whispered.

"I have a thermometer, and penicillin, and something Margret gave me to help the stomach. But how will we take his temperature? He will bite the thermometer in two."

"Let's see if we can get it under his arm. I'll hold him down." Caspar put his whole weight on Tod's good shoulder. For a moment he lay quiet, but as Claudia was about to insert the little glass cylinder in his armpit, suddenly Tod swung his wounded side over. Quickly she withdrew it.

Caspar said. "We might be able to do it up his backside. But listen, Claudia." He reached over and took the thermometer from her hand and put it back on the side table.

"What really is the point? We know he has a fever. We have the only medicine he's going to get—the penicillin. Unless we take him to a hospital. And if we take him to a hospital, it may be that we are only curing him for the purpose of getting him shot. So let's forget about the temperature until he has cooled down or—" Caspar no longer looked like a grown boy. "If we cannot save him we cannot save him. You know how to give the injection?"

Claudia nodded.

Together they turned him around. Caspar lowered Tod's shorts, and Claudia inserted the needle. For another hour Tod thrashed about in bed. Caspar and Claudia resolved on a watch system. She went off to the salon to sleep on the settee. Caspar, a book in hand, sat on the edge of the bed, alternately reading and wiping the perspiration off Tod's face. Once he changed the sheets. At four in the morning, he woke Claudia.

It had been so for nearly twenty-four hours. Late on Sunday they succeeded in taking his temperature. It was 105 degrees, and he was delirious. They resolved that on the Monday, Caspar would take sick leave; on the Tuesday, Claudia would do so. Their parents need not know, as they never called to speak to their children at work. They forced themselves to discuss the possibility that the man would die, and even focused on the problems of removing his corpse. It was a long two days.

When on Tuesday afternoon Caspar returned to Berchtesgaden, he found Claudia beaming. "Oh, Caspar, he's come out of it! His temperature is down to 101! And he is talking. Just a little. And he took some soup. His eyes are very sad, and he looks afraid."

"Did you ask him what the police want him for, Claudi?"

"Oh no, I wouldn't do that. Come and speak to him."

She took Caspar by the hand down the corridor, past the staff quarters, to the bedroom. Caspar entered it. Henri Tod was lying in bed, his eyes intelligent for the first time since he had fainted.

Henri began to speak. "I wish to . . . thank—"

Caspar interrupted him. Tod was speaking with difficulty. "Be quiet, friend; it is not right for you to make an effort. Not yet. You are getting better. Just tell us. What shall we call you? What is your name?"

For a moment Henri Tod's eyes narrowed suspiciously. But then, his head sliding back on the pillow, he whispered, "My name is Heinrich. I am pleased to meet you." With that effort, he closed his eyes, and was asleep.

On Wednesday morning Henri was talking, his temperature down to 100, and he assured them that he could easily look after his needs while they went off to work. They left a thermos of hot soup for him at his bedside, and reminded him to take the extra pills Margret had given Claudia. When they returned in the late afternoon Tod was asleep, but it was a serene sleep from which he woke instantly, announcing that that night he wished to join them at dinner. Claudia insisted on taking his temperature again, and when she read it she did not restrain her yelp of joy. It was very nearly normal.

They helped him from his bed, and for the first time in four days Henri Tod ate, however lightly. He did not have the strength to participate energetically in the conversation. He listened to them, and listened to the radio, and sometimes he smiled. He said he was feeling at once very weak and very much better. Caspar offered to massage him and he submitted, stretched out on the settee. Claudia volunteered to catch him up on the news developments of the past few days, and attempted to do so from memory. It was while she was reciting the litany that it came to her suddenly, with unmistakable clarity, that the young man in Berchtesgaden with them was Henri Tod. The most wanted man in East Germany; undisputed leader of the most fervent movement of mostly young Germans, East Germans and West Germans, in the recent history of the divided country. This was the man the paper and the radio had said was mysteriously missing, and might perhaps be hiding out in East Berlin. . . . She looked at Caspar, who was massaging as close as he could come to the back of Henri Tod's shoulder without causing pain. He looked up at her, acknowledging her signal. She pointed to the bedroom.

"I'll be right back, Heinrich. Getting some oil that will help."

"What is it, Claudi?" Caspar whispered, the door to the bedroom closed.

"Caspar," she hissed, muting her excitement. "Do you know who Heinrich is? He is Henri Tod."

Caspar's eyes widened. "How do you know?"

"I know."

During the next three or four days, Henri Tod was half the time asleep, half the time talking and lounging with Caspar and Claudia. From five on Friday through the weekend, they were both there uninterruptedly. It was some time during the long conversation on Saturday night that he perceived that his identity was known. By then the public flurry was considerable, and reading between the lines it was clear from radio announcements that the East German authorities suspected that Tod might well be hidden in East Berlin, that it was he who had been wounded the preceding Saturday. The possibility was even hinted at that Henri Tod had been killed. In anticipation of any move to make him a martyr and to keep alive the Bruderschaft in his memory, much radio time was given over to disparagement of Henri Tod, his background, his work, his associations, his methods. To these screeds the three would listen, mostly in silence. Occasionally Henri would say, after the broadcast was terminated, that he really felt obliged to tell them the truth about this Tod person and these allegations. But after two or three days of intensifying horror stories about what he had done, Claudia intervened. "Henri"—as they now called him—"you don't have to explain who it is that you are. We both know you now."

And they did know him, as few others did. Henri Tod recalled one night that he had never experienced sickness before. Much had happened to him, in a relatively young life, but never before had he spent a single day in bed. "I even still have my tonsils and appendix." The unexpected leisure, the sense of security in a little womb surrounded by hostile forces, caused him to be preternaturally relaxed, and even talkative, and so he recounted his thoughts, spoke about the past, about the years in the coal mines.

"Why did you go to the mines, Henri?" Caspar wanted to know.

He hesitated, but only briefly. "I went because I needed total distraction when I learned that my sister had been killed." He told them then that he had not permitted himself to think about his past, thinking only about what was expected of him as a physical laborer, and at night pursuing the thought of philosophers. "When you wrestle with Hegel you are too exhausted to concern yourself with your own thoughts. However," Henri said, sitting relaxed in the candlelight, on one of the armchairs opposite Caspar and Claudia on Hitler's side of the salon, "I became so much absorbed that I decided to go to Cambridge and pursue my studies under supervision. It was there that philosophy brought me to the conclusion that I needed to be politically active. I abhorred politics, but then—I remember the day, it was an afternoon, coming out of the Trinity College library, and I saw this young girl with books in her hand and two little pigtails coming into the library from the warm, moist freshness of spring, and I nearly froze, because for one moment I thought I was looking at Clementa grown up. It was an illusion, but I thought then that, of course, there's a sense in which Clementa *is* alive. Because there are other girls who are alive, of her age, perhaps even of a degree of her sweetness. And they are victims now, and will be victims tomorrow, of the identical passions that killed Clementa. I recognized then that there was nothing about Nazism in any sense distinctive. That its peculiar obsessions, the racism especially, were really only crotchets of the central disease—and that, of course, is the passion to govern others and to regulate their lives. That's when I decided I'd have to go back to Germany, the country that caused so much suffering, to try—*in* Germany—to help people to see that Nazism continues, only under another name."

Claudia was surprised to find that the effect of Henri on
Caspar was to wake in him, for the first time since they had
been together, something like a sustained interest in the
political situation. Henri of course was startled to learn that
his host at Berchtesgaden was not only the nephew of
Henri's principal enemy, Walter Ulbricht, but that Caspar
worked in such close quarters with Walter Ulbricht. There
was an evening during which Henri yearned to ask whether
Caspar would go so far as to cooperate with the Bruderschaft. The same evening during which Caspar, yearning to
do so, wondered whether it would be inopportune for him
to proffer his services to the Bruderschaft. It was that same
evening that Claudia told her story, and the bond that
annealed the three took shape, so that by Sunday night they
recognized that even if the words they had spoken had not
been spoken, they were joined together in a common enterprise of which Henri Tod was the leader.

From that moment on, until the following Thursday
when Henri Tod left, the time they spent together was, for
Claudia and Caspar especially, a time of exhilarating moral
excitement. They had now an entirely engrossing vocation.
Henri felt their excitement and shared it. Every day they
would listen to the news and comment on it, and discuss
plans and contingency arrangements and means by which
those who needed help could be helped. Henri warned that
they must, soon, come to West Berlin to live, that they
could not count on living forever at Berchtesgaden.

"Couldn't you arrange to hijack this car into the West for
us, Henri?" Claudia leaned over to pick up Henri's empty
plate. "You have the reputation of being able to do everything!"

Henri laughed. "If ever things go finally right in Germany," he said, contriving a synthetic solemnity in his
voice, "I will build you a private railroad car. Like this one,

if you wish. But not *this* one. This one will be exhibited in a museum. On either side of it, we will have displays of . . . the railroad cars that traveled to Auschwitz and Belsen and Ravensbrück—cars the owner of this railroad car had built when he was not preoccupied with building himself a private railroad car." Henri then looked up, and smiled.

"On the other hand, if ever it could be said that something has been exorcised, it could be said about Berchtesgaden that you two have rid it of its evil spirit."

"How was it today, Caspar?" Henri asked.

Caspar was at the other side of the polished table, wearing an apron. While listening to the radio, he had been helping Claudia with the potatoes. The smell of the pea soup in the galley aft, near the staff quarters, permeated the snug and luxurious drawing room.

"Pretty frantic," Caspar said, slicing the potatoes. "Uncle Walter had in three of the top people to rehearse how to clamp down. The idea is to start by chopping off only ten percent of the work permits, then begin turning the screws. They figure that the fuss generated by ten percent will be containable, and they can decide how far and how fast to go from there, depending on the level of public resentment."

"It's nice to know," Tod said, sipping on his cup of tea, "that public resentment means anything."

Claudia spoke. "You should see the reports my boss is getting about the train service. Yesterday one traveler, seventy years old, started to beat the conductor with his umbrella after the train had stopped for over an hour. The heat is awful right now. All the trains coming in are being instructed to be irregular." She got up with the panful of sliced potatoes and disappeared for a moment in the galley. "Next thing you know, they'll be giving out medals for Most Unpunctual Conductor of the Month."

"There's no talk, then, of a D-Day?" Henri asked.

"No," Caspar answered, opening a bottle of wine and pouring two glasses. "And I don't think he has a D-Day in mind, or he wouldn't talk about being flexible about the enforcement of the permits for foreign work."

"Speaking of trains, I'll tell you something odd; listen to this," Claudia said. "A report comes in from the division chief in Leipzig, and there's a covering letter on it to the boss. I know they're friends, because they've corresponded, and sometimes I put in a telephone call to the Leipzig man—his name is Sturming. Well, this report was on secret preparations being made at the Karl-Marx-Stadt Locomotive Works. They're making armored cars suitable for transporting prisoners."

Tod and Caspar fixed their eyes on Claudia. The report riveted their attention.

"The inventory is, as of this moment"—Claudia tilted her head back, and her light brown hair fell over part of her animated face—"thirty-eight cars, I think that's the exact number." She fished out a piece of paper from her purse. "Here, I copied it down: 'Cars suitable for transporting prisoners. Defined as cars that can be locked, that have minimal extra-utilitarian accommodations, and whose windows are barred.' Question: Who's going in those cars, where are they going, and when?"

Tod looked up. "That's important news. Either they're going to transport prisoners in large numbers to different camps—or they plan to have more prisoners. The type of German who lives in the East and desires to move to the West. Will you be seeing the follow-up correspondence on that?"

"I expect so. I open Herr Kohl's mail routinely, except letters marked personal from personal friends. There aren't many of those, and this report wasn't marked confidential."

Tod turned to Caspar. "How are they doing on . . . me?"

"There's a rumor out that your own people have been looking for you for several days. Uncle Walter and General Schlepper were discussing that this morning. Schlepper thinks you're not in East Berlin, and not dead. He thinks you may be out of the country for some reason or other, and there are strong rumors that you are in Paris to pick crumbs from the table of Kennedy-De Gaulle. Uncle Walter thinks you may have gone to Bonn to conspire with Adenauer about what he should say when he comes to Berlin—Uncle Walter never forgets the West German election is only two months off, and he likes to talk as if you and Herr Adenauer were political partners."

"I've never even met the Old Man," Henri said.

"They hope that they can pressure Willy Brandt to step up his criticisms of Adenauer. But they don't *know* where you are, and they're dying of frustration. Oh, I forgot!" Caspar walked over to his briefcase. "You'll like this, Henri. An artist's rendition of what they think you look like."

Henri Tod, Claudia looking over his shoulder, mused over a drawing of a dark-complexioned man in his thirties, with slender features, straight hair, fine nose, high cheekbones, and a trace of a cleft in his chin.

"Now, that is interesting," Henri said. "Someone has reported on my chin! Well, I've been seen by enough people. I'd say the picture was useful only in general circumstances. Not much use for specific identification. What kind of circulation are they giving it?"

"All the sector passage policemen have got one, and the railroad and airport people. They're also passing out the rumor that anyone who brings you in will receive a state bounty of 250,000 marks. They're not going public with that. I suggested it, but Uncle Walter said it sounded too bourgeois, the stress on the bounty. They're really hot for you, Henri. Wish Claudi were as hot for me."

She pulled Caspar's head back by the hair, and laughed.

"Now get over to the table, and I'll serve. I have something nice tonight."

Henri said, "You have something nice every night. That's why I had a little fever for so long. My constitution doesn't want me to go home and miss your meals! How do you manage? Do you suppose the Führer ate like this?"

"Of course not," Caspar said. "He was primarily a vegetarian, remember. I suppose he could have been induced to eat meat if he had been told it was human."

"I wonder where exactly he sat," Claudia said, looking about the dining salon.

"I know that," Caspar said. "It's in Father's notes. He sat in the corner there when the shades were up during the day. That was so nobody from the outside could see him. And when he had a staff meeting, or a number of guests at lunch or dinner, he sat exactly where you are sitting, Henri. Behind the closet, leaning up on the forward bulkhead, is a wooden section that attaches to this, making room for eight diners. Others invited to dine in The Presence clustered about those round table-desks over there"—he pointed to the far end of the drawing room, which dissolved into the green felt lounge-study. Claudia served the venison, salad, fried potatoes, pumpernickel bread, butter, and cheese, and set out a bottle of red wine.

Henri suddenly emptied his teacup, and poured into it a few drops of red wine.

"I want to make a toast. To the best foster parents I have had since I was a boy. May the God of Abraham bless you both, and may your countrymen someday know what you have done for me, and for them."

Claudia and Caspar sat, their heads slightly bowed. They didn't know whether it was right to take part in a toast when they were being toasted, this never before having happened to either of them. Claudia broke off the moment of embarrassment by lifting her own glass and saying, "And I want to return the toast. You have given Caspar and me more hope, and more brightness, in ten days than we found in many dreary years before we knew you."

Caspar raised his glass. But then, gently, he corrected her.

"More brightness, Claudi means, than at any time until she and I met." His eyes moistened as he looked at her.

"That was what I meant," Claudia said, shyly.

Caspar turned now to Henri Tod. Caspar didn't often use the idiom of candid idealism. But he found himself, almost instinctively, bowing to Henri Tod as if to a natural leader, a man of station; Caspar's superior.

In bed, the night before, Claudia had said to Caspar, "I would follow him anywhere."

Caspar sought to break the tone. "Not to bed, you wouldn't."

She smiled at Caspar and put her arms around him, holding him tight to her. "No, because it would be like sleeping with a saint, and you have hardly prepared me for that." Caspar slid his head under the covers. Claudia gave out a little playful shout. "Caspar!"

"Well, you said I wasn't a saint, so take that." She laughed again. "And that!" Soon she was no longer laughing but quietly moaning. "And that and that and that and that and that," he said softly, his exclamations now slow, rhythmic, as the sheets slid down from the bed, the bodies illuminated only in the light of the single candle by the bedside.

Moments later his head was beside hers again, and they nestled together, happier than they had ever thought possible.

18

"**I**s this the concierge? You have a message for Mr. Jerome?"

"How do you spell your name?"

"Jakob-Eda-Rosa-Otto-Marie-Eda."

"Just a moment. Yes. A Mr. Frank left the message that he will keep his appointment."

"Thank you."

"*Bitte.*"

Blackford thought it best not to travel directly to Vienna conspicuously, which he would be doing if he took the next flight out. He was booked the following day on the 9:30 flight to Frankfurt, where he would board the train. Meanwhile he needed to make a routine check with two informants, whom he saw respectively at five and seven. At 8:30 he had an engagement with Bruni. Bruni had left word that morning that he needed to meet with Blackford, suggesting a little coffeehouse conveniently located by the subway, near the Tiergarten. He was there when Blackford arrived, and he was munching on a cheese roll, a stein of beer handy.

Bruni, with his rimless glasses, heavy suit, and young yet jowly face, seemed ill cast as principal aide to the dashing head of the Brüderschaft. He had graduated as a doctor of medicine from Humboldt University in East Berlin. He was thereupon conscripted and sent as a lieutenant in the GDR army medical corps to an infirmary in Dresden. Here he had interned for a year under a quiet, elderly doctor whose

hands, at the operating table, grew progressively unstable
as he gave way to alcohol. As his only surgical assistant,
Bruni had twice now noticed obvious misjudgments, the
second of which nearly proved fatal to the patient, and
decided that his duty was to report the problem to the
adjutant at headquarters. The next day, orders were written detaching Lieutenant Bruni Lestig to duty at Bautzen, a
prison for political prisoners. There Bruni found that his
time was mostly devoted to attempting to repair the broken
bodies of those prisoners, bodies that frequently were beyond repair. As a clinician, he recognized that he was log-
ging valuable experience. As a moralist, he found it was no
longer possible simply to overlook the nature of what he
was engaged in.

He had, by considerable effort during the years of college
and medical school, forced himself to put politics in the
deep freeze of his mind. He did not remember when exactly
he made the decision to go over to the West. But perhaps,
he had told Blackford at an earlier meeting, it was when
they brought in the elderly woman. He declined to describe
her condition, but confessed that far from undertaking to
keep her technically alive, he had, after examining her,
given her a lethal dose of morphine. "I think it was about a
month after that that I sneaked into East Berlin while on my
vacation at Neuruppin."

When he reached West Berlin, Bruni could not turn
again to medicine. He found that any attention paid to the
anatomy recalled the grisly role he had played while prac-
ticing a profession he had sacrificed much to master.
Among the things he had sacrificed was attention to other
than biological kinds of health. Now his indifference to the
one kind of health heightened his interest in the other. It
was as his curiosity and concern for social health matured
that he encountered Henri Tod. A year later, Bruni left his
job as a junior manager at the Daimler sales office to spend
the whole of his time with Tod, to whom he gave himself

completely and who, above all other men in the society, Tod trusted.

Bruni motioned to the waiter; then, to Blackford, "You will join me?"

Blackford nodded. "I'll have the same. Do you have any news?"

Bruni's mouth was full. But he managed a "Yes," and Blackford waited until Bruni had washed his food down with a long, deep drink of beer. He reached into his pocket and pulled out an envelope. "Have a look."

Blackford read the note. It was handwritten, and signed, "T."

"Is this Henri's handwriting? I'm not familiar with it."

"Yes. It is his. I know it as well as my own."

The note said: "Bruni—I am all right. But it will be four or five days or maybe a little more before I can return. Meanwhile our friends must not have the impression I am out of action. Involve 'me' in something. I leave the details to you. Always, T."

"Have you figured it out?" Blackford asked, beginning on his own cheese roll.

"He is obviously in East Berlin, and almost certainly he has been wounded. There was a chase after the execution, we have verified. But he is apparently in friendly hands. He reasons that any suspicion that he is still over there will cause the kind of alert he doesn't want and maybe his friends, whoever they are, can't afford."

"Have you decided what to do?"

"Yes. I told Stefan Schweig this afternoon that I had a telephone call from Henri, that he was in Paris. That he had gone there to make financial arrangements and to get something on the Kennedy-De Gaulle meeting, which he would be bringing back with him."

"How's this news going to get back to East Berlin?"

"My dear Blackford," Bruni said, mouth full again, "surely you must know that that is no problem at all? Not all our friends in East Berlin are double agents. Stefan has been instructed to pass the word along to our contacts." Bruni took another swallow of beer, and then said, wiping his mouth with his napkin, "Now you must wonder why I have revealed these details to you?"

Blackford smiled. "Actually, Bruni, I hadn't really had time. But I suppose I would have wondered later on tonight. Go ahead, I'm listening."

"The first reason is that I trust you. But I don't give away state secrets—and my suspicion that Tod is probably crippled in East Berlin is as close to a state secret as I have ever known. I don't give away state secrets to people just because I trust them. I am trying to think ahead. I expect I shall hear from Tod again, and probably soon. He may want to come back even if he is less than completely well. I want you to make contingent arrangements if they should prove necessary."

"What do you have in mind?"

"An American officer. Say a lieutenant colonel. Someone in his forties. He's visiting in East Berlin. Say the Pergamum Museum, with another officer, call him the major. The major calls headquarters and reports he fears the colonel has had a heart attack, and they should send a military ambulance instantly. Ambulance arrives and takes uniformed colonel back into West Berlin. Only—of course—it's Henri. The real colonel, now in civvies, makes his way back routinely. Such an operation would take a little time to organize. It may be needed. We don't know how sick Tod is."

Blackford sighed. "That's not an easy one, Bruni. Officially, we work at arm's length."

"I know it's not easy. That's why I'm asking you to do it. I wouldn't expect Mr.—what do you call them, 'Mr. Joe Blow'?—to set up what I may need to set up. I do expect *you* to do it."

Blackford whistled. "All I am expected to do is to lay on the United States Army. Right?"

"Right. But only if necessary."

"There are a lot of interesting problems here, Bruni, and one mechanical problem. Which is that I've got to be out of town for two, maybe three days."

Bruni knew better than to suggest that Blackford postpone his trip, let alone ask why he needed to take it. But his disappointment was evident. "When are you going?"

"Tomorrow."

"Is there some way between now and then you can get the thing planned?"

"Sure. I could call Allen Dulles, I suppose. Where's the phone in here?"

Bruni did not smile. "Where Tod is concerned, I take no chances. He may be well on the way to mending. He may need special medical care. He may be mobile, he may not. There are more than thirteen thousand people per day that pass over and back to the Western sector, we both know that, all subject to detention and questioning. But if he is in a U.S. military vehicle, it is not lawful to stop it."

"Bruni, look. I'll try. If I could put off the trip tomorrow I would do so. That is impossible." He took a notepad from his pocket and tore off a blank page. "If the emergency does come, and if it comes before I return, call this telephone number and ask for Sergeant McCall. And say, 'Jerome told me to call.' Now I've got to get cracking to see what can be done. You can pay the bill. And by the way, Bruni, where *do* you people get your bankroll?"

Bruni smiled. "How do you Americans put it? 'Pennies from heaven'?"

"The way you all spend money, I could believe it. I'll report to Washington that Bing Crosby is bankrolling you. Good night, Bruni."

"Good night, Blackford."

Blackford walked out of the coffeehouse, then took a bus, and walked again close to where he knew that Rufus almost certainly could be found at this hour. At the corner he telephoned, let the phone ring four times, hung up. Then he redialed. At the first ring the telephone was answered. "It's me. And I'm around the corner. Can I come up?"

"Yes," Rufus said, and a half hour later, Bruni's problem was his.

19

Noon to midnight. Nice. Old Central Europe sort of feel to it. Frankfurt to Vienna, twelve hours. With roughly equidistant stops. Nuremberg. Imagine how long *that* show would have lasted if the goal had been to try *all* war criminals. Interesting question: Was Josef Stalin a "war criminal"? Blackford reflected on Henri Tod's point about the philosophers whose inverse taxonomic hierarchy ends up with worrying about such uninteresting questions as whether when you killed innocent people, you did so because you were a "Nazi" or a "Communist." It's what makes justice so slow in catching the point. To begin with, the Nuremberg trials were *ex post facto* legislation. Oh. So, if you're going to have *ex post facto* hangings, why not hang people who do those things that justify hanging them for doing? God knows, Hitler and his gang were such. But the effrontery! They were tried by, among others, judges deputized by Stalin, who on any objective accounting would have made the Guinness Book of Records as all-time mass killer of innocent people, though Mao Tse-tung was coming on fast. Idle thought department. The point, of course, was that Stalin had been among those who won the war. If Hitler had won it, no doubt he'd have tried Stalin. Though maybe he'd have tried him primarily for having collaborated, in his early years, with the Jew—Trotsky. Play with that. *"The defendant pleads, Honorable Judges, that he attempted to expiate his crime by subsequently sending an agent to kill the Jew Trotsky. That is an evasion. The fact of it is that Josef Stalin was a collaborator with the Jew Trotsky for a period of ten years, and nothing will do but that this honorable court pronounce a sentence of death, preferably by slow motion, like Soviet trains."*

Ideological daydreams department, Blackford thought. He was walking, an overnight suitcase in one hand, a briefcase in the other, through a part of the old city, or, more accurately, through the new part of the old city (not much had been left of Frankfurt after the Allied bombings) on a balmy afternoon, closer to summer than spring. He knew this section of the city, knew it well. That was another mission, and he thought wistfully that if Count Wintergrin had succeeded in his program to unify Germany he, Blackford, would not now be trying to do what he could to keep the American commander-in-chief one pace ahead of the Eastern juggernaut. Back then it could be said, in a way, that Count Wintergrin was taking the initiative: he wanted to unify something that at that moment was sundered—Germany. But now the Soviet Union wanted to unify Berlin. Or what, exactly, if not, exactly, that? How odd that all the world was wondering more: "What would be the American response?" than it was wondering, "What, exactly, will the Soviet Union do?" That it would be aggressive was accepted; discounted. That is what the Soviet Union *does*, don't you understand?

He walked by the Cathedral of St. Bartholomew. The sun was very bright, the temperature getting even warmer, but without any hint of tropicality. Here, in this city (the statisticians had figured it out), had been the densest per-square-inch bombing of the war—yes, Dresden and Berlin included. And here he was, an American, a former pilot in the American Air Force, wandering freely through Frankfurt, utterly unmenaced. The worry was not over the Americans who had fought a war and destroyed Frankfurt. The worry was about one of America's World War II allies. Would they do to Frankfurt—so painfully rebuilt, with its judges, its parliament, its free and unrigged elections, its prodigal

industry—what they had done to German cities so unfortu-
nate as to be located in the eastern half of the country?
Would they be given the chance, if the United States said
No, with nuclear resolution?

"Not if *I* can help it," Blackford said, and laughed. *I,
Blackford Oakes, promise ye yeomen of Frankfurt that, having won
my favor, you will be spared any danger from the barbarians.* Meanwhile, if you will excuse me, I have got to catch the train to
Vienna, because I have to bribe an unknown man on a
matter involving one young woman. *That is my last microcos-
mic concern, Oh ye Elders of Frankfurt. From that moment on, I will
look after your corporate interests.* Suddenly he ducked, because
a pigeon, flying only a few yards above, had dropped his
erstwhile belongings inches from Blackford's brown oxford
shoes, and, looking up, he knew with the certitude of a
former pilot that he had been between the crosshairs of the
Norden bombsight hovering over him. History records that
Blackford Oakes survived.

He arrived at the new railroad station, presented his
ticket at the gate, walked into the car whose number was
designated on his ticket, on to his compartment, and to one
of whose six seats he had contractual access to. In his briefcase he had Mommsen's *Römische Geschichte*, recommended
by Whittaker Chambers, but he had never got around to
picking it up until browsing in that bookstore in Berlin. It
gave a view of the political vectors of Roman culture, and
Chambers saw something of the same sort happening here
in Western Europe.

He was reading it when the train started out for Nuremberg. Three other passengers had entered the compartment, one of whom caught his eye. A fussy commercial
traveler, dressed in solid black with a gray tie as if he had
just attended a funeral. For him, travel was obviously something of a science. It required five minutes for him carefully
to stow his bags on the rack above; remove what he desired
from his lesser bag, which lay under his seat; regroup his

luncheon provisions, which had been packed in individual wrappers; take his ticket from his wallet and situate it in his shirt pocket, that he might more easily produce it when the moment came; remove his shoes, put on his moccasins, enter his shoes in the shoe stockings from bag two, place the shoes in bag one. Readjust the combination on the lock of his briefcase, before doing which he glanced, perfunctorily one must suppose, to his right and then to his left. He maneuvered his palm to cover over the combination lock, so that neither Blackford, seated on his left, nor the drunkard and his gabby female companion sitting opposite him might espy it. Then the briefcase was opened. From it a book was taken out, the jacket copy announcing a German edition of Professor John Kenneth Galbraith's *The Affluent Society,* though, Blacky saw quickly, the book inside was in fact the equally entertaining German translation of the *Memoirs of Fanny Hill.* The man sat down, finally, book in hand, and began to read. His posture was erect and if it had happened, at that moment, that someone had elected to take a comprehensive picture of Herr von Gruenigen, he'd have caught the portrait of a member of the upwardly mobile German commercial class that had prospered after the war.

The train was modern by American standards, the motion smooth, the service expeditious. In the dining car Blackford found himself placed by the steward opposite his fussy traveling companion, who nodded to him and continued reading his book while he ate. As did Blackford, while enjoying the Bavarian summer that slid by, with the occasional lake, the clean towns and hamlets, and the rich soil, carefully tended. Across the aisle and opposite him was a young woman who sat reading the latest issue of *Time* magazine, General Maxwell Taylor on the cover. She ordered a light lunch in English, and read listlessly, Blackford thought. She was dressed smartly in a light brown linen suit with a yellow silk blouse. On her ears were small pearls; her hair was soft and apparently untended, though it framed her face nicely and enhanced her profile. Impulsively Blackford took his notebook from his pocket and wrote: "If you are planning to go as far as Salzburg or Vienna, might we dine together? I am well behaved, I can translate for you, and later on if I can have *Time*, you can have Mommsen's *Römische Geschichte*, what do you say? I am sitting opposite you across the way. I am *not* the one with the mustache, who is eating pork chops. If the answer is yes, I'll reserve the table you're at for the second seating, at 7:30. My name is Jerome, first name Buck. My friends call me Bucky. You can call me Bucky after the first course, if we become friends. Advise."

He handed the note to the waiter, who presented it to the girl by merely swiveling about. Blackford noticed that she read it carefully. She did not look up. But she opened her handbag, took out a pencil and pad and wrote. She managed to engage the attention of the waiter and to direct the note to Blackford without once looking across at him.

Blackford read: "I'll decide after I know more about you. I am occupying Seat 3A in Compartment C, Car 326. During the afternoon, send me a note and tell me more about yourself. My name is Linda Lewis." Blackford was amused, finished his coffee, paid his bill, rose, and walked back without attempting in any way to arrest Miss (Mrs.?) Lewis's visual attention. When he reached the rear of the car he arranged with the captain to reserve the table, gave him two marks, took the reservation, and returned to his compartment.

They were in Nuremberg and would be here for eight minutes. In October of 1944 he had killed a German fighter pilot in a duel over Nuremberg. It had been his first of three aerial encounters. He closed his eyes and remembered the fear he had felt when he first saw the tracer bullets; in his bowels he felt the instinctive deep dive down for cloud cover. Before reaching the bank of clouds he spotted his assailant, bound for the bomber flotilla it was Blackford's job to protect, and so he pulled up, headed for what he recognized as an Me 109, and circled to come in between the sun and the plane. The German had begun to fire at the bomber, whose gunner was firing back. The angle was wrong, Blackford saw. As things stood at that exact moment, if he also began firing there was a fine possibility that an American bomber would engage in a suicide pact with an American fighter plane. So he pulled the stick sharply and rose, leveled, and then pushed down the nose of his Mustang and, the angle now changed, fired at the German. The German's response was a sharp left roll, a rotational loop, and now for the briefest seconds the adversaries were so to speak face to face: they might in another age in suits of steel have been riding armored steeds, holding lances and charging at each other. Blackford intuitively waited that definitive split second necessary to fine-tune his aim. The German fired and Blackford fired a half second later. The German's bullets missed Blackford's cockpit by half a foot. Blackford's bullets poured into the pilot's upper chest, and as he swerved to the right, Blackford passed his mortally wounded adversary a small room's distance away, and gazed for a tenth of a second at the lifeless features of a young man still, like Blackford, in his teens. Blackford's first kill. He wished it had been his last. But always it had been, in his case, a question of that man's life or Blackford's, if you didn't count the death of Count Wintergrin. Twelve months later, in October of 1945, five minutes away from the railroad station, the trial would begin against Hermann Göring, the head of the German air force, diminished on that other October day by one fighter, and one fighter pilot, *inter alia.* Twelve months after that, in the early hours of the morning, he was scheduled to hang, but two hours before the execution they found Hermann Göring in his cell, dead from self-administered poison.

Enough, Blackford thought, of gruesome reminiscence.

The incident in Nuremberg gave rise to a historic lead sentence in the United Press radio news in New York. Blackford remembered hearing a spirited young UP radio editor tell later how the Nuremberg executions were, "up-stairs" at UP, judged to be too important for the regular professional staff to handle. So the president of United Press, wearing a green eyeshade, had descended from the executive offices with his entourage into the radio press room in the New York Daily News Building, taking charge of the typewriter. And when the electrifying news came, he solemnly tapped out his lead sentence to UP's five thousand clients: "Hermann Göring cheated death today by committing suicide."

The solemn mood returned. One day one of the king's men meets the enemy in mortal combat in an engagement so routine that nobody bothers to notice who won, save the victim's family and the survivor. A few months later, the king himself is hanged. Or, in this case, call him the prince, since the king had killed himself off earlier, in that under-ground bunker. "Cheated death" by suicide. All of that in two years, Blacky thought, as the train pulled out. If they had kept Hitler in jail the full five years he had been sentenced to after his abortive putsch, instead of letting him out after nine months . . . might the gentleman on his right have been the aviator, unkilled? For that matter, would Blacky have any business in Vienna to take him through Nuremberg today?

But Blackford had things to do, and as they pulled out of Nuremberg—with two additional passengers in his com-partment, a middle-aged couple, the mother (grand-mother?) carrying a baby, asleep—he took a writing pad from his briefcase. He reflected that it had been over ten weeks since he had seen Sally. During that period there had been, at first, the ache so to speak *ad personam.* It was she he had missed, so sorely. But, gradually, Sally Partridge was missed not only particularly, but generically. How on earth did monks manage, he wondered. He began to write.

"Dear Miss (Mrs.?) Lewis:

You ask, and understandably so, Who am I? You instruct me to tell you more about myself.

Very well, but on the understanding that you keep the information to yourself.

I am the love child of the Prince of Wales and Tallulah Bankhead. I was born in 1925, and was kept hidden away on an Aegean island. There I learned to spear wild hogs, fight bulls, track snow leopards, and walk over burning coals. During the summers, my father sent the faculty of Eton to teach me Latin and Greek and history and science. During the winters, my father sent the faculty of Sandhurst to teach me the art of war. During the springs, my mother sent me hetaerae to teach me the arts of love. In the autumns, grandfather sent me to the Tower of London to study my ancestry. When I was twenty-one I was banished, provided with a little competence, and invited to make my own way. I have done moderately well, having acquired General Motors in the States, Aramco in Saudi Arabia, and the Eiffel Tower in Paris. I am bidding on the Bank of England, but will not have news until we arrive in Vienna whether I have got hold of it.

But if you will not dine with me tonight, I shall renounce everything and enter a monastery. Or, if you prefer, I could throw myself across the tracks, and those strollers who pass by before the great train shatters my flesh and bones will hear from my lips only the words, 'Linda willed it so.' "

Blackford put the paper in an envelope, on which he wrote out his car, compartment, and seat number. He walked to car 326 and gave the message to the attendant to deliver.

He heard back in a half hour or so.

"Dear Mr. Jerome:

I cannot tell you much about my parents, as I was a foundling. I was born with three arms and three legs, but the doctors did their work competently, and it is only when I am viewed from a certain angle that anyone can see that something is wrong. That angle is not at one hundred and eighty degrees, so at dinner tonight, sitting opposite me, you should not be distracted.

Yours. L.L."

He spent the afternoon reading, and, at Munich, reflecting on Hitler's putsch, two years before Blackford was born. In nine months, some people produce babies. In nine months, Hitler produced *Mein Kampf.* He wondered whether Henri Tod had anybody keeping an eye on the beer halls in Munich these days.

By the time he had got to the death of Julius Caesar they were at the border, showing passports to the Austrian authorities. When the train pulled out, the late eaters would be summoned for the second seating. The attendant with the bell walked through moments after the train began to pull out. Blackford put the book on his seat and went forward to the dining car, giving the yellow voucher to the captain, who seated him. He asked for the wine list, ordered a bottle of Austrian white, and was sipping it when she came.

It went wonderfully well. She was calling him Bucky even before they had done with the salmon. She worked for the United States Information Agency as a librarian. She was a Virginian, divorced—childless—from a husband "who was very sweet, but, really, he likes to drink more, actually, than he likes to do anything else."

"You mean literally anything else?"

She smiled. "I mean literally anything else."

"Is that why you didn't have children?"

Linda looked up at Blackford, and for a moment it appeared as though she might resume calling him Buck. She took the bull by the horns. "That really is none of your business, is it?"

"Well, you see, it *is* actually. I'm completing a doctoral thesis on the relationship between alcoholism and the birth rate. Did you know that in the Soviet Union the birth rate is actually declining? Is your husband—I mean, was your husband—a Russian?"

She laughed. The crisis was over. What did Buck Jerome do with himself? she asked as she sliced at her lamb chops.

Blackford was better schooled at answering that question than any other. Depending on who asked it, he accented, or did not bother to do so, the plausibility of his answer. When on business, he might give an answer so plausible that it had the effect of causing him to disappear into the furniture of the room. If the encounter was utterly transient, it did not much matter what he answered. On such occasions he was, safely, a lawyer, or an engineer. He preferred the latter to the former, if there was the risk that the questioner would spend more than a conversational moment or two with him and began to talk Blackstone. Blackford could handle engineering, inasmuch as he was an engineer. What he could not so easily handle were questions about what he was working on at the moment, where he was working— that sort of thing.

Linda was halfway between these extremes. It had to sound plausible, but need not be profoundly so. "I'm doing a study for the Relm Foundation on economic recovery and Marshall Plan Aid. I've got a couple of appointments in Vienna tomorrow morning, and am due back in London tomorrow night." She was only politely interested, which helped.

Both Blackford and Linda were in need of company, and they stayed in the dining car until it closed, and went then to the bar car, where they had coffee and an Irish whiskey. They had passed Linz and reached the outskirts of Vienna. Linda was candidly attracted to the informal American with the arresting face, expressive, relaxed, with the intelligent eyes, and the features so strikingly handsome in arrangement. Blackford enjoyed her greatly, and reminded himself how much more satisfying was the company of women than of men, particularly after prolonged celibacy.

Would she permit him to drop her off at home? Yes. Where was *he* staying? At the Regina Hotel.

Would he rather share her apartment?

That, he responded with a smile, was the most munificent offer since the Marshall Plan. He was positively joyful as he leaped up to assemble his bag and briefcase, saying he would meet her back in her car and help her with her bag.

In the taxi they chatted cheerful nonsense on the ten-minute trip to the Boltzmann Gasse, and she was laughing when the cab stopped and she fumbled for her keys. Blackford was at this point carrying three bags, she only Blackford's briefcase. Then suddenly she said to be quiet, she did not wish to wake any of the neighbors. So they rode whispering up to the sixth floor, and she opened the apartment on the right, flicked on a standing lamp in the living room, and disappeared from view. She returned in a dressing gown, with a tray and a bottle of wine. But the talk, suddenly, petered out. They drank from their glasses and looked at each other in the dim light. Blackford pointed, wordlessly, at one of the two doors that could be seen from the sofa. She smiled and shook her head, pointing her finger at the other door. He rose and entered a bedroom, lavender in sight and smell, into which the light from the living room only faintly penetrated. In a moment she heard him speak, asking her please to join him. They discovered a great, even urgent need for each other, and she was no less pressing than he as they met, tasted, devoured, and had each other, so to speak, by acclamation. Soon, he kissed her, and said that now he would bring the wine. She watched his body as he moved into the living room where the tray lay on the coffee table, and wondered whether, if he actually had been raised in the Aegean, this Bucky might not have rekindled jealousy in Olympus. They drank in the semidarkness, and soon reexperienced each other, with mounting excitement, with a passion unbridled, but never raucous.

He knew to make love without chatter, and also as they lay happily together later, without talking about future contacts; and she knew as much, so that neither his failure to initiate talk of a more enduring relationship nor her failure to inquire why he did not marred the serenity they now found. Somehow she knew he needed to leave the next day, and somehow he knew she knew it. So that there was no explaining done. And when in the morning she awoke, Buck Jerome had showered and dressed and made the coffee, and was looking about for something edible. She had intended, she said, to stop at an all-night delicatessen and buy fresh bread, but now all she could offer him was crackers and butter and honey, which was all, he said, he wanted, that and the peach he saw in the refrigerator which, having probed it, he pronounced *saignant*.

They walked down together. "Your hotel is directly in line with the embassy, so I'll drop you," she said. Once again they were silent, though one or the other would answer the questions of the talkative cab driver, or acknowledge, as required, his commentary. Blackford discovered only then that she understood German and could get by in it. When they pulled in under the portico of the hotel, Blackford passed his briefcase out to the porter, who had taken the handbag from the cab driver. He leaned over and kissed her lightly on the cheek. "You are a wonderful woman," he said, and she knew that he meant it, and so she went contentedly, if a little sadly, off to work. There would be one whole week's magazines to sort out in the library and the new books. She had slipped *Time* into his briefcase.

Blackford checked in at the desk, extending his passport. "Ah, Mr. Jerome, we expected you last night."

"The train was late," Blackford said, filling out the registration card. "Very nice train, though," he mumbled, and the clerk spoke about the weather.

20

At two in the afternoon on Thursday July 27, the sun shone over Vienna with only occasional interference from lazily scudding clouds that skipped about the Stadtpark as playfully as the children who frolicked with their toys, shouting out their pleasures and pains. The chestnut and oak trees of modest girth—fifteen years ago the young trees had been planted, replacing trees chopped down for firewood during the war—cast only the slightest vertical shadows, the sun being close, at this hour, to its meridian. Blackford Oakes, seated at one end of a park bench centrally located, was dressed in khaki trousers, a cotton sport shirt, and light navy blue sweater tied loosely about his waist. He wore dark glasses and was reading Linda's *Time* when he heard the man say, in German:

"I am Frank, Mr. Oakes."

Blackford looked up, but did not rise. "Ah yes, Mr. Frank. Well, we have both come a long way, so you may as well sit down."

Dmitri Gouzenko did so. He had on a light gray suit and a fedora, and he carried a briefcase. He was clean-shaven. About forty years old, Blackford guessed, of stocky build, but manifestly agile. His expression appeared well controlled, though his eyes were intense. A man of purpose.

"Shall we open the conversation by your giving me the money, which I shall put into this briefcase, handed to me a few days ago by your courier?" His German was fluent.

"I have the money here." Blackford pointed nonchalantly at the little duffel bag on the grass beside him. "I'll give it to you. But only after you tell me about Clementa Tod."

Dmitri paused for a moment. He deliberated whether to make a scene on the purely technical point, namely the promise that the money would be instantly forthcoming if he agreed to go to Vienna. It wasn't worth it.

"How did you come to know her, how did you learn her name, where is she, and how do you propose getting her to West Berlin?"

"Those are extensive questions, Mr. Oakes."

"I figure they could be answered in maybe five minutes. That comes to ten thousand marks per minute. Not bad pay for a Communist. By the way, your German is very good. Where did you learn it?"

"Mr. Oakes, I am not here to answer questions about myself."

"Your concern for your privacy certainly exceeds your concern for mine. Do you always put people's toothbrushes in your letters? Is that your signature?"

"Mr. Oakes, I am a soldier of fortune. Under the circumstances, I find out what I can. I do not doubt that you will endeavor to find out everything about me you can. I am, however, under no compulsion to cooperate in this enterprise."

"Fair enough, Frank. Fair enough. Okay, so I don't know anything about you, but we can go on and talk about Clementa. How long have you known her?"

"Mr. Oakes, my obligation is to satisfy you that I can deliver her. The question of how long I have known her is not to the point. However, I don't want to be unnecessarily fussy, so . . . I have known her for over two years."

"Circumstances, please."

"I committed an, ah, irregularity. Of a commercial nature. In Kiev, where I was then living. I was sentenced to five years in a camp at Vorkuta. During the last two years, I was assigned to the guards' section because of my knowledge of German. There I was used as a translator interrogating German prisoners coming into the camp, and for miscellaneous other duties, mostly clerical. It was then that I met Clementa Tod."

"What was she doing there?"

"You should ask, 'What is she doing there?' "

"Clementa Tod is still at Vorkuta?"

"That is correct."

"All right. What is she doing there?"

"She is acting as an assistant to the superintendent. She is the bridge between him and the personnel who look after the guards. I expect you know that she was at Auschwitz? Evidently it was not known to her family—to her brother—that the Russians liberated the camp before her scheduled execution. She was sent to Vorkuta in April of 1945, and has been there ever since."

"What is her sentence?"

"Originally, she was simply booked as an 'alien vagrant.' It was obvious that she had not been in collusion with the Nazis, so that when I became interested in her and got permission to see her records, I discovered that she had never in fact been sentenced to any particular term at Vorkuta."

"Why, then, is she still there?"

"Clementa Tod, I came to discover after a number of conversations, went into deep psychological shock on the day of her capture. The Nazis openly executed the couple that had been protecting her. Her brother was away in England. Her parents had been eliminated two years earlier. She was loaded onto a train the same day she was picked up. Yet she spoke very detachedly about her past. In any event, you are evidently not aware that prisoners are not released, under the Soviet system, unless they have someplace to go. Lacking any family or any home or any reserves, Clementa has no place to go."

"And how would you remedy that?"

"I would marry her. Then bring her to East Berlin. Then to you."

"What are you doing in Berlin?"

"I am not in East Berlin. I am in Potsdam. After I got out of the camp, I got my old job back. I translate and do odd jobs for the Amtorg Corporation, including purchases."

"Does that take you to West Berlin?"

Dmitri smiled. I can see where your mind is traveling, Mr. Oakes. "No, I stay in the Eastern sector."

"Except when you run out of toothbrushes, which is when you go to West Berlin?"

Dmitri smiled. "I am a man of business. I need occasionally to move about. But mostly I stay in the Eastern sector."

"Let me see your work permit for Potsdam."

"Ah, Mr. Oakes, to see my papers would require that you also see my name. And I see no reason to communicate that to you."

"What does Clementa know of her brother's current activities?"

"She was called in a few months ago when Henri Tod was becoming increasingly notorious and she was questioned. She has not exchanged any communication whatever with her brother since she last saw him in 1943. She has no address for him. She has no cousins, uncles, or aunts."

"How do I know she would come to Tod?"

"Henri Tod is the only thing she has in her whole life. They were exceptionally devoted as children. I mentioned to her the possibility of rejoining him, and she was ecstatic."

Blackford took the duffel bag and placed it on the bench between him and Dmitri. "Okay. We'll take a chance. You may as well take the bag, too. Transferring twenty-five thousand marks in cash in the park at midday might be spotted and thought to be aberrant behavior."

"I did not know we would be meeting in a park until I

talked with the concierge. My own briefcase is not entirely empty, by the way."

He leaned over and opened it. He took out another picture of Clementa, with another note to her brother scratched out on its back. "This is for Henri Tod."

"How long will this operation take?"

"Not too long, I should think. I can be in Kiev by Saturday. The paperwork at Vorkuta is minimal. I would hope to be back in Berlin within a week. I need to have a fresh address for you. The White House forwarding system is notoriously slow."

Blackford grinned, and wrote out a telephone number, tore the page from his notebook, and handed it to him. "I check this number a couple of times every day. I receive brief messages."

"Mine will be brief. It will suggest to which of the passage points I will bring Clementa, and when. Will you be carrying a duffel bag, or a briefcase?"

"You'll get your money, Frank."

"Well, in that case I can think of no other matter that requires discussion. Can you?"

"No. Only this. If, after you marry Clementa, you fool with her, Henri Tod will cut your balls off."

Gouzenko smiled. "Henri Tod cannot expect his sister, after what she has been through, to return to him a virgin. But my own interest in her is exclusively commercial."

Blackford got up. "Be seeing you, Frank. Both of you."

"Soon, Mr. Oakes. Goodbye."

21

Walter Ulbricht was by nature a volatile man, notwithstanding his carefully cultivated Prussian equability. He thought it proper in a leader to be publicly impassive. To be sure, he also thought it correct that revolutionary fervor on appropriate occasions be expressed, which is why when the time came, as it did every few months or so— mostly at public rallies—it was arranged that the public should be raucous in their support of Ulbricht, the GDR, the Communist Party, Stalin, Lenin, and Marx. On these occasions he could be seen to display a steely smile, half gold ever since his teeth had been redone in 1944 when he was a war refugee residing in Moscow, awaiting the liberation of Germany. On these days the roar of the crowd reminded unfriendly observers of the passion shown, not all that long ago, toward Ulbricht's predecessor as German leader—the point Henri Tod was always making, that the differences between the Nazis and the Communists were stylistic and theoretical and unimportant, their similarities being the cohesive thing.

In recent weeks Ulbricht had been training his nephew to take minutes. (*"You simply must develop orderly habits if you are to be of any serious use other than to indulgent uncles."*) Ulbricht was pleased by the progress his nephew was making. The first two or three sessions were marred by Caspar's penchant for interpolating his own comments or asides. Thus one day Colonel Hassel, the chief of the Vopos— short for Volkspolizei, or People's Police—had discussions with Caspar's uncle on how to deal with the East Germans who traveled to work during the day to West Berlin, returning at night. On their return, Colonel Hassel complained—usually after prolonged visits to West German bars—some of the Grenzgänger would pick political arguments, teasing and even vilifying the Vopos, and sorely trying their patience. Caspar recorded the discussion and wrote in parentheses, "Why not shoot them, Uncle?" The spirit was commendable, but, Ulbricht sternly explained, minutes of conversations between the chief of state and his subordinates were not invitations for the minutes-keeper to inject his personal views. Caspar bowed his head slightly, and said he understood. And although now and again he slipped, his minutes were by July very near to exemplary.

The reason this morning for Ulbricht's special excitement was the word from Khrushchev that perhaps the time had come for another meeting of the heads of the Warsaw Pact. Ulbricht's experience with Khrushchev was extensive enough to lead him to translate what Khrushchev was saying: He desired another meeting but he wished, for whatever reason, that Ulbricht request him to convene it.

He brought into the cabinet room that morning Erik von Hausen, his chief of staff; General Zippker, his chief of intelligence; and Professor Hans Wittvogel, who served him as general adviser. These were his most intimate confederates, and although Ulbricht did not hesitate to overrule them, he tended, in talking with these three men, to listen, and to weigh what they said.

They sat around the meeting table, Caspar in a chair up against the wall, taking notes on his stenographic pad.

"I think, gentlemen," Ulbricht began, having relayed to them the news of Khrushchev's message, "that this time we shall prevail. But I think it is important to give some thought to the communication Chairman Khrushchev evi-

dently expects from me. My impression is that he desires
something in the nature of an appeal to which he would be
seen as deferring, with qualifications we do not yet know. I
would suppose he wants something that goes beyond a
mere restatement of our difficulties in dealing with the
desertions to the neofascists. That complaint, however
acute the problem for us, is one he and our colleagues in
the Warsaw Pact are so accustomed to hearing, it is unlikely
that it would be possible to restate it with novelty or ur-
gency. We must not forget the rebuke of last March."

"Permit me, Herr Ulbricht"—Professor Wittvogel never
referred to him simply as "Walter" if there were others in
the room. "We must, I think, attempt to make congruent
policy here, anticipating Chairman Khrushchev. Remember, the Chairman does not let a day go by without warning
the West that he intends to complete a peace treaty with us.
He implies that were he to do so, the future of all of Berlin
would be a matter for us, the GDR, to decide. To be sure,
occasionally he equivocates. Last week, in speaking with the
American John McCloy, he made reference to how confident he was that the western part of the city could be kept in
some way distinct. What the entire world is wondering, and
the entire world—am I correct, General Zippker?—includes GDR intelligence, is *How far exactly does Chairman
Khrushchev intend to go?* If he indeed plans to conclude a
peace treaty with us, we cannot delude ourselves that our
subsequent dealings with West Berlin would be ours to
resolve, however 'sovereign' over all of Berlin the treaty
theoretically makes us. We would need a preunderstanding
with Moscow. Chairman Khrushchev does not, I assume,
know whether or at what point the Allies will use force to
resist us. He presumably knows that they will do so under
certain circumstances. Inasmuch as I think we all believe
that he does not desire war, he must control the circumstances that might lead to war."

"You are saying, then, Hans?"

"That Khrushchev may be waiting for us—for you, Herr Ulbricht—to communicate with him some such message as: 'Eventually you—the Soviets—will of course conclude a peace treaty with us. But more urgent for the GDR, at this moment, is to stop the flood of refugees. Accordingly, if you will back us in a limited venture, to contain the refugees, we will agree not publicly to press any immediate claims to sovereignty over West Berlin.'"

General Zippker interjected. "But, Professor, surely it is quite generally understood that we would not press claims over West Berlin that had not already been . . . authorized in Moscow? Surely it is quite obvious to the whole world that our military is not capable of taking on all of NATO?"

"I am making a slightly different point, Hermann. It is that Chairman Khrushchev may desire that we stake out a position in the presence of the Warsaw powers' leaders. And that position would be that we are prepared to settle for a compromise if Moscow will back us in the matter of the refugees. Otherwise, Chairman Khrushchev might be afraid of appearing to back down on his pledge to conclude a peace treaty that would leave the future of all of Berlin in our hands."

Ulbricht looked pensive. He leaned back in his chair. "Perhaps the safest way to proceed would be to address Comrade Khrushchev privately, and to enclose with that communication a projected draft communication to the Warsaw leaders. This would need to be accomplished in great privacy, because it is of course an invitation to the Chairman to edit our ostensibly spontaneous communication to him and the Warsaw leaders. Indeed, Professor Wittvogel, I think this important enough for you to convey to Moscow personally. Possibly you can take it directly to the Chairman. More probably, Gromyko will insist on its being delivered to him. I will have a draft of the proposed statement by the end of the morning, and you would all oblige me if you would meet me here again at three P.M. to review it."

"Of course, Herr Ulbricht," said Professor Wittvogel.

"To be sure," said Erik von Hausen.

"Indeed, Mr. Chairman," said General Zippker.

Walter Ulbricht called for his secretary, and waved at Caspar to leave, but suddenly thought better of it.

"No, wait. Listen to my dictation, and incorporate what I say in your minutes."

The secretary asked whether the Chairman, before he began, would take a call from Colonel Hassel of the Vopos. "He says it is very important, sir."

"Very well, get him on the line, but be quick about it."

And a moment later. "Yes, Hassel, what is it? Which one of the swine? Schweig? You have reason to believe he was with Tod that night, you say? Well don't tell me you have reason to believe he was with Tod, *find out* if he was with Tod. Surely I do not need to remind you how to do that. What you say? Ah. You overdid it. Maybe I *do* need to send you back to the academy. Does the doctor confirm that? Well, let him lie a few hours. If he does come to, go back to work on him. If he's still out by dinnertime, polish him off. Oh yes, take a photograph; send it to his parents. Save a copy for me. Very well." Ulbricht hung up.

"To Chairman Khrushchev, First Secretary of the Communist Party of the Union of Soviet Socialist Republics."

22

His mind wandered during the story about what had happened to Lady Anabella when she was packing up to move herself and the children to America for the summer. He was actually glad that the story was so protracted, because it gave him cover, and last night's speech was very much on his mind. It is a distinct disadvantage for presidents, he had begun to notice very early in his term, that they can't easily be inattentive, the reason being that they are hardly ever so situated as to be other than the center of other people's attention. Ordinary people, in the company of four or five or more persons, can more safely permit their minds to wander. Those skilled in doing so are, moreover, very good at evasive operations, and these he had practiced over his nonpresidential years, particularly on the campaign trail, and rather prided himself on his proficiency. But if every story is designed to catch the attention of the boss, and every piece of gossip is aimed at his special titillation, to say nothing of the ponderous proposals which are sculpted exclusively for the boss's examination, he being the only person whose reaction to them counts—what is one then to do, except listen, or run the chance of coming very close to being excommunicably rude, as if to say, "Nothing you utter can possibly be funny, interesting, or profound, and therefore I do not deign to listen"? Fortunately, in this case it was family, so that in fact the long story was primarily addressed to his wife . . . How he had worked on that speech. Any speech, he reflected, that in part satisfies Acheson *and* Fulbright, from both of whom he had heard congratulations, was at least high diplomacy. But how had it really gone over in Moscow? Oh, they were saying the usual things, but had they got the message? What message? Waal . . . His train of thought was interrupted. He was dragged directly into the discussion, a point of controversy having been brought up. His views having been solicited, his opinion was given, and it was the consensus that he had acquitted himself marvelously . . . What message? They were in the private quarters, and his wife said it was time to look in on Caroline, and there were general movements suggesting the diaspora for which he longed, so that he could complete his thinking. That damned fool Fulbright, saying on "Issues and Answers" that he didn't understand why the East Germans didn't just go ahead and partition the city, that being after all their right. Jee-zus, you would think a Rhodes scholar would have got that straight by now, that the East Germans don't *govern* East Berlin: under the treaty and protocols, administrative control of the Eastern sector was given over to the Russians only subject to corporate understandings, one of these being continued right of access by all Berliners to all of Berlin, by all occupying powers to all of Berlin; and, incidentally, under the protocols no German in military uniform was even allowed to set foot inside Berlin, for God's sake. He was interrupted. Yes, he agreed, as he prepared to usher Anabella to the elevator, it had indeed been an extraordinarily rich season for people dying. No, he had never actually met Ernest Hemingway, though they had corresponded. No, he had never met Augustus John, and there was a lot about him, he thought to himself, that he admired that had nothing to do with art. Yes, he knew Ty Cobb had died; in fact he had dispatched a telegram to Ty Cobb's widow professing that in his youth he had worshipped her late husband, which wasn't strictly true, because he was as uninterested in baseball when Ty Cobb was making home runs, or whatever, as he was today. Indeed they would see Anabella again soon at Hyannis Port, perhaps this weekend, no doubt arrangements have been made, don't hesitate to let us know if there is anything you need. Whew . . . What message? He went into the Lincoln bedroom, where the Emancipation Proclamation had been executed, and sat down. What message? Well, he had defined the threat to Berlin. To Berlin? Well, no. He had said, "West Berlin." The people he associated with had pretty well got him into the habit of talking about "Berlin" as West Berlin. He had to face up to it that the cable that had come in from General Watson, U.S. Commandant in Berlin, had nagged him. General Watson said all the usual, pleasant things about a presidential speech, but paused to register his dismay that the President who had referred every few seconds to the city had in every single case referred only to West Berlin. Did this communicate to the Russians that United States concern was exclusively for West Berlin? He had defined the threat, and elaborated what were U.S. interests in West Berlin. I mean in Berlin. He had gone over all that—the integrity of NATO, the whole bit. Then came the stick: He asked Congress to mobilize certain military units. How can you get any plainer than that, Nikita, you old fart?—and indications from congressional leaders were solid. Hell, 85 percent of the people, in the last Gallup, said they were willing to risk war to defend Berlin. Then he had finished with the carrot. He was entirely willing to negotiate differences with the Soviet Union. That would give Khrushchev, if he wanted it, the excuse to delay on his ultimatum, right? That, backed up by the mobilization. It certainly had not helped that Britain's defense minister Harold Watkinson had said he didn't think it was necessary to send a division right now to Berlin—the Brits are under strength as it is in West Germany, with fifty instead of fifty-five thousand men there. And the French! De Gaulle has pulled two of his four divisions out of Ger-

many to help out in Algeria. To help continue French
colonialism—watch it: De Gaulle may be listening. He
would not find that at all funny. Anyway, the Soviet Union
has got to have the impression we are standing by our guns.
Where are our guns? Oh yes, in Berlin. Where in Berlin?
He found he did not really want to answer that question, so
he interpreted a voice calling out in the hall as if directed at
him, though he knew it was the butler who was being called.
So he showed up, and said he was terribly sorry he had
been absent—he thought dear Elsie had left the White
House along with the other guests. By all means dear Elsie
should stay on, have a nightcap or whatever; he was going
to have a Coke himself, which order he gave to the butler,
who was standing there, since he too knew that it was he,
not the President, who had been summoned.

23

Blackford had been gone a mere forty-eight hours, but right away he noticed that the strain in Berlin had mounted. Ulbricht had ordered the number of Vopos regulating the transfer points to be increased by a factor of six. The commuters were beginning to feel seriously threatened when they went out in the morning to work. And those who set out accompanied by their baggage and obviously intending to stay in West Berlin were being harassed almost to the point of physical detention.

And Bruni had been right. The day after Blackford left he had heard again from Tod, and this morning yet another communication, this one advising Bruni, using the code only the two of them knew, that he was to meet an emissary at Residence Four at ten o'clock, and that she was absolutely to be trusted. Tod's handwriting, well known to Bruni, appeared on the back of a picture postcard of a slight, pretty girl, perhaps twenty-two or twenty-three, dressed in a bathing suit and laughing as she stood on the beach of what appeared to be a lake, laughing at something someone was doing, or not doing.

"She came promptly at 10:05. I got right to the point and asked where Henri was. She replied by asking me for some kind of proof that I was Bruni. That stumped me. I don't tattoo my name on my chest. Then she made it easier for me. 'What did Henri tell you once about your name?' I remembered," he laughed. " 'He told me he thought Bruni was a nickname for Brunnhilde.'

"So she relaxed right away. She told me that Henri had indeed been shot that Saturday, but that he had got away, and she and her 'companion' were looking after Henri; that at first he had had a considerable fever, but they had got some penicillin, and his strength has been going up and his fever down. It was thirty-eight degrees this morning—"

"How much is that in real money?" Blackford interrupted.

"That," Bruni reflected, "is about one hundred degrees Fahrenheit. Then she said he was busting to get back here, but also, the girl said, mostly because he was getting very useful information which he wanted to get to us right away, but didn't want to convey it through a third party, even through the girl herself."

"Does he want us to go in and get him?"

"I told her we had contingency plans for getting him out. But then what I did was write down a medical questionnaire on the basis of which I can do a better job of diagnosis. I told her we ought to get a blood sample. I gave her a twenty-minute lesson on how to do it, and had her experiment on me. She says she has a friend, a nurse, former roommate, and she's quite sure she can get Henri's blood over to her and have it examined for infection. She's coming back over here tomorrow morning, and on the basis of the information she brings I can make a pretty good judgment as to whether we're better off letting him sit it out there for a few more days, or whether we ought to take the risk of bringing him in and giving him treatment here.

"Meanwhile," Bruni picked up a clipping, and handed it to Blackford, with a bow of the kind one makes when one expects one's achievement to be applauded, "here's an account by Spartacus." "Spartacus" was the principal hatchet man-toady-gossip columnist in the East Berlin *Neues Deutschland*. In today's column his readers were informed that Henri Tod had run off to Bonn to conspire with the government's "Nazi generals."

"Nice going."

"I don't suppose I should ask *you* what you have been up to?"

"That's right," Blackford said. "You shouldn't." He smiled. You will know, pretty soon now. Unless, Blackford thought, Mr. Frank turns out to be nothing but a con man. A con man twenty-five thousand marks richer than he was yesterday morning.

Henri Tod was at once restless and elated. Saturday night he had very nearly been apprehended and very nearly been killed. He was saved—by a young confidant of Walter Ulbricht who proceeded during Henri's convalescence to bring him not only medicine for his wounds, but news of that very morning's most intimate meetings between Ulbricht and his confederates. When he first saw the minutes of Friday morning's meeting, Tod was breathless with excitement. In Caspar Allman he had a direct link with the inner mind of the enemy. Could the whole business be a flamboyant, spectacular charade? Only if he, Henri Tod, had plotted, last Saturday night, to grope his way, in the dark, to come to rest at a remote siding of the Berlin Ostbahnhof, at this particular car, at this particular moment.

By the end of the first week, he had come to trust Caspar, as also Claudia, wholly, subject to his adult lifetime's presumption against imparting to anyone information it was not necessary to divulge. Their loyalty and courage was one thing. But there was in Caspar a quality, probably ineradicable, of devil-may-care, which was attractive, even endearing—but which could conceivably bring down the entire operation. "Caspar," he had said from the sofa, after coming upon the section in the July 28 minutes in which Caspar had interposed the suggestion that perhaps one means of demoralizing the commuters would be to have one commuter per day disappear inside a trapdoor at each passage point, "Caspar, you *mustn't do* this kind of thing. You must strive to be absolutely sober, and indispensable to your uncle. If he ever gets impatient with you, remember, he can still appease your mother by giving you a soft job in the bureau of taxi licenses. It doesn't have to be a job in his own office. *Please* don't take such chances."

"Okay," Caspar grinned, his feet stretched out on Hitler's best coffee table. "On the other hand, it wouldn't do, would it, Henri, for me to change too suddenly? Might make him suspicious?"

"You uncle is suspicious as a matter of principle. Don't worry about that. Worry about provoking him."

Claudia returned with the news of her meeting with Bruni, warned that she had got just the morning off, pleading that she had to accompany her mother to her dying aunt in the hospital at Gross-Ziethen. She pulled out the little hypodermic needle and rubber tubing, and with some trepidation—this was more difficult than injecting penicillin into muscle tissue, she proclaimed, never before that morning having taken blood—went through the motions Bruni had taught her. "I'll take this right away to my friend," she intoned as, slowly, she drew back the plunger, pulling Henri's blood into the little glass cylinder. "And tomorrow—that's when I'm supposed to be picking up my mother at Gross-Ziethen—I'll bring back word from your friend Bruni."

Tod was satisfied. He yearned, above all else, to see the minutes, a report, of the meeting at which Khrushchev's response to Ulbricht was rendered. And, alone now in the coach, beginning his tenth day in Berchtesgaden, he reflected on the arrangements that would need to be made in order to get, every day, Caspar's information while protecting the most valuable pipeline anyone, surely, had ever had in the history of intelligence to the enemy's deliberations. *"Worry only in part about the enemy's capabilities. Worry about the enemy's intentions.* '' Who first said that? Was it Julius Caesar? Cato? Alexander? It could have been Abel, who knew the power of Cain, but did not know his intentions, and then suddenly it was too late.

24

Bruni had carefully studied the results of his remote-control medical diagnosis. He satisfied himself that Henri was healing and did not need dramatic medical care. That finding released Blackford from any obligation to plead with Rufus and the U.S. military for heroic clandestine intervention. On the other hand, Bruni did not judge Henri ready to proceed instantly to make his own way back to West Berlin, involving, as such a journey would, makeup, tension, oblique routing, and the possibility of en route harassment. He conveyed to Claudia his most urgent recommendation that Henri remain where he was for three or four more days. Henri reluctantly agreed to do so, but was cheered on learning from Caspar that Khrushchev had summoned, most secretly, the leaders and the first secretaries of the Warsaw Pact to Moscow and that they would be departing that very day.

Just before leaving, Caspar told Henri, his Uncle Walter had come up with a fresh idea for complicating border arrangements. Polio! "Where was polio when I needed it most!" Caspar imitated the accents of his uncle, who cared about the devastations of polio only if he, or Stalin, contracted it. Ulbricht, in consultation with his kitchen cabinet, had decided that an "epidemic" of polio in the GDR justified extravagant care to prevent its infection of the Federal Republic. "If Uncle Walter really thought those cars and trucks were carrying polio germs into West Germany, he'd be giving them a police escort." And then a West German paper, with a name the pronunciation of which Caspar plea-sured himself in repeating in heavily accented British, imi-tating the BBC announcer who had quoted from it, the *Bundesnachrichtendienst,* had predicted that the closing of the sector boundary in Berlin was imminent. Inasmuch as, in his celebrated press conference of June 15, Ulbricht had in as many syllables told the questioning reporter that no such thing as a dividing wall was in prospect, the East German press derided the prediction.

Nevertheless, there was reaction from the Allies. Whether in specific response to the prediction of a parti-tion in Berlin, or simply to give the appearance of coordi-nated activity, Washington issued an order. And the U.S. Army Commander for Europe ordered all U.S. military not on leave to return to military quarters by midnight. Six nights per week. On Sunday, they could stay out until 1 A.M. Henri Tod told Caspar of the bitter comment after Hitler's march on Poland, which followed his march on the Sudetenland, which followed his march on Austria, that whereas Chamberlain took his weekends in the country, Hitler took his countries on the weekend.

On the third day, having got word from Claudia of Henri's growing strength, Bruni authorized Henri Tod to leave his quarters and come home, taking, of course, due precautions. Tod planned to leave on the S-Bahn at 10:15 P.M., which was the hour when the substantial post-theater traffic returned home from the East to West Berlin after the show, stretching to 11:15 for those who wished to dally. The trains at that hour were shortened, and patronage dense, so that there was little risk of being conspicuous. As ever, a member of the Bruderschaft would stand by, in the event that anyone approaching their leader behaved men-acingly.

It was, Henri reflected as Claudia struggled to put on makeup that made him appear a man of sixty-five, as sad a night as he remembered since that awful evening after

which, he knew, he would be separated from his beloved
Clementa. It was almost inconceivable to him that in twelve
days he'd have forged ties so strong as those he felt now
toward this slim, competent, pretty, quiet girl who had
risked her life to help what was then a stranger. And, looking back from the improvised makeup room by Claudia's
galley to the imperial sofa on which, as not unusually, Caspar stretched out, Henri reflected that the Prussian knout
had not driven away from Germany whatever it was that was
responsible for creating the elfin charm of Till Eulen-
spiegel. Caspar was there, playing with the shortwave radio, but he was not really concentrating on it, because he
too felt the keenness of an impending separation that
would almost surely be permanent, unless he and Claudia
decided at some point themselves to leave, in which case, of
course, he would begin his new life by signing on as a
member of the Bruderschaft. In Henri he had found a
somewhat older man who had given him the only complete
human satisfaction that Caspar had ever had from another
man. When in the late afternoons Caspar hurried over toward Berchtesgaden, taking the usual devious routings, to
tell Henri what had happened that day, he felt a sense of
accomplishment, of usefulness, he had never felt before;
that and the pleasuring of Henri Tod were a perfect combination. In the days that lay ahead, the procedures had been
specified by which Caspar would continue to relay his intelligence. But it would never be the same as it had been these
past days, with Claudia listening, dressed in her apron and
cooking in the galley, and darting out to hear Tod's incisive
comments.

Henri would be lying on the couch, his arm in the sling,
facing Caspar, who alternately sat and darted about to help
Claudia, but always reacting in some way to what Henri was
saying. Henri would discuss with Caspar the political impli-
cations of this or that projected move by his Uncle Walter,
or whatever.

Then there were the discussions at dinner, everything from the fate of Germany to the experience of this or that friend, something heard that very day by Claudia at work, or by Caspar; and Henri would reach back and tell them tales of this person or that, known to him. He knew name, rank, and serial number of everyone in the huge East German bureaucracy. He knew relationships—who was sheltered by whom; who was secure, who less so, in Ulbricht's esteem. He spoke as if he were the official, inside historian of the German Democratic Republic.

And all of this in the sealed-off, profanely comfortable, regally appointed railway car within which the great malefactor whose only competitor in Europe had been Josef Stalin had ridden up and down Germany for four years, giving orders by telephone and teletype in the instrument room aft to bomb more civilians, kill more Jews, draft more young Germans, scorch more Russian earth. From this car, during substantial intervals, Hitler had run one side of an entire world war.

And lately from this car, Caspar suddenly permitted himself to believe, a tiny little counterrevolution against tyranny had been commanded by the leader of a band of young Germans who would not accept things as they were.

The thought of Henri leaving—Henri, the center of that movement; and a human being whose personal qualities had overwhelmed, equally, him and Claudia—made him inconsolably sad; almost irresponsibly sad, he thought as he struggled to control his emotions, drinking yet another glass of the Ukrainian champagne he had spent his week's savings to buy for tonight.

The time came. Caspar would lead him to the S-Bahn. Claudia would stay behind. During the preceding three days Henri had performed exercises rigorously, so that when for the first time he stepped down from the platform, he felt physically competent. Less so emotionally. He had embraced Claudia, but had spoken not a word. He thought briefly of his leave-taking from Clementa. He embraced her again, and this time said that they would see each other again, very, very soon; though not again, he supposed, at Berchtesgaden.

Tod's return was not uneventful. The car which, by pre-arrangement, he entered was, as projected, crowded. But as it approached the border a burly Vopo got in and began asking for papers. These were produced sullenly, and the Vopo sergeant became progressively gruff in manner. He came to Tod and stuck out his hand. With one hand on the railing to keep his balance, Tod produced his identity card with the other. The sergeant stared at it. Behind him, in a disguised treble, a passenger let go an obscenity about Ulbricht and his whores. The Vopo wheeled about but could not identify the taunter. In retaliation he turned back to Tod and shouted, "You. You will get off at the next stop with me, and answer some questions." The next stop being the final stop in East Berlin before the crossing, the moment was tense.

"What's going on here?" A large gray-haired man emerged from the crowded corner of the car. "Sergeant"—the stranger flashed his credentials before him—"I am Colonel Himmelfarb, Volkspolizei. What exactly is going on here? Who was the man who insulted Chairman Ulbricht?" Colonel Himmelfarb had managed to place his large frame between Henri Tod and the sergeant, and now there was considerable bellowing, and the colonel asked that the passengers behind where the sergeant had been standing identify the mischief-maker. During the hubbub, Tod slid slowly away, and when the train stopped at Friedrichstrasse he stepped out on the platform as though it were his destination. The tumult in the car meanwhile subsided after the colonel had given the passengers a lecture on civic responsibility. Tod caught the next train into the Western sector. A small convoy of waiting, nervous friends discreetly led Tod as close to his personal quarters as he permitted. Only Bruni knew that he lived at 28 Kurfürstenstrasse, to which he accompanied him. Henri was tired now, suddenly, after his first protracted exertion, so he asked Bruni if he might postpone until tomorrow an account of everything that had happened during the fortnight, and why he felt it so important that he return quickly. Bruni readily assented, but said that before leaving he would insist on taking Henri's temperature and pulse, and putting him through a mild neurological examination. Henri sighed and said very well, and together they climbed to the attic of the little house on Kurfürstenstrasse, the first two floors of which had never been rebuilt since the day when the SS had stormed in to search it, after arresting its owner at his office. Colonel von Stauffenberg had been taken away to be tortured and executed for the crime of attempting to kill Adolf Hitler on July 20. Intending to burn down the entire house, they had left flaming torches, but a kindly and officious neighbor had got there in plenty of time to restrict the damage to the first two floors, which were gutted. But the scaffolding was solid, and the third floor was entirely habitable, and that was where Henri lived, proud in the knowledge of who last had lived where he now lived alone, monastically, in three rooms, the walls of two given over to volumes of philosophy, the other to research materials that gave to the leader of the Bruderschaft most of anything he needed to know about the geography of Berlin, or the background of the tyrants who governed it.

He submitted acquiescently to the quick examination. Bruni pronounced himself pleased by heartbeat, temperature, and pulse. They shook hands warmly, and Henri turned on the radio before sleeping, and heard that Mayor Willy Brandt had conferred with the three Western commandants about countermeasures against East German harassments of the workers who came to West Berlin to work, and that the three Western commandants had sent off a note to the Soviet commandant in East Berlin protesting the interference in intercity travel. Whatever was coming, Henri thought as his fatigue began to overcome him, was coming now fast, very fast. Eyes closed, he reached for the electric cord, fingered his way to the switch, doused the light, and slept, his first night in almost a fortnight asleep on a bed that had not been Adolf Hitler's.

25

Tod slept soundly and awoke refreshed, though for a fleeting moment he found the absence of Claudia and Caspar almost intolerable. He boiled water while washing and dressing, took tea and a dry cracker, and, after the routine exploration out the window, walked down the circular iron staircase that permitted passage through the two gutted stories, and walked out the door, headed, as by arrangement, for Number 12. There Bruni was waiting, and three other young men, the high command of the Bruderschaft.

Tod had carefully thought out the means by which he would get communications from Caspar. The use of the telephone was excluded: Ulbricht had cut off municipal intercommunication, so that a West Berliner could not now telephone across the street to an East Berliner to whom from his balcony he could wave, save by telephoning Copenhagen and putting through an international call.

It would need to be done by foot, and at the current political tempo it would need to be done once or even twice per day. Caspar had undertaken to do a paraphrase of the information he gleaned, unless there was detailed information that needed to be got through. Tod's decision was to send a courier from West Berlin into East Berlin, rather than ask Claudia to come west. Under no circumstances, he instructed him, was Caspar to risk passage into the West, particularly if he had on him any information that might prove troublesome. Ulbricht, without apology or explanation, was now ordering a thorough body search of up to ten

percent of westbound Germans. But the Berlin Ostbahnhof, where their Berchtesgaden lay, was situated directly
opposite a passage point. The courier would need only to
go to Oberbaumstrasse, cross the street, enter the station
through its main entrance, at the opposite end of the deserted sidings with the abandoned old coach cars, including
10206. Just to the left, after passing through the principal
entrance to the station, was a row of locked compartments
where travelers could leave, overnight or for a full day, a
small suitcase. It was agreed that after Caspar's return from
his uncle's office he would type the précis of the minutes at
home, on his father's typewriter. He would then meet Claudia, who would put the message in an envelope and deposit
it in one of the lockers. Provided the locker was every day
fed two 10-pfennig pieces, it would not attract the attention
of the inspector, as the timing mechanism would not indicate that its lease was overdue. But in the event something
should go wrong with that mechanism, causing the inspector with his passkey to open the locker, he would find in it a
brown paper bag, two cans of biscuits, and a half pint of
schnapps. Such a parcel as might routinely be left by any
East German traveler. He would not be tempted to explore
in the further recesses of the locker, where an envelope
would repose, in which plans for the future of Berlin were
to be found.

Before leaving the station, Tod had rehearsed his hosts
in the details of the operation, and Claudia had without
difficulty got a locksmith to duplicate the key to the locker
they would use. They then were left with one key, while Tod
took the second. His courier—he would alternate Georgi
and Roland—would inspect the locker during the rush
hour between seven and eight in the morning, and again
during the rush hour between five and six in the afternoon.

At first Tod had thought not to tell anyone the identity of
his informant. But by the time he arrived at Number 12 he
had decided that Bruni must know, in the event that Tod

met with an accident. So when he briefed his companions on the new informant, whom he designated as "Wotan," he shielded—and of course they understood—Wotan's identity. He would tell Bruni later in the day who Wotan was.

And so he told his companions, during the briefing, that he had reason to believe that as they spoke, Ulbricht was in Moscow, conferring with Khrushchev and leaders of the Warsaw Pact. Moreover, the purpose of that meeting was to come to a resolution involving Berlin. He also believed that Ulbricht intended to plead one more time for Russian approval of Ulbricht's plan actually to partition the city, denying to any East German access to West Berlin, and vice versa. He would, he said, expect a report on that meeting very soon, and that would be the moment when the Bruderschaft met their ultimate test.

The day was spent going over reports on the day-to-day doings of the Bruderschaft during the fortnight interval he had been gone. There was much to cover—details of hardships, of treachery, of sadism, of exploits, of rescues effected. The apparatus comprised now several hundred men and women, every one of them save Bruni fully employed in other work. Every one of them accepting assignments from headquarters and routinely risking imprisonment and life to further the objectives of the society. At four, Bruni insisted that Tod take one hour for a nap, to guard against a setback from overwork. Tod walked up to the little bedroom on the second floor and fell instantly to sleep. He would meet with Blackford Oakes at six.

That morning, six days after the Vienna meeting, Blackford had received in the mail, postmarked the previous day in East Berlin, the first communication. "Frank" had married Clementa, got her out of Vorkuta, and brought her to his apartment in East Berlin. But much to his surprise, she had flatly refused to cross over into West Berlin save in the company of her brother. "The problem, Mr. Oakes, is that Clementa Tod has complacently accepted the Soviet version of what is going on in West Germany, and her childlike fear of the Nazis, well justified as we both know, operates now to frighten her. Because for fifteen years she has heard it said about West Berlin and West Germany that the two areas are governed by Nazis and crypto-Nazis. I have tried very hard to persuade her that certain exaggerations of a political character are necessary in such adversary circumstances as divide East and West. But she will not budge. Her brother Henri needs to come here, and then, on his recommendation, but only on his, will she leave her sanctuary. Needless to say I am anxious to expedite this business. I have gone to considerable trouble to earn my purse. So kindly arrange as quickly as possible to send Mr. Tod over with the balance of the money, and the exchange can then be made. You can communicate with me by mail to this address, or you can telephone me, directly or via Copenhagen, at the above number. Your servant, Frank."

Blackford went to Rufus. After Rufus had finished reading the letter, Blackford spoke. "I would now put the odds at ninety-five percent that our friend Frank is working for the KGB. Do you agree?"

Rufus reflected. "I'd say more like eighty percent. The young woman's fear is plausible. I assume that Mr. Frank, whose telephone number and address we now have, has taken pains to establish a convincing cover. Still, we have assets in East Berlin, and the Bruderschaft is heavy with them. So let's begin by asking for a quick investigation into the background and the occupation of Mr. Frank."

"Suppose he checks out? I mean, satisfactory cover?"

"Then," Rufus said, "we will put him to the acid test."

"How?"

"A friendly gentleman will approach Mr. Frank and advise him that he has very wealthy clients who are willing to pay one hundred thousand marks if Mr. Frank will lead

Clementa Tod to a designated location in West Berlin that night at, say, ten o'clock."

"Rufus, you're a clever bug—gentleman. There's only one hole, of course. It's that hypothetically he could be on the level as a mercenary, yet honest about original commitments."

"Could be. But his reaction to the offer when it is made will probably give us the information we need. Meanwhile, Blackford, we can no longer keep the news from Henri Tod. It is for you to handle this."

And it was for this purpose that Blackford had, through Bruni, sent word to Henri Tod that he must see him that very day, and the date had been set for six o'clock. Blackford was both eager to give Henri the news, and apprehensive about the effect of it on a man who had not seen his sister in eighteen years, during the last sixteen of which he thought her dead.

26

Tod slept for nearly two hours, but he woke refreshed and anxious to visit with Blackford, who was there waiting, in the living room of Number 12, seated and reading *Der Spiegel.* The two young men greeted each other warmly, and Henri asked the housekeeper for tea. By prearrangement with Blackford, Bruni said he needed to go out on an errand. It had been agreed he would not return until seven.

Henri sat down and motioned Blackford to do so. "I have some very interesting information. A new informant. Ulbricht has gone to Moscow." Henri told him as much as he had told his staff. Blackford resolved as soon as possible to telephone Rufus. Without giving details of where he had been or who had tended to him, Tod told Blackford the story of the past fortnight. "I was very lucky," he said, contentedly. "And there will be much to do in the next few days, I would guess. But we will know more soon."

"I've been busy also." Blackford began cautiously. He rose then, and turned toward the bookshelf. He did not want to be staring at the face of his friend if the news proved too much to handle. Blackford had also decided to pace the narrative.

"Henri, I have here a photograph, with writing on the back of it, which you must look at." He handed over the picture, and then turned back toward the bookshelf. He heard nothing from Henri. And then the muffled sobs, deep as from the center of the earth. Blackford turned his head. Henri had put the sofa's pillow on his lap, and now his face was buried, his shoulders heaving. Blackford spotted the housekeeper, the door beginning to open. Quickly he intercepted her, taking the tea tray and thanking her. He set the tray down on the table, and put his arm on the shoulders of his friend, whose sobbing continued.

"There is more to tell, Henri. When you are ready."

It was another minute or two, and again Blackford, having poured the tea and set a cup on the coffee table in front of Henri, was back looking at the book titles.

"Where is she?" He heard a voice as of a stranger.

"She has been at a camp, in Vorkuta."

"Tell me."

"It all happened two days after you were shot. With that photograph came this letter." He turned, and handed it to Henri.

"Thank you, Blackford. You can sit down. I will be all right."

Blackford asked, "There is no question in your mind about her identity?"

"It is she. Only she could have written that message. Besides, though she was fourteen when I saw her, the face is the same. She is so beautiful," he added, as if speaking to himself.

"Yes."

Henri read the letter signed "Frank." "What then did you do?"

"I conferred with my principal, and we decided that in your absence—and at that point we had no way of knowing how long it would last—we had better proceed to pick up the trail." Blackford described the initial meeting and the precautions that had been taken. He described the exchange in Vienna. "At that point I was prepared to proceed on the assumption, however unlikely, that our friend Frank, as we designate him, was an independent man of affairs, an operator who somehow managed to find me in West Berlin. We all know that sort of thing is possible."

"And now?"

There was no way to prolong it, Henri might as well know now where the girl was. Blackford handed him that morning's communication. He read it.

"In Berlin! At Friedrichshain! It is the far end of Berlin, but not more than one half hour from the border, by the S-Bahn. I must go," he stood.

So did Blackford. His voice was stern. "Now sit down, goddam it, Tod. *Sit down!*" Henri did so.

"I began to explain why I now incline to believe that Mr. Frank is an agent of the KGB. It is too neat. She will only leave for West Berlin if you lead her here. Ha. And what makes us so sure that once you are there, *you* will be permitted to leave? And are you ready to jeopardize needlessly the Bruderschaft and all who have sacrificed for it, depending on you? Another thing: How can we be sure that your sister was in fact brought from the camp? These are matters we simply have to explore. If your sister remains separated from you a few more days that is a small price to pay—"

"Small price?" Henri's eyes widened, and he clenched his teeth. "Small price? For Clementa to think I put anything on earth higher than ransoming her from the hell she has been living in since 1945?"

"Now listen, Henri. Your sister is apparently under a number of misapprehensions, just to begin with. The perspectives are wrong. But nothing would hurt your sister more than to find herself an instrument in your own undoing. Among other things, we need to shield her from that."

At this moment, without knocking, Bruni came in. He turned to Henri, as if unaware of what had been happening, and said excitedly, "We have the first message from Wotan!" He handed Henri the unopened envelope. Henri sliced it open and read aloud:

"How are you, my friend? C. and I both miss you very much. Your bed is made up for whenever you want to come back. Big news. The boss returns late tonight. I will know soon after midnight what you wish to know. I'll try to get word to our niche early in the morning. —W."

"And, Henri, it's going to take us more than twenty-four hours to get answers to the questions that need answering before you begin to consider traveling to East Berlin."

Henri turned to Bruni. "Do you know about—"

Bruni interrupted him. "Yes. I am very happy for you, Henri."

"All right." Henri was addressing Blackford.

Blackford turned to Bruni. "Let's go across the way. We have things to check on, and there is room here for a division of labor."

They went out. Before closing the door, Blackford looked over at Henri. He was seated, staring at the photograph.

27

Nothing was so secret as Walter Ulbricht when he was being secretive. Had it been feasible he'd have elected to schedule all meetings at midnight in pitch-dark, wearing blackface in a cellar. Accordingly, his airplane from Moscow, bearing him, his deputy premier, and two deputy advisers, put down at Schönefeld Airport at one in the morning. Although the chances that anyone would, at that hour, at that place, espy Walter Ulbricht descending from the plane were, to say the least, remote, Ulbricht descended the gangway wearing a mask, a balaclava and a Russian fur cap. Caspar, who was a member of the tiny delegation that met him, wondered whether, thus disguised, his uncle ran the risk of being shot as a bank robber, but followed the lead of his elders by keeping absolutely quiet. Without saying a word, Ulbricht made the rounds, shaking the proffered hands of the four people entrusted to meet him, and silently followed the Vopos, who had instructions to escort the masked gentleman to the offices of the Chairman.

Inside the Chancellery, Ulbricht took off his face mask and stuffed it into his pocket. Come, he waved to his companions. In his office he rang to the sleepy attendant. "Bring two bottles of champagne." He went to the chair at the head of the table, gestured to their places his chief of staff, his chief of intelligence, his chief of police, Professor Hans Wittvogel and his nephew, in his accustomed spot against the wall, with his notebook.

"Gentlemen," he said grandly, "this is a historic occasion. I announce the liberation of Berlin!"

At exactly that moment a sleepy older man scuffled into the room with a tray bearing champagne and glasses. Ulbricht stopped talking, and no one else spoke while the butler wrestled with first one, then the second champagne bottle. The cork from the second flew out at great speed and collided with the chandelier in the ceiling, causing a glass sprinkle over the table. The butler looked dumbly at the debris, the champagne bottle still in his hand. He mumbled that he would go fetch a towel. "You clumsy idiot!" Ulbricht exclaimed. "Get out of here! I will call you if I need you. Caspar. Get paper from the bathroom, wet it, and wipe away the glass." Caspar got up and was back presently with the paper. The four men were sitting silent, waiting for the table to be cleared so that they might safely get to their glasses, which the Chairman had filled. Caspar wiped the pieces into a wastebasket under the table.

"Gentlemen," Ulbricht said grandly, "this is a historic occasion. I announce the liberation of Berlin!" He raised his glass, and the others followed suit.

"Oh my but it was gratifying," he said, his thin lips glistening as he savored his triumph. "And how they changed their tune when Chairman Khrushchev made his speech! It was grand to hear Zhivkov pronounce that, in retrospect, events in Germany seemed to augur a renewal of a fascist offensive, and that under the circumstances it was wrong for the Warsaw powers to tolerate the refugee flow. And," Ulbricht laughed, if that was the word to describe the sound, "old Gomulka, announcing that in his judgment it was the responsibility of the Warsaw powers to protect misguided citizens from taking steps which they were bound to repent. And so it went. One after another! The same people who in March voted against us!"

"What did Chairman Khrushchev say in his speech?" the professor asked.

"He said that, in his judgment, it was the responsibility of the Soviet Union, in concert with those members of the Warsaw alliance who agreed to do so, to provide moral backing for a solution to the Berlin problem. That it would need to be East Germans who effected my plan, but that he favored joint approval of our plan—up to a point."

"Up to what point?" Colonel Hassel looked up.

Ulbricht put down his glass. "The Chairman explained that it would not be wise to proceed with my plan if the Allies reacted with . . . force."

"What kind of force?" Colonel Hassel pressed.

"The Chairman was not talking about a United States military policeman with barbed wire cutters or a fire hose, or that kind of thing. That kind of thing we must expect."

"Well what kind of thing *was* he talking about?" Colonel Hassel pressed.

"Tanks." Ulbricht's voice was now much quieter.

"How many tanks?" Colonel Hassel persisted.

Ulbricht put down his glass. "If any tank runs over our barricade, we are instructed . . . counseled . . . to retreat." Ulbricht's voice began to trail. "Chairman Khrushchev said the Soviet Union would need to proceed with reference to the comprehensive responsibilities of the Soviet Union to the Warsaw powers."

"You mean to say"—Hassel was not going to let it go—"that if an American tank runs over our barricade, Khrushchev will not come to our aid?"

"That is what I mean to say," Ulbricht said acidly. *"However,"* he brought buoyancy back into his voice, "the Chairman says we are not to concern ourselves, that he has weighed the character of the President at Vienna, and studied carefully his television speech of last week, and has got reports from agents in the field. He is convinced that if we make no move against West Berlin, and none against the convoys that provision West Berlin, the President will turn his back on East Berlin."

Colonel Hassel shrugged his shoulders. "Yesterday Willy Brandt gave a speech. He said we would not dare partition Berlin because Berlin was an 'indispensable safety valve' and we would not risk the popular explosion that might ensue—"

"I'm good at handling popular explosions," Ulbricht snapped. "It's the tanks I don't want."

"That wasn't my point, Mr. Chairman. My point was that I can't see how Brandt, who is after all running for political office in one month, would say something like that unless he knew that the Allies were planning to resist."

Ulbricht waved his arm and very nearly shouted. "I don't care what Willy Brandt says. I don't care what Konrad Adenauer says. I care only if American tanks come on the scene, and I am convinced that Chairman Khrushchev is correct, that they will not do so. Now I say by God let's toast to the liberation of Berlin, so let's by God do what I say, all right, Hassel?"

"Yes, Mr. Chairman."

"Now, we have been stocking material, as you know, since March. The plans for Operation Chinese Wall are in your hands, General. We have the barbed wire, many thanks to the British who manufactured it. We will travel from sawhorse traffic interrupters to concertinas of barbed wire to concrete stanchions. And beginning on the third day, if our work has not been definitively interrupted—and believe me, gentlemen, it will not be—we will begin constructing a 45-kilometer wall which will be impassable."

"Have you decided," the professor spoke up, "when D-Day is?"

"I have. I deem it imprudent to reveal the day. You will have forty-eight hours' notice. You must go to work as if D-Day were the day after tomorrow. We shall begin by stopping the subways and the trains at 0100 on D-Day. Troops will be brought in to help the Vopos with the barbed wire. Beginning at daylight, the acetylene torches will begin drilling the holes." Ulbricht, a teetotaler, reached for the champagne bottle. "I am going to drink to D-Day, and a Berlin made safe from the traitors who wish to flee it."

The Chairman rose. "Gentlemen, good night. We shall meet every morning, beginning on Tuesday, at eight, when I expect reports of the progress of the various bureaus."

They said good night. Professor Wittvogel caught the eye of Ulbricht, and lingered. "Walter," he said, sitting in the armchair next to the doorway as Ulbricht, yawning, sat opposite him, "did Khrushchev tell you in front of the other leaders that he defined a single tank as a 'force' that would cause him to counsel withdrawal?"

"No. That was in a private conversation after the meeting had been disbanded. Why do you ask?"

"Chairman Khrushchev does not enjoy backing down. It is hard to understand how it is that he let our Warsaw partners go out with the impression that he would back us up unless the Americans moved in overwhelmingly, while indicating to you that one or two tanks and the operation was off."

"Yes, I suppose so. But Chairman Khrushchev clearly believes that the presence of a single American tank is an indication that the entire force of NATO, and ultimately the strategic weapons of the United States, will support the resistance to our wall. He does not expect this to happen and neither do I."

"And neither do I, Walter. But just on a hunch, if the American tanks do show up a week from Sunday—look after your personal safety."

"You are saying, Hans?"

"I am saying Khrushchev will be looking for a scapegoat."

"Why me? The Warsaw partners endorsed my proposal, unlike last March."

"Your thoughts, Walter, as I warned you as a student in the university, are sometimes hampered by a bourgeois affinity for reason. If the operation fails, there will be the need for a scapegoat. Chairman Khrushchev will take care to exclude himself. You will recall that he contrived to cause you to petition for the Moscow meeting. Enough said?"

Ulbricht got up. "I appreciate your personal loyalty, Hans. Don't worry."

28

It was a very late night for Caspar. Ulbricht had instructed him to prepare the minutes of the meeting in Ulbricht's secretary's office, rather than use the pool typewriter he shared with three other aides. "This time, make no copies. Just put the original in a sealed envelope and leave it right on my desk."

Caspar sensed that this was the moment to take liberties. Instead of supplying Henri with a paraphrase of the minutes, he resolved to give him a carbon copy. He emerged at 4 A.M. with four sheets of paper in his pocket, in an envelope on which was imprinted "Office of the Chairman, Democratic Republic of Germany." In his left pocket he carried an unmarked, unsealed envelope. If by any remote chance he was stopped and searched, he would identify himself and advise that the document he was carrying was a confidential document of his uncle's that he had been up late working on. When he reached the lockers, he would take the document from the official envelope and insert it in the unmarked envelope in his pocket, destroying the official envelope.

But go, at four in the morning, to the Ostbahnhof's lockers? He deemed this provocative. Not earlier than 6:30, he reflected. By then the traffic would have begun to move. But not later than 6:45, because Henri's courier came as early as 7, and on no account must they meet or must there be any delay in relaying the tidings of the evening. But to go home, a distance of sixteen blocks, enter his house, sleep, wake, wash, and return by 6:30 meant not only to risk awakening his mother, but also to reduce his sleeping time by the one hour the round trip would take him. The answer was, clearly, to rest at Berchtesgaden.

And so he slithered into the old sidings via the usual entrance, the same door through which Henri had come the night he was wounded. He walked silently the well-trod route. When he turned at the fourth siding he began reflexively counting the cars as he walked down. 10206 was the fourth. He got there, took the key from his pocket, and opened first the platform door, then the door leading to the car. He lit a single candle, next to Hitler's bed, set the alarm clock, reflected on the convulsive events one week hence, and wondered, among other things, what, if anything, would happen to Berchtesgaden, and soon he was asleep.

It was 8:15 when Roland delivered the envelope to Bruni, who opened it and, without a word to the housekeeper who was serving him breakfast, tore out the door. He knocked his code on the door. Henri promptly opened it, then read the document and said to Bruni, "I must go quickly to Oakes. Trail me—just in case. No chances on this one." He went to the telephone and dialed Blackford's number. Without identifying himself, he said, "I am on my way to see you. Wait for me," and hung up.

At Rheinstrasse, Blackford was waiting. His right hand trembling, Henri gave the envelope wordlessly to Blackford, who said, "Come on in." As he started to read, he led Henri to the kitchen. While still reading, he poured a cup of coffee, sat down at one of the kitchen chairs beside his own unfinished cup, and finished reading.

"Great God, Henri. Who in the hell is your mole? Mrs. Ulbricht?"

"You know I can't tell you, Blackford."

"I know that *ordinarily* you couldn't tell me. But this time you have to tell me. Don't you know how much hangs on the reliability of this document?"

"It is reliable."

"Thanks, Henri. Now all we need to do is convince the President of the United States. Look, for this one I'll need you to come with me to my superior." On principle, Rufus avoided meeting other than with his own agents. He especially did not want to meet Henri Tod, wanted, in the Eastern Zone, for murder, among other things. Blackford knew Rufus well enough a) to break the rule, and b) to do so without consulting him. "Let's go," he said.

29

Cool young man, Oakes. You'd think the President of the United States, the Chairman of the Joint Chiefs, the Vice President, the Secretary of State, the Director of the Central Intelligence Agency, the National Security Adviser to the President—did I forget anybody? Caroline didn't drift in on this meeting—oh yes, the Secretary of Defense. McNamara would love that, remembering everyone there, forgetting the Secretary of Defense. All of us in the Situation Room, which by the way why in the hell didn't I choose a larger room? In there like sardines. Oakes talked, if anything, as if we were classmates. Well no, that's not fair. As Bobby says—oh, forgot Bobby. Of course Bobby was there. As Bobby would say, protocolwise he was okay. Master spy Rufus is a pretty impressive guy, Allen was right about it. And Oakes absolutely swears for that Tod man. I don't doubt Tod believes those minutes. As a matter of fact, I don't doubt their authenticity. Boy, how we went round and round on *that* point. The Oakes guy, I bet he makes out. Mm. He came pretty close to advocacy, though his job was just to answer questions about Tod and his contact. Jesus *Christ*, that's got to be one for the history books. His own fucking nephew! "Mr. Chairman," I'll say to Khrushchev next time we summit, "Mr. Chairman, do you have a nephew whose father you executed? Because I have a *wonderful* idea how you can make amends. You *don't* have such a nephew fitting that description? Well, I tell you what, Mr. Chairman, you pick any nephew, and you go ahead and

execute his father, then you'll have a nephew you need to
make amends for, right? There's a simple solution to every
problem. All we need to do is to think positive, right?" . . .
Oh shut up. So after a half hour on the authenticity of the
document we dismiss Tarzan and Boy, and then oh God. I
set the rules. Look—I was right about this, Bobby agreed
right away, so did McNamara. You set out a premise and
move or you don't move, but you don't question the premise. I was right to say: Goddam it, we've decided it was
authentic, now let's think the problem through on *that* assumption. Otherwise we'll sit here and find ourselves arguing all over again whether the minutes are the real thing. I
didn't look at Dean, I looked in the opposite direction, but
Dean knew I was really looking at him. I don't think Dean
really cares much about Berlin, or, for that matter, about
Germans. That was a nice line of Clemenceau's—was it
Clemenceau? "I feel so attached to Germany I think there
should be at least two of them." Might use that one, one of
these days. If I had invited Acheson into the meeting he'd
have come out for three American tanks going over the
Berlin barbed wire and not stopping until they reached
Moscow. Khrushchev told Ulbricht that if the barbed wire is
run over by American tanks he is to call off the operation
because of the Soviet Union's "comprehensive obligations
to the Warsaw powers." That's a nice way of saying that he
doesn't really want to tangle with us. So Lemnitzer says,
What if Khrushchev changes his mind? We have twenty-
seven tanks in the American sector. The Russians have over
one thousand squatted around Berlin. But Khrushchev
wasn't telling Ulbricht and the gang that he couldn't lick
our Berlin military, even if you add a couple of British
bicycles or whatever they have out there—not much, McNamara says—and add whatever the French have that they
haven't flown out to Algeria—add all that up and *still* they
can clobber us in no time. But that isn't what Khrushchev is
afraid of, apparently. He's afraid of a *casus belli*. Good thing

they put that in Latin. Sounds too scary in English. I wonder if I could decline *casus;* I got pretty good marks in Latin at Choate. Casus, casi, casum, no, there's something in between. Caso? I'll ask Jackie. Maybe Vienna wasn't as bad as I thought. Maybe he thinks I'm looking for an opportunity to wipe out the Bay of Pigs. Could be. Bundy's right, of course. Even the Moscow meeting was only three days ago, and the partition is coming up fast—wish we knew exactly when; there's still time for the generals around Khrushchev to push and shove and make him change his mind. If they can get into the act, they will. They could persuade him that world opinion would weigh in on their side if the Russian tanks, say, met our tanks deep inside East Berlin. I know I know—old Acheson must have told me this five thousand times—the Soviet Union has no right to do what's being done, but the fact of it is that East Berlin has for all intents and purposes been Soviet territory for ten years. That's the way the world would square off on this business. And what's the flip side? Suppose they do cave in? So the escape valve business goes on, and we continue to get the refugees. Into West Germany. And East Berlin tries to keep them from leaving by becoming a pleasant place to live. But that means West Germany has to become a pleasant place to live, otherwise people would leave East Germany and go live in East Berlin. But if East Germany became a pleasant place to live, then people would leave Bulgaria and Czechoslovakia and Romania and Poland. Did you ever see a dream walking? . . . I was right not to take a vote. There was sentiment there to go in with a few tanks. It would have been a hell of a show, all right, if the barbed wire people had slunk back to their dungeons, big cheers in Berlin, but we'll get big cheers in Berlin—in West Berlin, as I said on teevee last week—whenever we go, so long as we keep West Berlin open, and this we're going to do. The alternative? Sounded good, but you got to be careful. Guns of August sort of thing . . . Was kind of startled, coming out, to see the spymaster and Junior still there. Who told them to wait? Did *they* need to know our decision? The spymaster already told us we needed to protect our source; what other business do they have that kept them waiting there, like ambassadors waiting for a yes-no? On the other hand, you don't like to be rude. When I *think* of all the people I haven't been rude to I'd like to be rude to, like that asshole who runs Chicago. I wasn't going to start out being rude by being rude to Superspy, who's a terrific asset, Allen says, and his brightest kid. Well, hardly—he must be thirty. So I stopped and shook hands. But I didn't say anything about what we were going to do, just that we were considering the question. Oakes looked awfully let down. Well, so am I, in a way. But damn, it's a relief if that's all K has in mind for East Germany. Yes yes, I'm just putting on my tie. I'll be with you in a minute.

30

On the flight Washington-Paris-Berlin the coach section was uncrowded, so Rufus took the three seats directly ahead of Blackford, allowing them both to stretch out. Rufus had been in session with the Director after leaving the White House, a meeting from which Blackford had been excluded. On the way to the airport Rufus had said nothing about what he had learned at that meeting, and they had to hurry to catch the flight. Rufus, one hour after takeoff, was reading De Gaulle's *War Memoirs*, Blackford the latest issue of *National Review*. They were over Nantucket when Blackford bopped Rufus on the head with the magazine open at a page on which Blackford had circled an editorial and scratched on top: "Rufus, read this. Buckley is almost always right. But on this one he doesn't have the right nephew advising him." Rufus picked up the magazine and read an open letter:

"Ambassador Mikhail Menshikov

"The Soviet Embassy, Washington, D.C.

"Last Saturday you told some fellow diplomats at a Washington cocktail party that Americans will not fight for Berlin. Well, it isn't true. How do we know it? Because we are Americans, and only Americans can know truly how wrong you are. It is not a distinctive American heroism that we are laying claim to. Probably we are no more heroic, nor less, than this people, or that. Nor do we want war as a means of exporting our well-being—and yet we know there are others who would go to war to export, and share, their misery. We would not die for Berlin *merely* to save Berliners —that would be un-American, as the saying goes. But we are all agreed, right across the political spectrum, that Berlin's freedom is inexorably tied to our own freedom, that a single axis connects the two and that if you disturb it at one end, you must disturb the other end. That, and let us be very plainspoken here, is a basic strategic intuition, and the assumption underlying our country's foreign and military policies.

"We are saying something much less grand than that freedom is universal, or indivisible, or whatever. Berlin is different. You Communists certainly know that. To the extent Berlin is coveted by you, it is coveted also by us. For you it is a bone in your throat; for the West it is a regenerating fountain whence flows hope for millions. For you Berlin is a bourgeois enclave which must be wiped out. But for us it is the critical salient we cannot surrender. For you it is a mirror, which throws incandescent rays east and west, opposing, against the potency and spirit and well-being of life under freedom, the hideousness of life under Communism.

"And then, apart from all of that, the laws of nations uphold our right to stay in Berlin. And, finally, we have pledged, through Presidents Democratic and Republican, that we will not let the people of Berlin down.

"Examine, then, your assumption. A lot hangs on that reexamination including, quite conceivably, your life and ours.

"Yours truly, The Editors of *National Review.*"

Blackford saw Rufus's hand crooked over the back of his seat, waving a piece of paper. Blackford leaned forward and retrieved it. Rufus had scrawled,

"Like everybody else, NR anticipates a threat against West Berlin, which isn't going to happen."

Blackford turned the notepaper over and scratched out, "Rufus. Are we going in with the tanks on D-Day?"

From where Blackford sat he could see that Rufus was pondering whether, or perhaps how, to reply. But a minute later his hand stretched up over the back of his seat with the notepaper. Blackford took it.

Under Blackford's query he had written, "No."

One more time Blackford scratched out a comment, which just fitted in the space under the word "No." He wrote: "Whittaker Chambers died last month. I think he was right that he left the winning side to join the losing side."

Rufus terminated the colloquy with a note on a fresh piece of notepaper. "Despair, Blackford, is a mortal sin."

31

At nine o'clock on Thursday morning, Henri received the news from Caspar. The date and hour had been set: 0100 Sunday August 13. Less than seventy-two hours.

Never had three hours taken so long for Henri Tod. Blackford's flight was due in at eleven, and he would reach Henri by twelve or shortly after. And he would bring, Henri supposed, the tidings from Washington for which he longed. He managed during those three hours to look only three times at the picture of his sister, though he did go back to write yet another few pages to the letter he had begun the day he heard. The document was now forty pages long. He would finish it, he pledged, that night, and have it delivered to her. But he would first consult Blackford, as promised. At ten minutes to twelve he left his rooms and walked the six blocks to Number 12. Ten minutes later, a taxi brought Blackford.

Henri knew the moment he saw him. He would not have needed to say, "The answer is no, Henri. The President isn't sending in the tanks." Blackford added, "And if you don't mind, I don't want to talk about it. I'm going to go get some sleep. I'll check on the phone and see if the information is in on Clementa's custodian. If it is, I'll get back to you. But it may not be till tomorrow."

"Thank you, Blackford. And my news is that the wall will go up at 0100 Sunday."

"*This* Sunday?"

"Yes."

"You will be interested to know, Henri, and this is obviously confidential. At Washington we were told that the intelligence services of France, Great Britain, and, yes, the United States, informed the foreign ministers at their get-together in Paris last weekend that there was no indication whatever that partition was being planned."

Henri managed a smile.

32

"Why is supper taking so long?" Caspar looked over from the radio at the end of the sofa in Berchtesgaden.

"Because tonight we are going to have a special dinner."

"Why? It's not your birthday, Claudia. Is it mine?"

"You can be very silly, Caspar."

"Well, then, why are we having a very special dinner?"

"Because I feel like it."

"Well, that's a good reason. Come to think of it, you don't really need an excuse for a specially good dinner, do you? It's always a good idea. But rather a bore to bring in all the makings, isn't it?"

"I have it pretty well down to a system. Caspar, I went *over* today, and I came back with a ham. You ought to see what the stores there have. It's like Christmas."

"Henri told me I was not ever to go over, you know that."

"Henri is quite right. But I want to talk to you about something after dinner."

"Sure, what?"

"I said after dinner. Anything special on the news?"

"Yes. The great Rudolf Nureyev has just defected, in Paris."

"Who is Rudolf Nureyev?"

"*Who is Rudolf Nureyev?* Who is Napoleon Bonaparte!"

"Come on, who is he?"

"He's only the world's best ballet dancer."

"Have you ever seen a ballet?"

"No."

"When did you hear about the great Rudolf Nureyev?"

Caspar giggled. "Tonight. Over the radio. Anyway, I'm glad. Aren't you?" Claudia had sat down at the little table, decorated with three candles and two apples, one facing Caspar's plate, one facing Claudia's. Each had been made to look like a human face, by means of raisins and cherry stems and careful peeling. Caspar cried out his pleasure. "They're beautiful!" He leaned down and kissed her, and slid into his seat. Hitler's seat.

It was the finest meal he had ever had, said Caspar an hour later, "and that includes one of Uncle Walter's banquets I was invited to two years ago." Claudia was pleased, and emptied the wine bottle into Caspar's glass.

"Come on, let's go to bed. We can clean up later."

As was their habit, Caspar went into the stateroom first, arranged the lighting in the way he knew Claudia liked it. She came in, in her nightgown, from the bathroom. She smelled like apple blossoms, but then she always did. Caspar was stirred, and quickly they were embracing. He felt the special intensity of her embrace and returned it, his passion now overwhelming. Claudia gasped, and when it was over clasped him to her, her arms around his neck.

"Darling, darling. I can't breathe."

She loosened her hold on him, but just a little. "Caspar, there is something I must say to you."

"Well, silly, say it."

"We must leave."

He sat up. "Leave . . . Berchtesgaden?"

"No. Leave East Berlin."

Caspar was thoughtful, but said nothing.

"We know now it may not be possible after Sunday."

"But—what would we do?"

"What did the thirty thousand who left in July do?"

"Well, yes. I suppose we could find jobs. I don't need to worry about my mother. What about yours?"

"She has been urging me to leave for over one year."

Caspar said, "Don't you think we ought to check it out with Henri?"

"I think we should tell him; I don't think we should give him a veto."

"No, I suppose you're right. On the other hand, if the Americans do what we expect them to do, Sunday won't mean anything."

"Your uncle will find some other way of stopping the traffic. Caspar, let's just agree to go on Saturday night, as if we were going to a movie over there—and then just not come back. Henri would look after us."

"Yes, he would. I don't worry about that." He sighed. "Oh dear, how I shall miss Berchtesgaden. Claudia! I just had a wonderful thought. Couldn't you, since you work for the director of the railroads, issue an order that car 10206 should be hauled out of the sidings, and railed over to West Berlin? Tell them it is in exchange for a traitor, or something like that?"

"You *are* a silly ass, Caspar. Now. We will stop by on Saturday afternoon and say goodbye to Berchtesgaden. And it will just be a happy dream."

"How long does it take to get a marriage license in the West, I wonder, Claudia?"

"Why do you wonder?" she smiled, now the coquette.

"I was just wondering, that's all. You don't need an excuse to get a marriage license, do you?" And he returned her embrace, and inhaled her apple blossom, and reflected on how deeply he loved her, and how happy he was when in her company, and how in West Berlin they would insist only on this, that they work together wherever next they worked.

33

Blackford had been asleep a half hour when the telephone rang, just before one in the morning. He had that afternoon slept two hours, then attended to his rounds. The report on Frank proved nothing much. His real name was Dmitri Gouzenko, he had not lived in Berlin up until about a month ago, so that he might indeed have been at the camp in Vorkuta. And he was attached to the Amtorg Trading Corporation in the foreign merchandising division, and he did inhabit 117 Frankfurter Allee, and there was, at that address since last Tuesday, a young woman registered as Mrs. Gouzenko. If he was KGB, which Blackford continued to believe was the case, Dmitri was being thorough. Blackford had attempted to reach Henri to give him this information, and indeed told Bruni, to whom he had been put through, that the matter was of some importance. He was surprised that Henri did not get back to him, but reasoned he would do so in the morning. Still tired from his trip, he had gone to sleep just after midnight. Now, awakened by the phone, it required a few seconds to orient himself. He dreamed he was in an airplane.

"Yes," he picked up.

"It's Bruni. Number one priority. It is 12:47. Can you meet me outside at 1:04? I'll be in a blue two-door Fiat."

It was Bruni all right, no question about the voice. Bruni had been in this business for several years. But Blackford had been at it for ten years. And certain things certain people in this business do not do. Like go out of their houses into a strange car after midnight.

"Bruni, sorry, it doesn't work that way. And you've made things tough on me, because if someone is standing beside you with a gun pointed at your head, he is obviously also after me, which is going to bring on a sleepless night."

"Dammit, Blackford, I'm here alone. This is terribly important. I wouldn't wake you otherwise. Our friend needs you right away."

Blackford thought, and relented in part.

"Listen, Bruni. You go and park that Fiat of yours. In fact, at this hour you can even leave the motor running. Then come into my apartment. *Then* I'll go out with you."

Bruni swore. "All right," he said. "Please be ready."

Blackford dressed, checked his pistol, turned off his light, looked out the window, and waited. Just after one o'clock a car stopped, a single figure emerged, and he heard the ring above the doorway, apartment 3C. He pressed the buzzer to open the door at the apartment entrance, opened his own door, turned on the lights in the living room into which the apartment door opened, and retreated into the bathroom. From there, with its light off, he could see his living room but not be seen. There was an almost soundless knock and Blackford, pistol in hand, called out, "Come in, Bruni."

It was he. Blackford stepped out. "Where are we going, Bruni, and what's up?"

"Henri wants to tell you himself. He asked me just to bring you. Please do hurry."

Blackford deeply trusted Henri and Bruni. He put down his firearm, tucking it back into the pocket of his raincoat in the closet. "Okay. Let's go."

Bruni drove to Lepsiusstrasse, yet another safe house, one Blackford didn't know. Number 8, Bruni said. The car was parked, and they walked across the street, dimly lit by the streetlight on the corner. Like so many Berlin dwellings, it was new in appearance. Probably it had been built since the bombings, or at least rebuilt—but solid; dark red, it appeared in the dim light. The door opened before they could knock. It was Henri.

"Thanks, Blackford. Come with me, please, to the cellar office." A figure loomed between them and the cellar door. "Oh, meet Mateus. Mateus used to work for my father."

Blackford found himself shaking hands with a large, muscular man, bald, in his late sixties, wearing an open shirt and faded brown slacks. Henri had not given Blackford's name, and now said, "We're going to meet downstairs, Mateus. If I need anything, I'll ring." Mateus nodded.

They walked down stone steps. At the bottom Henri flicked on a light illuminating a whitewashed corridor. A few feet to the right of it was a heavy wooden door. "They used this as a bomb shelter," Henri said, opening the door and flicking on another light. The interior was small but comfortably furnished, a straw mat on the stone floor, a desk and a cot on the far side and, visible because its door was open, a little, utilitarian bathroom.

Henri sat down at the desk and began instantly to talk.

"Blackford, my men are going to run the blockade on Sunday. In United States tanks. Wait, listen. I was able to organize this afternoon and evening. I have rounded up six men. Three of them drove tanks during the war. Another three work during the day in the armory, two in yours, one in the British armory. My men are Bruderschaft, of course. They understand what it is we are up to. They will assemble at your armory at the McNair Barracks. On Sunday, one of them assures me, the probability is that the situation there will be pretty sleepy. The MP at the gate we may have to overpower if he is suspicious. Though Sunday is not the day for tank testing, it is plausible that orders came in during the night to test tanks that may be suffering from mechanical problems, and because of the general emergency conditions this is being done on Sunday, rather than on Monday. The tanks will leave in a single file. When they reach the Brandenburg Gate, they will fan out in formation and trample over whatever the Vopos have constructed. Having done that, the tanks will swing around and head back for the armory. No one will have been hurt. The Vopos aren't going to fire from their armored cars at tanks. But the partition of Berlin will have been frustrated." He paused. "We call it Operation Rheingold."

"Go on," said Blackford.

"I want you to help us."

"How?"

"We have an agent in East Berlin. He knows how to tap one of your codes. If you can arrange for a bogus instruction to come in on that code as if directed to General Greenwalt telling him to proceed with plan A3, and to send three tanks in to destroy the blockade, I can arrange for that intercepted message to get through right away to East German and Soviet intelligence. That would convince them the U.S. military isn't going to tolerate partition. And when the tanks materialize, they'll know it for certain."

"When do you see that message coming in?"

"They're going to begin, as you know, at 0100. That's 7 P.M. Washington time. I would recommend the cabled instructions coming in at, say, 4 A.M. That allows approximately three hours for a) news of the partition to get from the border to the U.S. military here, b) a cable to Washington, c) a couple of hours' deliberation in Washington, and d) returned orders. To designate the maneuver with a code name 'A3' also suggests it is the contingency plan to cope with this maneuver. Will you help? I am talking about the future of Berlin and of millions of Germans. I may be talking about the future of the West."

Blackford stood up. "Henri, *Henri.* I'm with you and you know it, but the answer's got to be No. How in the hell *can* I? I'm an American citizen and an agent of the Central Intelligence Agency, and we get our instructions from the

President of the United States, and he gets his from Congress, and Congress gets its from the voters. Now you people have put on one hell of a show. But you also write your own rules. You go out and kill people as required. I'm not saying the people you do this to don't deserve it. I'm not even suggesting that if I lived here I wouldn't join your organization. I'm just saying that I'm an American citizen, and when I got into this job I made certain *commitments*—"

Tod interrupted him. "Blackford, I know about the nature of formal obligations. I also know that you are something of a moralist. So, why can't you satisfy your conscience by resigning from the CIA? Now. Before you help us? The Agency would no longer have any claim on your movements and you would be freed to advance—history."

"Henri, that sounds good. But really, it isn't. I'd be using skills the CIA taught me, contacts the CIA has set up for me —including you. I'd be an accomplice in a venture that involves stealing American tanks and writing American foreign policy in defiance of constituted authority."

There was silence. Then Henri Tod spoke. His voice was even, the tone almost casual, but his message rang through, like a machine gun hitting only bull's-eyes. "We're going to do it anyway, Blackford. If you helped, it would make it safer for everyone. With that cable from the Pentagon backing the tanks, Ulbricht's enterprise would collapse. I think it will anyway, with just the three tanks. All I can say is, I'm disappointed." Henri reached over his desk and pressed a buzzer.

"And there's something else I have to say, Blackford, and I'm very sorry about this. You can understand, though, that I can't let you leave now until Sunday. After Rheingold."

Blackford sat down on the edge of the bed. He smiled. "Well, well. Maybe it would be safer still if you just killed me?"

"Don't say that. Even in jest. The Bruderschaft does not kill people like you."

"Is this"—Blackford gestured toward the room—"to be my quarters? And"—he pointed to Mateus, who stood now inside the door—"that my guard?"

"Mateus will look after you."

"I will need some books."

"There is a library upstairs. Mateus will bring you books."

Henri rose, as did Bruni. There was an awkward moment, the moment when, under normal circumstances, both he and Bruni would have extended their hands to say good night, but now they wondered if the gesture would be reciprocated. Blackford, recognizing the problem, took the initiative, extending his own hand, which first Henri, then Bruni took. They were on their way out.

"Henri?"

He stopped at the door.

"I got the report on Mr. Frank. I tried to get you earlier. His name is Dmitri Gouzenko, he does work at the Amtorg Trading Corporation, he cropped up in East Berlin only a month ago, and last Tuesday a young woman who goes by the name of Mrs. Gouzenko began to live in his apartment."

"Thank you, Blackford."

Blackford said nothing, and the two men left. Mateus spoke:

"I am to get you some reading matter. Do you wish anything to eat or drink?"

"Yes, I'd like—" but what was the point in wisecracking with Mateus? "Yes, I would like a scotch and soda."

"Very well, sir."

He left the room, and Blackford could hear the lock turning.

He went instantly to inspect the door. It was a conventional door constructed from heavy wood, with rails, stiles, and six panels. The door lock was of heavy brass. Blackford turned the doorknob, which moved the latch bolt, but, of course, Mateus's key had moved the dead bolt into the striker plate on the doorframe—the locked position. Right above the doorknob was the keyhole, in its own cylinder. So that the model was clearly of the kind that provided for a key to be used on either side of the door. He looked about him to see whether there might be means of overpowering Mateus. It would not be difficult to make a bludgeon out of one of the legs of one of the chairs. Yes, he could do that. He could also simply try to overpower Mateus. The guard was big and heavy and powerful, but Blackford was well trained. He reflected on this alternative. But first, he thought, it would pay to check on Mateus's style, and this he would be able to do soon now, when he brought down the drink and the books.

He heard the key turning and Mateus's voice through the wooden door. "Sir, please open the door, and then step back and stand in front of the desk with the door open."

Blackford opened the door and found himself facing the muzzle of a Luger. Obediently he stepped back five paces, and now there were twenty feet between him and Mateus. With his left hand Mateus carried a suitcase which he deposited to the left of the door, his eyes always on Blackford, his pistol pointed at him. "I am sorry about this, sir, but my instructions from Herr Henri are very explicit. It won't be for very long, after all. Every time I come to the door, we must proceed as we have just done. You must not come within reach of me. Now I will fetch you your drink." He went out again, locking the door.

Blackford went to the suitcase and lifted it up on top of the desk. It contained six books, a dozen magazines, an unused toilet kit, three pairs of shorts, T-shirts, socks, a sweater. He would be a pampered prisoner. All he needed to do was find a way to outwit Mateus before Sunday. Or overpower Mateus.

He decided he would begin by cultivating him. But in stages. This was, after all, two-thirty in the morning.

He heard Mateus's voice, and went, with ostentatious docility, through his ritual. Open the door; step back in full view of Mateus, who is there with his pistol aimed at my stomach; come to a halt by the desk.

Mateus, with one strong hand, deposited a tray on a side table by the armchair opposite the door. On the tray was a full bottle of scotch, an ice container, and a large bottle of soda. Blackford moved as if to go to the tray.

"Stop, sir! That's right. You must not be in the same part of the room as I am in." Pistol pointed at Blackford, Mateus backed out of the door, swung it closed, and Blackford heard the key turning. And, through the door, "Good night, sir. There is a buzzer on the desk if you should need anything. Don't hesitate to call me. Ring when you desire your breakfast."

"Very well. Good night, Mateus."

"Good night, sir."

34

$\mathbf{M}$argret Nilsson had succeeded in arranging her schedule at the hospital to coincide with Franz's as much as possible. She was with him as an assistant when he did surgery, and the chief nurse indulgently gave Margret primary responsibility for the care of Franz's patients, which made for additional moments together. Several times a week Franz would call for Margret to come to his office to take postoperative notes on a patient, and it was made known that when Franz was dictating, he was on no account to be interrupted; and, with a leering smile here and there, the staff went along. So what business of theirs was it that Franz also had a wife and little girl? He did his work, so did Margret. So let them go ahead with their amorous dictation, even if during hospital hours.

But the existing relationship was not what Margret wanted, and Franz often told her how unhappy he was at home without Margret, and how unsatisfactory his wife was, and Margret said that they must go away together and live a normal life instead of continuing the imposture. But go away where? West, of course.

Franz agreed but said there was a money problem. He could not in good conscience go without leaving provision of a sort for his wife and child, and he set the sum at ten thousand marks that he must leave her, in the form of civil settlement—alimony, so to speak. The difficulty lay in amassing such a sum of money, on his paltry savings. Margret said she could come up with twelve hundred marks, and perhaps borrow as much as another eight hundred. But that, together with what Franz had in savings, came to only one half the figure they so desperately needed.

It was one morning after a passionate interval with Franz during the dictation hour, when yet again they had wondered how they could find the necessary money, that Margret stopped at the post office. She was there to buy a stamp with which to mail a letter to her sister in Leipzig, where Margret had grown up and gone to school with Claudia. There was a line behind the counter where stamps were sold, and while waiting in that line her eyes traveled to the post office bulletin board. She noticed a sign that appeared fresher than the others, no doubt only recently posted. It announced a government award of five thousand marks to anyone who gave information resulting in the arrest of any seditious enemy of the republic. The terms were of course general, but Margret found her heart racing. Five thousand marks.

She had sensed that the two times Claudia had come to her—the first to obtain penicillin, the second to pass along a vial of blood for examination—Claudia's vaguely stated reasons why she had not gone directly to a doctor, or to a hospital, indicated that she was hiding something. Which meant hiding somebody. Hiding what? Hiding whom? Well, she thought, surely that is the business of the government to discover, not me?

She read the sign again carefully. Her responsibility was merely to provide the police with leads, not to do anything more than that. "Confidentiality is guaranteed," the sign went on.

Margret resolved to discuss the matter with Franz at their next private meeting, early that afternoon. She liked Claudia. But she loved Franz. And it was not right, in any case, for her to run the risks Claudia had imposed on her. Would she, she wondered, now need to give a reason for not having gone earlier to the police with information about the penicillin and the blood?

She would need to have an excuse that sounded reasonable. On the matter of the penicillin, she supposed it would do merely to say that Claudia was under the impression that as a nurse, Margret could get the penicillin free or at small cost, and that Claudia had distinctly given her the impression that it was for her own use. But the blood . . . She perked up. Why not say that Claudia had confessed her private fear that she had contracted a venereal disease, but was ashamed to go to the regular doctor to find out? That struck her as plausible and imaginative. But why then did she choose this moment to go to the police? Why, because it had suddenly occurred to her that Claudia had asked not only for a reading on venereal disease, but for a full analysis of the blood, so that now Margret wondered whether there might be involved some fugitive from justice . . .

She would try it out on Franz, which she did, and he thought it not only prudent, in the event that suspicion might at some point attach to Margret for dispensing drugs without authority, but also a capital idea for raising the necessary money which, the moment it was handed over, would free them to go off to the West and live happily ever after.

Caspar was both sad and excited. He had taken the greatest care to assemble in the laundry bag he carried every week to the laundress what he wished to take with him to the West. He reasoned that if he and Claudia traveled on the S-Bahn with the Saturday afternoon traffic the chances were slight that, carrying only a laundry bag, he would be stopped and examined. And even if that happened, his escape would not necessarily be aborted. For one thing, he was, after all, the nephew of Walter Ulbricht, and he carried a formidable identification card designating him as a clerk

attached to headquarters. His last name wasn't Ulbricht,
but in a pinch he could let it be known who he was and
where he worked. All he and his girlfriend were doing was
going to West Berlin for a couple of days, and taking a few
souvenirs for friends.

He had tucked into the bag his father's letter, freshly
sealed in an envelope. A few photographs, his father's portable typewriter—that was by far the bulkiest item; indeed
the only bulky item—and then underwear, shirts, an extra
jacket and pants, socks, all of these carefully rumpled to
look as though they were being taken to be cleaned or
pressed. No matter.

And then he had written a letter which his mother would
discover later that night or the following morning. He had
been careful not to disclose in the letter that he had any
premonition, let alone specific knowledge, of the events
planned for just after midnight, and of course not a hint of
his knowledge of Operation Rheingold on which he had
been personally briefed the night before by Bruni. Henri
had been asked by his tank commander what exactly would
be the deployment of the East German armored cars that
would reinforce the barricades, and exactly how far away
were the reserve Russian tanks to be situated, and Henri
had judged that only a knowledge of why this information
was so necessary could justify the intensity of Caspar's
rather dangerous search for the answers, and for that reason had dispatched Bruni to talk with Caspar. It was merely
a happy coincidence that he and Claudia thought to leave
East Berlin only a few hours before leaving East Berlin
would cease to be possible—unless, of course, Henri succeeded with Rheingold. He told his mother he was unhappy
with the diminishing freedom of East Germans, that he
would make every provision for her if she elected to join
him, that he would write regularly, that he loved her very
much, that he intended to marry Claudia, and that his very
first child he would name after her if it was a girl, and after

his father if it was a boy. He sealed the envelope and, with tape, affixed it to the mirror of the bathroom outside his bedroom, knowing that only when his mother came looking for him would she notice it.

He glanced at his watch. He would rendezvous with Claudia at Berchtesgaden at five, and already it was a quarter past four. His bundle was by no means too heavy to walk with, so that rather than while away twenty minutes and then take the bus, he decided to walk. His mother was out of the house, so there were no problems going out with his laundry bag.

He went to the alleyway off Warschauer Strasse and sidled up to the abandoned door which opened, as always. He glanced about him, but there was no one in sight. So he turned left, and walked in the dim light toward siding number 4, and up to car 4. He took the laundry bag in his left hand and with his right hand positioned the key. But the door was already open, which meant that Claudia had already arrived. It was wrong of her to forget to lock the door, even though she expected him, and even though this would be their last time there. He climbed the platform stairs and turned to the car door, which was also open. Never mind—after today it would not matter. He proceeded down the familiar corridor toward the living quarters. It was totally dark. He called out, "Claudia?" and was instantly blinded by a searchlight. From behind, he was struck above the kidney by a club, and he fell to the floor.

The blow was the gentlest thing that happened to Caspar Allman that long evening. Four hours later, Walter Ulbricht invoked his authority as commander in chief personally to give the orders to the firing squad, and Caspar had to be seated and tied to the chair by the wall because he could not stand, or even sit, without slumping. Claudia was then brought out, manacled, and placed, standing, beside him, to go down with the same volley. They looked at each other. He could not speak, and she chose not to. Ulbricht was in any case delayed for only the very few minutes he needed to confer telegraphically with Ustinov and to call up the Soviet military commander to advise him instantly to telephone his American counterpart in the Western sector to warn him to be prepared for something the Bruderschaft were calling "Operation Rheingold." He entered the military courtyard briskly, and took in jubilantly the sight he saw. Let all his enemies perish so, he thought, as he gave the command to the firing squad.

35

Blackford was surprised when, late in the afternoon, he heard the key turn and saw not Mateus, but Henri Tod come in through the door. Mateus, following his master, took note of the warmth with which Herr Henri greeted Blackford. There was no pistol this time, presumably on the assumption that if Blackford attempted anything the two were enough to restrain him. Henri saw that Mateus did not quite know what was expected of him, so he told him to lock the door from the outside, that Henri would ring for him when he was ready to depart. Henri sat down in the armchair opposite the door, while Blackford lay propped up on the bed.

"I'm not here to try again to persuade you, Blackford. By this time tomorrow, Operation Rheingold will have been done, and if it works, it could be the turning point of the Cold War. I am not here to proselytize. But possibly I will not see you again. Because tomorrow, after it's over, I am going for my sister. I reason that whether our plan works or doesn't work—and I am confident that it will work—tomorrow will be just tumultuous enough to make it the ideal day to go for her and snatch her away in the confusion."

"How will you get her across the intersector boundary if they've got it closed up?"

"I won't have any trouble. I have West German papers, and they precisely don't *intend* to mess with West Germans, Casper told Roland this morning; they want us in West Berlin, not East Berlin. I don't know what kind of papers

Clementa has. We were both born in Hamburg, so she's
properly a West German. She may have some sort of a
Russian document, if she went and married that Gouzenko
man. Besides, we're talking about eight in the morning,
nine o'clock at the latest. Even if we failed, which I repeat
we will not, there is no way by then that the Vopos can
hermetically seal 45 kilometers. There are weak points
where, for a day or two, the problem will be a few strands of
barbed wire.

"Oh. I haven't told you, Blackford, what they plan. I got
hold of a copy of Operation Chinese Wall. There has not
been anything so elaborate since the Maginot Line—"

"Equally impregnable?" Blackford asked.

"You Americans make the mistake constantly. The Maginot Line was never penetrated. It was circumvented. The
wall they plan to build, if they follow the 1950s specifica-
tions, includes everything you can imagine. A high concrete
structure, with spikes, broken glass, machine-gun turrets,
thirty meters of no-man's land, mined; hunting dogs pa-
trolling a narrow alley on either side of the strip; then a
smaller wall, again with barbed wire and broken glass, and
electrical trip switches and flares. It would take a while to
raise that structure throughout the city of Berlin, Blackford; but it would then be as impenetrable as anything can
be created by the mind of man. . . . But they will not build
it—not after Rheingold, they will not. And anyway, we were
talking about me and Clementa. If things went bad, at worst
we could swim across the Spree. Clementa and I swam a
great deal during the two summers in Tolk. How wonderful
the prospect is! But as I say, I shall be preoccupied with her.
Perhaps she will need medical attention. I plan to devote
myself entirely to her until she is well, so that I may even
take her away, perhaps to London. But eventually I will be
back here, probably with her, to resume the work of the
Bruderschaft."

Blackford looked at the darkly handsome, animated face of Henri Tod and felt the excitement he felt.

"You've got a remarkable organization, Henri, I have to compliment you on it."

"Thanks. We have helped a lot of people."

"Yes. And you've also done a little bit to relieve the population problem."

Tod smiled. But quickly added, "Wherever there has been any doubt, we have not harmed anyone. And remember that simply because tyrants rule over one half of Germany, it does not follow that those tyrants exercise legitimate civil authority."

"Let's not go into that. You are a trained philosopher. I'm only an engineer. —So I may not be seeing you? For a while. Which reminds me, are you going to take twenty-five thousand marks with you tomorrow?"

"Yes. I see no moral point to be served in welshing. If he's KGB, then my problem becomes simply to rescue my sister, instead of merely ransoming her."

"Tod, do you mind my asking you where you get your money?"

"Yes. Because although I trust you, you might disapprove; and it would make you uncomfortable just to know."

"It makes me uncomfortable not to know. But then, it's just curiosity."

Tod looked over at Blackford, lying on the bed helpless, his hands linked behind his head. On impulse he spoke up. "Would you promise me you would not reveal the answer to your question?"

"I promise you."

"A member of the Bruderschaft is employed by the Marshall Plan people, in the division that holds your counterpart funds. You have nearly two billion marks of credit in that fund. Well, subtract from that two billion marks about two million marks, which we have embezzled. Our moral justification is that we are serving your purposes and giving you"—Henri lapsed now into English—"positively the biggest bang for a buck, as they say in America."

"Well, I'll be damned. You have embezzlers, tank drivers. Do you by any chance have any alchemists in the Bruderschaft? You could do away with Third World poverty, and get a Nobel Prize."

Tod stood, and smiled. He walked over to the desk and pressed the buzzer. Almost instantly the door opened and Mateus came in. Tod approached Blackford and embraced him. "Will you wish me luck?"

"Yes, Henri. I am morally free to wish you luck."

Tod walked out of the room.

An hour later, Mateus brought in Blackford's dinner. And Blackford embarked on his plan.

"Why don't you sit down in the chair over there, Mateus, and talk to me. It is lonely, eating alone."

"Well, sir, very well." He locked the door, waited for Blackford to fetch the tray from the coffee table back to the desk, then sat down, putting the pistol carefully in front of him on the side table.

"Help yourself to a little scotch"—Blackford pointed to the bottle on the ledge by the chair.

"Thank you, sir. This will be an exciting night. I am going to listen all night long to the radio."

"How I wish I could also. It will be a historic night, Mateus, no doubt about it."

"Well, sir, perhaps I could arrange it so that we could both listen. Yes, I think that should be possible."

"Mateus, tell me. Do you by any chance have any vodka? I am inclined to have a drink of vodka with my dinner."

"Vodka! When you can have scotch, sir? But of course, that is no problem at all." He retrieved the pistol, inserted the key in the lock, but kept his eyes on Blackford the entire time, as Blackford nibbled on the peanuts that had come in a corner of the tray. "I will be right back."

In a few moments the voice came, and Blackford went through the drill. Open the door, peer at the pistol, retreat to the desk area. Mateus came in, smiling, pistol in one hand, vodka bottle in the other. He finessed the rules to the point of taking the vodka over and depositing it on the desk, but his pistol hand was always level.

"Ah, thank you, Mateus. But tell me, did you forget about the radio? It is almost nine o'clock."

"The radio. Of course." Once again, the same ritual of withdrawal. As soon as the door was locked Blackford took the bottle of vodka into the bathroom, emptied it, and filled it with water.

In a few minutes Mateus was back. Genial, but, as required, formal in his attention to duty. "I think, sir, that under the circumstances it would be better if you were to plug the radio in, and perhaps attach the antenna to the pipe there," he pointed to one of the several pipes that traversed the ceiling.

"Of course," Blackford said, attending to the details.

"I am not sure, sir, what the reception down here will be like. But we will see."

The reception was gratifyingly good, and they heard the usual Saturday evening fare, flicking from station to station.

"Do have another drink, Mateus. It will be a long evening. I'm going to have another vodka," at which he poured his water glass half full. Mateus looked up, arched his eyebrows, and poured himself an equivalent amount of scotch.

"Tell me, Mateus," Blackford said, relaxing on the cot, the pillow set up to support his head and shoulders, "tell me, how long did you know Henri's parents?"

Blackford struck oil. It was a gusher. Mateus, it transpired, had gone to work for the Toddweiss family just after the First World War, in which he had fought. The highlight of his social history had been an encounter with an Austrian corporal. Yes, the one and only Austrian corporal.

"You mean to say, Mateus, that you knew Adolf Hitler as a corporal?"

Mateus could not have been more gratified to have been asked that question, to which he had given the answer perhaps one thousand times. He described in great detail what Schicklgruber, as he referred to him, looked like, what he said, the circumstances of their encounter ("Oh, sir, he was very imperious, even then"). Blackford poured himself another half glass from the vodka bottle. ("I don't want to be asleep when Operation Rheingold comes about," he commented. "No, sir," said Mateus, doing as much with the scotch for himself; "I'll see that you are awake.") Mateus had then returned to Hamburg, and a friend of his who worked for the Toddweiss family recommended that he seek employment there as a groom, since he had had cavalry training in the army. "The Toddweisses were fine people to work for."

"Then you knew the family even before Henri was born?" Indeed he had known the family *well* before Henri was born, Henri not having been born until after the Toddweisses had been married for five years.

As the time went by Mateus's voice blurred, as did Blackford's. He persevered with his bottle of vodka; indeed an unstated competition had begun, reaching the point where Mateus thought it would be impolite not to keep company with "my host. Or perhaps, sir, I should not, under these lamentable circumstances, refer to you as my host. On the other hand, sir, I should not want so to presume as to ask you to think of me as *your* host." To which Blackford replied, with a little blear in his voice, that he did not remember ever having a more attentive host, and that he was fascinated by what he had learned of the background of the Toddweiss family, and what happened after Henri was born, and Hitler—Schicklgruber—was elected?

It was just after one in the morning that the first indication came that something unusual was going on. Mateus's hand on the radio dial had become a little unsteady, and he found it progressively difficult to manipulate the dial in such a way as to go from station to station in pursuit of fresh bulletins. Blackford poured from what was the bottom third of the vodka bottle, and Mateus instantly followed suit.

"Here's to Rheingold, Mateus."

"To Rheingold, sir."

Blackford chugalugged. So did Mateus.

"Keep the radio on, Mateus—" Blackford's intonations were progressively hortatory, and Mateus found himself responding, and doing, as Blackford indicated.

"Yes, sir, I will do that."

"Because, Mateus, I think I am going to catch just a little catnap before the excitement. Just ten minutes, that is all. But you must keep listening. But before, I think I will just have one last toast to Rheingold." He poured himself a glassful this time, watching the level on the vodka bottle sink to below the label.

"I would not let you drink alone, sir," Mateus said, taking all but a few ounces of what was left in the scotch bottle.

Blackford closed his eyes and began a slow snore, his face turned down, his chin on his chest. He was gratified to see, out of the corner of his eye, Mateus take the last of the scotch into his glass, but was alarmed at the thought that he might then decide to go back upstairs. In the event he did so, Blackford would wake up, profess renewed interest in the radio, and demand more booze.

What happened was that Mateus's head began to nod. Within a very few minutes his head lay over the back of the armchair and he was snoring, mouth wide open, one hand on the glass, beside which lay the pistol.

Blackford waited a few moments, at which point his confidence was complete. He rose, and walked over toward Mateus. He leaned over and gently removed the pistol and put it into his pocket. He was now in command. But he did not want to gloat over a Mateus awake and aware of how he had tricked him. And he especially did not want to have to fire the weapon at the old man. The problem would be to get the key from Mateus's pocket without waking him. He was glad to see that it was on a chain attached to a loop on his belt. The radio was now abuzz with reports from the intersection boundary. A breathless commentator was describing the rolls of barbed wire outside the Brandenburg Gate, the rapidly congregating crowd of protesters, the armored cars with riflemen, weapons poised, looking over the crowd. Mateus's body slumped to the right, and it was in his right pocket that the keys lay. Blackford studied the conformation of Mateus, and resolved that he had no alternative than to pull gently on the chain and hope that the keys would slide up Mateus's pocket without waking him. He pulled with infinite care, a half inch at a time. Mateus registered nothing, and the keys, reaching the wider part of the pocket, began to follow the tug more easily. In a moment they dangled under the key chain. The radio spoke of the shouts of the crowd at the Vopos, and of the human wall of Vopos giving protection to the work squads that were laying the barbed wire concertinas. Whether to withdraw the key, or attempt to disengage the chain from the belt loop? . . . He would find it easier, Blackford decided finally, to unclip the entire key ring from the chain. With infinite care, he did so. He was safe now. It did not matter if Mateus did wake up. Besides, there was always the pistol. He tiptoed to the door, and slipped in the key.

He began to turn it, after which the door would open, letting him slip out. At just that moment he heard the radio announcer say excitedly, *"The Vopos have fired tear gas at the*

*West Berlin protesters! The protesters are shouting . . . and chok-
ing from the gas . . . They are shouting now at the West Berlin
police to protest. There's a flag flying there with huge lettering. It
says, 'America. Where Were You When We Needed You Most?' "*

Blackford had ceased all movement, listening to the announcer. Now he found himself letting the doorknob
spring back, slowly, to its closed position. America, where
were you when we needed you most? Well, Herr, er,
Friedburger, I was, you see, in a cellar, and I was playing it
real smart, persuading this here old German guy—he was
in WWI, and he knew Hitler as a corporal, you bet—that I
was blasted out of my mind and he didn't need to guard me,
he could go ahead and plop down the scotch, and after a
while I was able to sneak around him and pull the keys out
of his pocket and rush to the door! Yessir, there's no moss
growing under my feet; my name is Blackford Oakes,
maybe you've heard . . . ? Read any spy stuff? Well, we act
anonymously, but, you know, every now and then word *does*
get out, nothing you can do about it, understand? What was
I escaping from? Well, I was escaping to perform my mission. My mission. M-i-s-s-i-o-n. To do what? Well, to go to
the Americans and warn them. Warn them. Warn them
about what?

Blackford stood before the door now, for a full minute.
He breathed heavily.

And then, slowly, he withdrew the key, walked quietly
back to Mateus, carefully refastened the key ring to the
chain, eased it into the flappy part of Mateus's pocket, and
replaced the pistol by Mateus's glass. And went back to his
cot.

What would he do now? Nothing of what was coming in
over the radio could he in any way affect. Perhaps he should
write a letter to Linda Lewis, at the USIA Library in Vienna,
and tell her that he had thought of her often with delight,

not only biological. Yes, that would take his mind off what was going on, and in any case was true. The radio announcer reported that a West German smoke bomb had been dropped in front of the demonstrators, robbing them of any sense of direction. "Both sides," the announcer said, "appear determined not to use force." Right, thought Blackford. The Communists will not use force to deter the Westerners who seek to deter the Communists from taking the offensive, and the West will not use force to deter the Communists from proceeding with their offensive. East-West relations, they call it. Coexistence.

"Mateus!" he called out.

There was no answer.

"Mateus!" he shouted.

No answer.

He reached for one of the books, took sight on Mateus's stomach, and let fly. With a start, Mateus woke up.

"Yes, sir, yes, sir. I must have gone to sleep myself. What can I do for you, sir?"

"I have run out of vodka. Kindly fetch me some more."

"Right away, sir," and Mateus went out, pistol in hand, keeping his eyes all the while on his charge.

36

It was just after dawn that Günther Saxon, followed informally by six men dressed in work clothes, four of them carrying lunch pails, reached the MP gate outside McNair Barracks.

"Hello, Joe," Saxon said in broken English. "What iss ze hurry? I get telephone call, round up the crew, check tanks, even on Sunday you bet."

"Big trouble at the intersection border, Günther. The usual crew?"

"Plus coupla special mechanics, Joe. We must check all ze tanks."

"Good luck, Günther." The corporal motioned Günther and his men past.

They headed, at leisurely gait, left toward the large armory. When they were hidden from view, and before reaching the armory itself, Tod, wearing mechanics' fatigues and a fake mustache, addressed them.

"All right," he whispered. "Everyone knows what he is to do. God bless you all." Tod saluted his men and then struck off to the canteen, where he would monitor the proceedings.

Günther led the men toward the door at the side of the hangarlike armory. It was pitch-black inside. But Günther knew where the light switch was. "Hang on, men. I'll get the lights." The sound of the switch was quickly followed by floodlighting of the vast armory. He looked dumbly at twelve American G.I.'s with machine guns in a semicircle around Günther and his men.

Tod waited inside the commissary, open twenty-four hours every day, sipping a cup of tea and keeping his eye on the window through which he could observe the armory. They had calculated it would take less than five minutes to start up the three lead tanks, swing open the two huge apron doors, and come rumbling out. It took less than five minutes to see coming, not out of the apron doors, but from the little side door into which the men had entered, a squad of soldiers with machine guns, leading six members of the Bruderschaft, their hands clasped behind their heads prisoner-fashion, toward an office building.

Henri Tod stared at the remains of Operation Rheingold. He could not move from the stool he sat on. His vision faded, and he was again a schoolboy, quite drunk, talking to the prefect, Espy Major, and telling him that all Germans weren't bad, really, Espy. In fact, he leaned forward, causing the attendant behind the canteen to lean away slightly. His lips were moving, and he was saying to Espy, Look, I have a sister, and two foster parents. Listen to *this*, and tell me if you do not agree that there are some good Germans?

"Sir. Sir? Can I get you something else?"

Tod came to life and spoke now in his St. Paul's English. "No. Thank you very much. I must have been daydreaming." He nodded his head, looking through the window to the deserted drilling area, and walked out.

Mateus's orders were to release Blackford at nine. He opened the door, this time without the prescribed ritual, and both men concentrated on the radio, which told Blackford the whole story. "The West Berlin authorities have issued a warrant for the arrest of Henri Tod. Tod is alleged to be the leader of the Bruderschaft, the clandestine organization of anti-Communist Germans. United States military authorities have said that when Tod is apprehended, the trial judge advocate will wish to question him concerning his activities. Asked whether these included activities relating to the closing of the border last night, the authorities replied that they would not comment on the matter."

Blackford said to Mateus, "I must speak to Herr Henri. Drive me instantly to his quarters."

"Oh sir, I cannot do that. He does not permit anyone to know where he lives."

"Goddam it, Mateus, I am attempting to save the life of your master. Now will you do as I say, or shall I visit him in prison and inform him that I could not help him because you were frozen by old orders?"

Mateus thought for a moment. And then, "Follow me, sir."

Outside the safe house, Mateus motioned Blackford into a small station wagon. He drove him, without a word, to Kurfürstenstrasse. "There, sir." He pointed to Henri Tod's building. "Herr Henri lives on the third floor."

Blackford opened the door and climbed the staircase through the gutted stories. There was no answer when he rang the bell, and the entrance was locked. He wondered whether to break the lock. Instead he walked back to the station wagon to speak with Mateus. Did he have a key? Mateus reluctantly acknowledged that he did, and led Blackford back into the house, up the stairs, and opened the apartment. Blackford made a single telephone call, to Rufus. He did not tell Rufus everything. He did not tell him from where he was calling. And as he put down the telephone, Henri Tod was at his side. Blackford turned to him. Henri was pale, but apparently composed.

"Did you hear the radio coming here?" Blackford asked him.

"No."

"I take it Operation Rheingold was aborted?"

"It was. And I do not know who betrayed us."

"Are you aware that orders are out to arrest you?"

Henri Tod's eyes widened. "Did you give those orders, Blackford?"

"Henri, for one thing I don't have the authority to give those orders; for another I am unlikely to give them. They are orders from the civil government. We must assume that Operation Rheingold was exposed, that your part in it is also exposed as having been central, and that somewhere in the books there is a law against taking tanks that belong to the army of an occupying power with the intention of marching against another country and maybe starting a world war."

"East Berlin, Blackford, is not another country."

"All right, all right, I'm sure your lawyer will make that point. Meanwhile, are you prepared to go to jail?"

"I am going nowhere except to East Berlin, to Friedrichshain, where I shall take Clementa away."

"Where will you go then?"

"I have not given that matter any thought."

"Well you had better begin by giving that matter thought right now." He motioned to Mateus. "Bring coffee, and a roll." He sat on the corner of the desk and removed his jacket. It was already very warm.

"Now listen, Henri. With the collapse of Rheingold, and with orders for your arrest, it seems to me that that's the end of Bruderschaft. Oh, it may build up again, somewhere along the line. But for now, it's dead. And the only chance it has of ever building up again is for you to survive this mess. So what I propose to do is to . . . transcend . . . the authority of the government of West Berlin and get your ass out of this place if I can, and I think the thing is to try to get to Vienna."

"I am going nowhere without my sister."

"Your sister has a much better chance of uniting with you if you leave for Vienna and let her be our responsibility.

The chances are overwhelming that she is sitting right now surrounded by KGB agents."

"You heard what I said, and I do not wish to discuss it."

Henri Tod stood up. His complexion was still white, but his manner was sober, authoritative. He had said the final words he intended to say on the subject.

Blackford made rapid calculations. Either Henri was off-his-rocker determined to go after Clementa, in which case the mission was quite simply suicidal, or else he was determined to go after Clementa, but would listen to reasonable arguments about how best to do this. Blackford decided to try.

"Henri, now listen. You do, I assume, admit at least the possibility that Clementa is being held by that Gouzenko man as a part of a KGB operation to get hold of you, correct?"

He was relieved to hear Henri say, "I not only think it is likely, I think it is probable."

"Why then are you going?"

"I am going because at this point I am not interested in anything other than my sister."

"But if you are interested in your sister, what is the point in walking into an ambush which neither you—nor she—will survive?"

"We do not know anything that surely, Blackford"—Henri had risen, and was checking out a pistol—"and besides, there is always risk."

Blackford knew Tod when he was determined, and his mind raced furiously on the possibilities. He could arrest Tod there and then. Yes, he could . . . True, he thought, this was the least likely moment the Communists would expect to see Henri Tod arrive at the remote apartment building where the sister was being kept. Tod's timing was as good as could be, this he acknowledged. True, there was the theoretical possibility Tod could bring it off. He paused, but he knew it instinctively, knew that he would not

let this man go alone. Blackford's presence would not
hugely maximize the chances of so reckless an operation's
coming to success. But the odds would increase. Better if
they had a half-dozen Bruderschaften with them, but what
the hell, better if they had an armored U.S. battalion with
them. But this was hardly the day to conscript help. He
turned to Tod:

"Then you would agree that in approaching Frankfurter
Allee we should proceed as if it were a military operation?"

"Why do you say 'we' should proceed?"

"Because I'm going with you."

"You are not going with me."

"Look, Henri, I'm giving you a choice. Either I accompany you to East Berlin, or you accompany me to jail."

Henri looked about him, but saw only Mateus whom he
could command. For all intents and purposes, the Bruderschaft no longer existed. He was a general without an army.

"Why do you do this, Blackford?"

"Because I choose to, no further questions. Now concentrate. Everyone in Berlin is listening to the radio right now,
has been since 1 A.M. The probability that the people squat-
ting around Clementa have heard that there is a warrant
out for your arrest I would judge at approximately 99 percent. Agreed?"

"Agreed."

"So, number one, you are apprehended."

"Blackford, please. Speak plainly."

"We need to get word to the radio stations that you have
been apprehended and that you are in jail. That will have
the effect of disarming the gang around Clementa, if we are
correct that that is what we are to expect."

"I understand your reasoning."

"Now, I could telephone to the embassy, tell 'em I have
you by the hand and am taking you in to the police. But
there are lots of reasons why that is not the ideal way to do
it."

"I understand. The word should go out from the West German police without your involvement in any way."

"Either from the West German police—or from RIAS, the West Berlin radio station."

"How RIAS?"

"Routine. Scoop. They find out you have been arrested and they report it."

"How do they find out?"

"Come on, Henri. A couple of hours ago you were in charge of a clandestine organization of hundreds of people."

"Forgive me. Of course. And I know the man. News Department, RIAS. He is a member of the Bruderschaft. I need merely to telephone him."

"Okay. You will telephone him. Five minutes before we leave here."

"When do you propose that we leave here?"

"In five minutes."

Henri Tod picked up the telephone book and dialed a number. He asked to speak to Roman Haldi. Haldi on the line, Henri gave a code and the telephone number Haldi was to call back from a public telephone booth. It was less than three minutes. Henri gave his instructions. Five minutes later RIAS's commentator, broadcasting—among hundreds of reporters and radio and television commentators who had been flying in from all over Europe since shortly after midnight—opposite the Brandenburg Gate, reporting on the gradual consolidation by the East Germans of the obstacle that would soon become a wall, interrupted his narrative. "FLASH. The word has just come in that Bruderschaft leader Henri Tod has been apprehended and is being taken to police headquarters. Asked to which branch of headquarters he would be taken, authorities declined to give an answer, citing reasons of security. We'll keep our eyes on that story, and now back to the Wall as, already, they are beginning to call that concentration of barbed wire and concrete stanchions going up . . ."

"That was fast work, Henri," Blackford said.

"I am not yet entirely without resources," Henri answered.

Blackford had on him the papers he required: an American passport, a letter or two attesting to his responsibilities in the insurance company that ostensibly employed him. Henri Tod deliberated for a moment, choosing two of a half-dozen passports in his hidden safe, one certifying him as a U.S. citizen, the second as a West German. Blackford selected a Luger from Henri's armory. Henri also took an automatic, small binoculars, a canister of tear gas, and a smoke bomb. They put all the paraphernalia in with assorted towels and underwear into a laundry bag, got into the car, and directed Mateus to one of the remoter passage points at the Oberbaumbrücke.

Although this was at the far south end of the city, the commotion had reached the bridge. There was heavy activity with construction workers bent on planting the barbed wire and the concrete blocks. But virtually all the administrative concentration was on westbound traffic. The Vopos had been cautioned not to interfere with eastbound Americans, and accordingly, when Blackford and Tod showed U.S. passports, the guard nodded them on.

"But you will not be permitted to take your automobile," he said. "Those are orders."

Blackford tried arguing with him, but it didn't work. He turned to Mateus, told him to wait for them back at the apartment, nonchalantly reached for the laundry bag and, conversing uninterruptedly with his fellow American, walked across into East Berlin carrying a bag with two false passports, two pistols, binoculars, one smoke grenade, and one tear gas grenade. Two blocks into the city, they looked for a taxi. But on August 13, 1961, there were no taxis. Blackford hailed a passing vehicle. "Sir, my sister is very ill, and I need to go to her. Please"—he passed the driver a hundred-mark bill—"drive us to the corner of Frankfurter Allee and Proskauer Strasse." The driver obliged.

At the corner, Blackford and Henri entered the café they knew to be there, two blocks from Clementa's apartment house. They sat down and ordered coffee and beer. Several dozen men and a few women were silently staring at the television set on top of a battered old phonograph.

And now Henri Tod took over. "You agreed, Blackford, that the operation will be under my command. You have most thoughtfully made it easier than it might have been. I will repeat now our understanding."

He looked at his watch. It was 10:12. "At 10:25 we will leave the café. We will arrive outside 117 Frankfurter Allee at 10:33. We will enter the apartment house together, and walk up the staircase. At the third floor, you will stop. I will climb to the fourth floor, and will ring apartment 4B. When the door opens, I will simply demand my sister at gunpoint, and if I find there only the Gouzenko man, I'll drop this sandwich pail with the money in it. In fact, I shall permit him to open and examine it.

"If there are KGB there, I expect to catch them off balance. But in any event I will give the signal for you to come up and give me cover. Are we understood?"

"Those are the arrangements," Blackford said. "And you know what, Henri, we may as well enjoy our beer and coffee. Our schedule permits us thirteen whole minutes to do so! Oh goodness, how leisure time can spoil a man!" He lifted his glass to Henri; and, for the first time since leaving the armory that morning, Henri Tod smiled.

Dmitri Gouzenko, for the obvious reasons, did not have his radio turned on that morning. He had a gramophone, and Clementa and he were listening to the music of Richard Strauss soon after they had breakfast, as she washed the dishes. Every half hour or so Dmitri would leave his apartment and cross the corridor, as he had been doing now for over a week, ever since they got there, explaining to Clementa that across the way was the office to which he reported and from which he received instructions, but that it was otherwise uninteresting, not worth her visiting; besides which, it was for men only. Clementa was entirely unconcerned, attending to her sewing—she had embarked on an ambitious petit point for Nina's birthday, and was intermittently reading a Dostoyevski novel. Dostoyevski was all she ever read, and she did the cycle in eighteen months, beginning it all over again. She never tired of it, besides which, she said, she had always forgotten the plots by the time she turned back to them.

Across the hall, where Glazonouw and Shelepin were on duty, the radio was very much on. They listened to RIAS, though they would check every hour or two on the East Berlin station. And when the bulletin had come in an hour before, that Henri Tod had been arrested, Glazonouw had taken the unusual liberty of knocking on the door of Gouzenko, who instantly came out, and the three of them huddled together.

Clearly the ambush was no longer relevant. Henri Tod had been told that he and only he could entice Clementa to follow him to West Germany. Now not only was there a physical obstacle to any such journey, but Henri Tod was in jail. Operation Tod was—defunct. To be sure, this would need to be certified by headquarters, and headquarters, on this day, Gouzenko guessed, was not to be easily distracted from its principal concern, which was with the hectic activity of the Wall. "The thing to do is just to sit, and relax. Figure it will be another twenty-four hours, maybe a little more, before we are officially relieved of duty," Gouzenko said.

Quite right, except that in the commotion they had not reckoned on Helmut Bollinger, and Bollinger, sitting alone, twelve hours every day, until relieved, ten days in a row, in the little room on the sixth floor directly across the street, had no radio. His relief corporal, Sebastian, had taken it out to be fixed three days before, but it was not yet returned. So that he had nothing to do, hour after hour, except his duty; and that was to peer out the window, binoculars in hand, in the event that any unusual or suspicious person or persons approached 117 Frankfurter Allee, which was exactly how Bollinger would describe these two men, one dressed in fatigues, the other in slacks, neither of them familiar, who now approached and, obviously unfamiliar with the apartment house, closely scrutinized the directory in the hall.

Bollinger was glad to have a reason to relieve the tedium. He took the telephone, dialed the number of his confederates across the street, and said, "Two men. Strangers. Careful." Instantly Glazonouw and Shelepin were back at their battle stations.

The two men walked wordlessly up the dingy stairs to the third landing. There Henri Tod nodded at Blackford, who stopped and bent down as if to tie his shoelace, while Henri proceeded up another flight.

He turned left, facing the door to apartment 4B. With his left elbow he depressed the buzzer. In his left hand he carried the lunch pail with the money. In his right hand, the pistol. He heard a voice.

"Who is it?"

"I have come to see Madame Gouzenko."

Those words, the last Henri Tod ever spoke, were answered by a rain of bullets. Blackford leaped up the stairs in time to see the door opening. He fired six times, bringing down the two killers. Instinctively he sensed the nature of the deception. He bent down quickly, grabbed Henri's unfired pistol, and with all his strength aimed his foot at the door to 4A. The door, splattered by the same bullets that had penetrated Henri's body, flung open. Pistol in hand, he found the weapon aimed straight at and six inches away from the body of the man of Vienna, Mr. Frank. Blackford's blood was boiling, and he knew that life would not again give him such satisfaction as now he would get from pressing the trigger at the man who had managed the ambush of Henri Tod. It was then that he spotted her, sitting on the couch.

She could only have been the sister of Henri Tod. She looked up at him, her face oval, eyes dark, her hair framing the face and features of a madonna. She said nothing, continuing to sew; while Gouzenko slowly backed toward her, his hands held high.

Blackford thought breathlessly. He needed to move quickly, but he needed above all to establish one thing. He said, simply, "Clementa?"

"Yes," she replied, "and who are you, and why is there so much shooting again?"

He said, purposefully, "Is this man, Gouzenko, your friend?"

She replied, "He is not my friend. He is my husband. He is the father of our little girl. Please, sir, do not harm him."

Blackford was breathing hard. He took a full minute to compose his thoughts.

"Gouzenko," he said, "I am leaving here with—the body. I propose to take it back to where he was born, to get him the kind of burial he'd have wanted. I expect you to do nothing for one full hour, allowing us to get across. Is that . . . an understanding?"

"That is an understanding, Oakes."

Later, Blackford would have difficulty in reconstructing what he then did, but at the time his motions came as reflexes. He walked to the middle of the road and stopped the first car that approached, an old Opel four-door sedan driven by a large middle-aged man wearing a black derby. He approached the driver.

"I am sorry, sir, this is a military emergency." He pulled out his pistol, directed the driver to the hallway of the apartment house, and instructed him to take the corpse by the legs. Together, they lifted Henri Tod onto the back seat.

"You will find your car on applying to the Volkspolizei late this afternoon," he said, driving off.

He headed right for the Brandenburg Gate, never mind the lesser passage points. When he was within a hundred yards of the barricade he was overwhelmed by the spectacle —the platoons of construction workers, the armored cars, the sirens. Across the burgeoning partition was what looked like the whole population of West Berlin, crowds which now included, front and center, the hastily assembled military band playing patriotic anthems. He forced his car right to the passage point, which had had virtually no traffic until now. He leaned out of the window, stuck out his American passport, and said to the captain (normally, it would have been a corporal), motioning behind him with his other hand, that he had a dead man in the back seat. His tone was straightforward, impatient, businesslike, imperious.

"Corpses traveling between sectors must be moved by certified morticians, pursuant to regulations."

"Fuck regulations, captain." It was hard to make himself heard because the band was now playing "Deutschland Über Alles," and the amplified sound made conversation difficult. "This man"—he shoved Henri's West German passport in the captain's face—"was married to my sister. *You* take the stiff if you want. What a goddam mess. Do you also want the widow's telephone number? This is the last domestic scene *I'm* getting into. Goddam it, will you raise that bloody gate?"

The captain peered at Blackford, hesitated a moment, then looked to the right at the construction workers with their ear-shattering acetylene torches, to the left at the armored cars moving about, raising and lowering their cannon, and across the way at one hundred thousand West Germans and the military band. "You may not take the vehicle through. *That* is strictly forbidden," he growled.

Blackford looked up at the captain with impatience. Wordlessly, he opened the door at his side and got out. Then he opened the back door, reached in, and dragged the corpse out onto the pavement. Bending his knees, he now grabbed one arm of Henri Tod and hoisted the corpse over his shoulder. He began walking toward the barrier. "Tell those bastards to let me go by," he muttered to the captain, who nodded to the intervening guards, who moved the wire, to permit the final passage home of Henri Tod.

37

It had been set up as a buffet. There were, after all, twenty people invited. An unexpected guest had been the Director of the Central Intelligence Agency, who briefed the President on events that day in Berlin, bringing him up to date on what the President had got at noon, over the telephone, from the Secretary of State, the Secretary of Defense, and the National Security Adviser. Mostly his guests were social friends, but because one of his advisers was vacationing at nearby Wellfleet, he had asked him to come, and his wife. And, from down the street, they had invited Judy Garland and her husband, on the strict understanding that they would not fight with each other even if the party lasted until ten o'clock.

The children had been the center of attention—not only the infants, but the boys and girls, most of them nephews and nieces ranging in age from eight to sixteen, who had been racing during the day in the regatta. The shrieks and yells of the returning sailors, the boisterous swimming and the tennis playing—it had been a fine, full day. And now the children were packed off, the scene was stilled, and the senior party had their drinks, and chatted. It was 8:30 before the food was brought out and they filled their plates and sat randomly.

Around one card table, the President sat with the Director, the President's assistant from Wellfleet, and Judy Garland. The President was distracted, and although he responded to all remarks addressed to him, those who knew him well knew that he was not really engaged in the conversation.

It was dark by the time the coffee was served, and the chatter was everywhere, like the sound of crickets. Suddenly the President lifted the glass of white wine that sat in front of him, which he had not touched during the meal. He caught the eye of the Director and said, in a voice so quiet as to stress the privacy of the communication:

"Let's drink to Rheingold."

The Director raised his glass in acknowledgment.

"Too bad," the President added, putting down his glass.

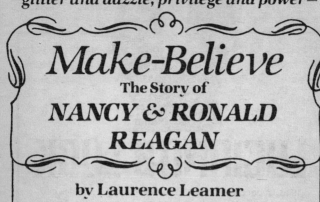

LUCIANO'S LUCK

1943. Under cover of night, a strange group parachutes into Nazi occupied Sicily. It includes the overlord of the American Mafia, "Lucky" Luciano. The object? To convince the Sicilian Mafia king to put his power—the power of the Sicilian peasantry—behind the invading American forces. It is a dangerous gamble. If they fail, hundreds of thousands will die on Sicilian soil. If they succeed, American troops will march through Sicily toward a stunning victory on the Italian Front, forever indebted to Mafia king, Lucky Luciano.

A DELL BOOK   14321-7 $3.50

JACK HIGGINS

bestselling author of *Solo*

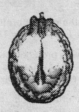

The ROBERT LITTELL
Amateur

"One of the best. A thoroughly professional and sur-prised-filled work."—*Los Angeles Times*

"Taut, chilling plot and a protagonist as memorable as one of Len Deighton's or Le Carre's George Smiley." —*The New York Times Book Review*

When terrorists murdered his fiancée, Charlie Heller decided to penetrate the Iron Curtain with the intent to kill. But in a world of professional killers, his chances of success were one in a million.

A DELL BOOK $3.50